THE H

They were companionably silent for a few minutes as they sat there and watched the fire. Flames like this were so different from the ones she usually dealt with, Annabel thought.

"Annabel."

Cole's voice was little more than a whisper. Annabel lifted her head and turned it toward him. Their faces were scant inches apart now. She could see the muscles in his jaw, the tiny creases around his eyes that came from wind and sun and laughter, the strong line of his mouth, the softness of his brown eyes.

And with that, she pressed her lips to his . . .

Praise for Elizabeth Hallam's
SPIRIT CATCHER

"An engaging, warm-hearted story of justice triumphing over the odds and love crossing all barriers."

—*Romantic Times*

"*Spirit Catcher* is a timeless and haunting tale of love. Their passions will keep you riveted with emotion, and the pages turning long into the night. Don't miss this splendid tale of love!"

—*The Literary Times*

Jove titles by Elizabeth Hallam

SPIRIT CATCHER
ALURA'S WISH
YESTERDAY'S FLAME

YESTERDAY'S FLAME

Elizabeth Hallam

JOVE BOOKS, NEW YORK

This is a work of fiction. Names, characters, places, and incidents are either the product of the author's imagination or are used fictitiously, and any resemblance to actual persons, living or dead, business establishments, events or locales is entirely coincidental.

YESTERDAY'S FLAME

A Jove Book / published by arrangement with the author

PRINTING HISTORY
Jove edition / February 2000

For information address: The Berkley Publishing Group, a division of Penguin Putnam Inc., 375 Hudson Street, New York, New York 10014.

The Penguin Putnam Inc. World Wide Web site address is http://www.penguinputnam.com

ISBN: 0-515-12750-7

A JOVE BOOK®
Jove Books are published by The Berkley Publishing Group, a division of Penguin Putnam Inc., 375 Hudson Street, New York, New York 10014.

PRINTED IN THE UNITED STATES OF AMERICA

10 9 8 7 6 5 4 3 2 1

This book is dedicated
to all the firefighters who
put their lives on the line
every day to protect ours.

Yesterday's Flame

Chapter 1

"NOW *THAT* IS what I call a handsome man."

Annabel Lowell said distractedly, "What? Where?"

"That man right there," her friend Vickie Pasetta said, pointing.

Annabel turned, expecting to see Vickie indicating some tourist who had wandered into the San Francisco Fire Museum. Instead, she saw that Vickie was pointing at a large framed photograph on the wall. A brass plaque above the photograph read *Engine Company No. 21.*

Annabel frowned. "What are you talking about?" she asked.

"Right here." Vickie stepped closer to the photograph and reached out to actually tap with a fingernail the glass that covered it. "This guy. Don't you think he's good-looking?"

"Hey, don't touch the exhibits," a deep voice said from behind the two women. "You'll get us kicked out of here."

"And it would break your heart to get banned from the Fire Museum, wouldn't it, Earl?" Vickie said over her shoulder.

"Well, yeah," Earl Tabor said as he slouched up next to

Annabel and Vickie. He was a big, affable bear of a man with a beard and rather long brown hair. "I won't deny that I'm a fire buff *and* a history buff. C'mon, girls. I want to take a look at that Amoskeag pumper they've got on display."

"Go ahead, you two," Annabel said. "I'll catch up to you. I'm sort of a third wheel on this date anyway."

"It's *not* a date," Vickie insisted. She glanced at Earl. "No offense."

"Oh, none taken," he assured her. "I'm confident you'll come around sooner or later." He took her arm, not so much in a romantic fashion as out of sheer boundless enthusiasm for a subject that fascinated him. "Wait'll you see this Amoskeag. It's really something the way it's been restored. . . ."

Vickie cast an imploring look back at Annabel, who just smiled at her and then turned back to the large photograph her friend had pointed out to her. She wanted to give her two best friends some time alone together; Vickie could deny it all she wanted, but this *was* a date, and there were definitely sparks between her and Earl, mismatched as they might seem on the surface.

But in spite of her motives, Annabel found herself growing interested in the photograph. She had been a member of the San Francisco Fire Department for several years before going to work for the U.S. Forest Service as a smokejumper, and the photograph was a bit of history.

It showed the men of Engine Company Number Twenty-one standing in front of their station, gathered around a horse-drawn steam pumper. The firemen—in that day and age, nobody would have called them "firefighters"—were wearing military-style uniforms and round caps with short, stiff leather brims. The one Vickie had pointed to was standing at the end of the group, a serious expression on his face. He *was* pretty good-looking, Annabel supposed. Tall and broad-shouldered, with a lean waist. It was hard to tell much about his body because of the uniform, but

Annabel would have been willing to bet that his legs were trim and muscular if he had spent much time in San Francisco. Muscular legs were a by-product of navigating the city's famous hills. The uniform had several decorations on it, probably medals of commendation, and a pin of some sort was fastened on the lapel of the jacket, reflecting brightly in the sun.

The fireman's face had a rugged cast to it. A strong jaw and chin, and eyes that looked out at the camera with honesty and intelligence and courage.

She wondered who he had been. He was surely long dead, since *April 17, 1906* was written in the lower-right-hand corner of the picture. Almost ninety-five years had passed since then. It had been a whole different world in those days. . . .

Of course, things had changed quite a bit just in her lifetime. For one thing, back around the time she'd been born, in the seventies, there had been very few women in the SFFD, and for another, there had been even fewer female smoke-jumpers. Her dad, a captain in the department, had surely never even considered the possibility that someday his little girl would grow up to follow in his footsteps and fight fires.

Annabel had surprised Mike Lowell quite often over the years.

"Taken right before the earthquake," Earl said, breaking into Annabel's thoughts.

"What?"

Earl pointed a strong, blunt finger at the photograph. "I said it was taken not long before the earthquake. Those guys probably helped keep all of San Francisco from burning down."

"Why do you want to go to Fisherman's Wharf to eat?" Vickie asked, changing the subject. "We're not tourists, you know. We actually live here in San Francisco, Earl."

"I know, but the food's good there," Earl said.

"Why don't we go to my cousin Donnie's restaurant on

Columbus Avenue," Vickie suggested. "The caponata . . ." She kissed her fingertips. "The best you ever ate. And it's right around the corner from the apartment."

Earl shrugged his massive shoulders. "All right, whatever you say, Vickie. As long as I get some of that focaccia bread."

"Sure, sure." Vickie looked at Annabel. "You ready to go?"

Annabel turned back to her friends, the photograph that had interested her a moment earlier now forgotten. "I guess so," she replied. "If you're sure you've seen enough of the museum."

"We can always come back another day," Earl suggested. "What do you say, Vickie?"

"We'll see. For now, just feed me."

They caught a taxi on Bush Street, just outside the museum, and headed for North Beach.

Annabel loved the neighborhood, nestled as it was in the irregular triangle between Telegraph Hill to the east and Russian Hill and Nob Hill to the west and southwest. She had moved into a little apartment in an old building just off Columbus Avenue when she went to work for the SFFD, and when she moved to the Forest Service and was assigned to the smoke jumpers' base up in Redding, she saw no reason to give up the place. True, the Service flew her and her fellow smoke-jumpers all over the western half of the United States to fight forest fires, but in between jobs and training exercises, she could live wherever she wanted. Earl, her best friend in the elite unit, was the same way. He hadn't grown up in San Francisco, as Annabel had, but he had always wanted to live there.

"Why don't you drop me off at City Lights?" Annabel suggested as the cab cruised up Columbus Avenue. "The two of you can go on the restaurant."

"Are you sure?" Vickie asked.

"Yeah, I want to poke around in the bookstore for a while, then I'll walk home from there."

"Look, if you're worried that three's company," Vickie said with a glance at Earl, "don't be."

"Sure, come along with us," he urged.

Annabel shook her head. "No, I just don't feel like eating yet. I'll fix something later, or go down to the deli."

"Well, if that's what you really want . . . ," Vickie said.

"It is," Annabel said.

She stepped out of the cab when it pulled up at the curb in front of the famous City Lights Bookstore. She was pleased with herself for playing matchmaker. Vickie and Earl were perfect for each other, if only Vickie would open her eyes and realize it. Earl had come to that conclusion the first time he had visited Annabel's place and seen Vickie coming out of the apartment across the hall. Vickie didn't believe in love at first sight, however, so she was being stubborn about the whole thing. At first she had worried that she would be cutting in on Annabel, until Annabel had assured her that there was nothing romantic between her and Earl. They worked together, they were good friends, and that was as far as it went.

As Earl said, sooner or later Vickie would come around, Annabel told herself as she closed the cab door and leaned over to say goodnight. She waved, and then they were gone, carried on up Columbus Avenue.

Annabel went into the small, triangular-shaped building that housed the bookstore and spent the next hour browsing through the shelves on its three floors. Her father had had a good collection of Beat Generation literature—though he never would have admitted as much to his friends at the fire station—and as a teenager Annabel had read Ginsberg and Ferlinghetti and Corso and *On the Road* as well as Norman Maclean's tales of fighting forest fires. Today she bought a couple of books and then walked around the corner to the apartment house.

As she did so, she heard the keening wail of a fire engine several blocks away, and out of habit her muscles stiffened in readiness. It took a conscious effort for her to relax. She didn't have to climb into her suit and grab her equipment. Wherever the fire was, other people would deal with it.

She let herself into the building lobby and headed for the stairs. Footsteps filled the stairwell, and a man appeared at the first-floor landing. He was blond, fairly attractive, and looked to be about five-eleven, only an inch taller than her. Annabel didn't remember seeing him around the building before, and she felt the city dweller's natural wariness around a stranger. But he smiled at her and said, "Hi. You live here?"

"That's right," Annabel said cautiously. "How about you?"

"Just moved in this afternoon. I'm Kyle Loftus." He stuck out his hand.

"Annabel Lowell," she said as she took his hand. His grip was firm, and it didn't linger. Annabel chalked that up as a mark in his favor.

"Annabel," he repeated. "That's sort of an old-fashioned name, isn't it?"

"My father was an old-fashioned guy."

"Well, it's a pretty name, too. Say, can you show me a good place to eat around here? I haven't had a chance to stock my refrigerator yet."

That was fast, Annabel thought.

"There are a lot of restaurants in the neighborhood," she told him. "Almost any place you look there's somewhere to eat. And it's all good."

"Oh," he said. "No recommendations in particular?"

"Nope, I'm afraid not."

"Okay," he said. He lifted a hand in farewell as he headed for the lobby door. "See you around the building, I guess."

"Sure," Annabel said. She turned toward the stairs and didn't watch him leave, but she thought she felt him glance back at her.

She had certainly shot him down in a hurry, she told herself as she climbed the stairs. And he had seemed like a pretty nice guy, too. But it didn't really matter. For all of her matchmaking where Vickie and Earl were concerned, the last thing Annabel wanted in her life right now was any sort of romantic relationship. They never worked out. Men were attracted to her because of her looks, but sooner or later they started telling her how she shouldn't risk her life fighting forest fires. They tried to take away from her the things that meant the most to her.

She wasn't going to let that happen again. Once burned, twice shy, that was how the old saying went, and Annabel knew that like most clichés, it had a kernel of truth at its core.

She would rather face a wildfire any day than a man who wanted to change her.

Later that evening, Annabel dozed off on the sofa with one of the books of poetry she had bought at City Lights draped across her lap. A shrill ringing woke her, and she sat up straight, thinking at first the noise was her doorbell. Probably Vickie, she thought fuzzily, wanting to tell her how the rest of the evening had gone.

As she put the book aside and stood up, she realized the ringing wasn't the doorbell at all, but rather her cell phone. She had taken it out of her purse when she got home and placed it on a small side table. She had to keep it with her at all times, as well as spare batteries, because that was the number her boss at the Forest Service used to call her.

And Captain Ed McPhee never called unless it was urgent.

Annabel scooped up the phone. "Hello?"

"Mount Diablo State Park," Captain McPhee's voice said curtly in her ear. "Practically in your backyard, Lowell. We're backing up the state boys. How soon can you get over there?"

"You don't want me to come up to Redding?"

"You can get there quicker if you go straight to the fire. You'll coordinate with the state firefighters on the ground."

"I'm not jumping?"

"Not this time. We'll be in the air by the time you get there."

Annabel felt a pang of disappointment. Most people would think it was crazy to want to jump out of a plane and parachute down into the middle of a forest fire, and Annabel agreed that it took a certain type of personality to do such a thing. But those who had never experienced it could never know the exhilaration of such a moment, either.

"What about your buddy Tabor?" Captain McPhee went on.

Annabel hesitated. It was almost midnight, and while there was a possibility that Earl might be across the hall in Vickie's apartment, Annabel didn't want to be the one to interrupt whatever might be going on. "I'm not sure where he is," she told the captain. "You'd better call him."

McPhee grunted. "All right. I'll radio you from the plane in an hour."

"Right. I ought to be there by then if the traffic's not too bad."

"Just be there," Captain McPhee said. He broke the connection.

Annabel thumbed the "End Call" button and turned to hurry into her bedroom, where she kept a spare set of all her gear.

Less than ten minutes later, wearing the yellow fire suit and black helmet, she trotted across the street to the parking garage where she kept her Jeep. She had her breathing apparatus and radio slung over her left shoulder and in her right hand carried her Pulaski, the half-hoe, half-ax that was every smoke-jumper's friend. Her long brown hair was tucked up underneath the hard plastic helmet. To anyone watching, she must be a strange sight, she thought.

As she pulled out of the parking garage a couple of minutes later, she saw Earl running along the sidewalk. He spotted her Jeep and waved his arms. When she pulled up next to him, he piled in.

"Can you swing by my place so I can pick up my gear?"

Earl lived on the waterfront, not far from the Embarcadero. It wasn't very far out of the way. Annabel nodded. "I see Captain McPhee caught you," she said. "Were you still at the restaurant?"

"Naw, we were at, uh, Vickie's place. You should've knocked on the door when you went out."

"I thought about it. I just hated to interrupt you."

"You wouldn't have been interrupting anything," Earl said grumpily. "I was just telling Vickie about the earthquake."

"The one in '89?" That catastrophe had been before Annabel's time on the SFFD. She'd still been in high school, in fact. Senior year.

"No, the '06 one. The big one."

Annabel shook her head. "That wasn't the big one. The big one's still down there somewhere in the ground."

"Yeah, but it was bad enough. Did you know that the quake busted all the water mains, so the fire department had to pump in water from the bay. . . ."

Annabel tuned him out as he continued talking about the historic earthquake in 1906 and the massive fires that had followed it. Earl knew more about such things than anyone else she had ever met, and he talked about them to anyone who would hold still. Annabel had learned to listen to him without really listening.

Say she had gone out tonight with her new neighbor Kyle Loftus, she thought. They could have ended up back at her place. Not in bed, of course. Some people might accuse her of being reckless because of her profession, but some things she took slowly and carefully, and sex was one of them. But she and Kyle *could* have been in her apartment, having coffee or some wine and talking, and then the call from Captain McPhee would have come, and Annabel would have rushed off to fight a forest fire at Mount Diablo. . . .

What would Kyle have thought of that? she asked herself. Probably the same thing that most men would have thought under similar circumstances: that she had lost her mind.

Earl thundered into the old row house he was in the process of restoring in his spare time and then hurried back out with all his gear. Annabel had left the Jeep's engine running while he was gone. As Earl struggled into his fire suit in the passenger seat, Annabel headed for the Bay Bridge.

There was traffic at any hour of the day or night, but it wasn't quite as heavy now, a little after midnight, as it might have been earlier. The lights on the Bay Bridge sparkled brightly in the darkness. Annabel's foot was heavy on the gas pedal as she sped through Oakland and Berkeley and then curved southeast toward Mount Diablo and the sprawling state park that surrounded it.

"Look," Earl said after a little while, and Annabel knew what he was talking about. Her experienced eyes had already spotted the distant reddish glow in the sky. She rolled down the window beside her and sniffed the air. Smoke. Faint, but there.

The telltale signs of the fire—the glow in the sky and the smell of smoke in the air—grew more distinct as Annabel and Earl approached the park. Annabel felt her heartbeat racing faster than normal. It was an unavoidable reaction. Before the night was over, there was every chance in the world that she would be putting her life in danger.

It had been a while since she had been to the park, but she hiked there two or three times a year and knew the layout fairly well. She headed for the north entrance. The park headquarters and ranger station were actually closer to the south entrance, but Annabel would have had to backtrack to get there if she came in from the south. She wished she knew exactly where the fire was located.

The portable radio that was attached to the Jeep's dashboard crackled into life. "This is Tango One-Niner," Captain McPhee's voice said. A slight roaring in the background came from the engine of the smoke-jumpers' plane. "Lowell, are you and Tabor there?"

Annabel gestured for Earl to take the radio. He picked it up, keyed the mike, and said, "This is Tabor, Cap'n. Lowell and I are approaching the north entrance of the park."

"Good. Proceed to the ranger station and act as liaison with the State of California firefighters."

Annabel said, "Ask him where the fire is."

Earl relayed the question, and the captain replied, "It's confined so far to Mitchell Canyon, but with the way the wind's blowing, it may threaten the summit."

"Any civilians in the way?" Earl asked. Both he and Annabel knew there was a museum and restaurant in the old stone building atop the summit of Mount Diablo.

"Not at this time of night, thank God. At least that's what I'm told."

Annabel felt a surge of relief. Fighting forest fires was difficult and dangerous enough without having to worry about rescuing any civilians who might be caught in the path of the flames.

"The state crew is already working on a firebreak between the canyon and the summit," Captain McPhee continued. "We're going in on the far side of the fire just in case the wind shifts. With any luck, we'll have it contained by morning."

"All right, Cap'n," Earl said. "Any further orders?"

"No. Good luck, you two."

"Thanks, Cap'n. Good luck to you, too. Out."

Earl hung the radio back on its hook. "Well, that doesn't sound too bad. Ought to be a piece of cake, in fact."

"We'll see," Annabel said. She didn't trust any fire to be easy. She had seen too many of them that had appeared to be under control break and run wild again.

The gate at the north entrance to the park was open. Annabel wheeled the Jeep through it, then followed the twisting road toward the ranger station. Mount Diablo itself loomed above them to the left, its rounded, heavily wooded slopes blocking out much of the glow from the fire now. The smoke smell was stronger, though, indicating that the wind was still carrying the flames up Mitchell Canyon toward the summit.

The ranger station and park headquarters were beehives of activity. Fire trucks and Jeeps were parked everywhere. Firefighters were wetting down the buildings of the compound to protect them from any airborne sparks that might float this far from the fire. Men and women in fire suits and helmets, as well as others in the uniform of the State Parks and Wildlife Service, hurried here and there. Annabel parked her Jeep where it would be out of the way, and she and Earl hopped out. Carrying their Pulaskis and other gear, they stopped the first state firefighter they encountered. "Who's in charge here?" Annabel asked, raising her voice to be heard over the general hubbub. She could also hear the distant crackling and roaring of the forest fire itself.

"Captain Skinner," the firefighter replied, pointing to a balding man in glasses, a windbreaker, and a hard hat. The windbreaker had *State Parks and Wildlife* stenciled on its back.

"Thanks," Annabel said. She and Earl hurried over to intercept Captain Skinner.

"—teams on the north end!" Skinner was calling to someone. He turned to the new arrivals and frowned slightly at Annabel. "Don't I know you?"

"Annabel Lowell from the Forest Service. We met at a joint firefighting exercise last summer," Annabel explained. "This is Earl Tabor. We're here to coordinate our people with yours, Captain."

Skinner grunted. "McPhee and his boys are already aloft?"

"That's right. They should be jumping soon, if they haven't already."

"Blast it! I was just handed a weather report that's got me worried. We've got a front that was stationary about to start moving again. The wind shift line should pass through the park in the next half hour to forty-five minutes, and there's a strong pressure gradient. It's liable to throw that fire right in McPhee's face."

Annabel felt a cold chill go through her. "Have you advised Captain McPhee of this?"

Skinner shook his head. "Negative. We're on the wrong side of the mountain to contact him. It's blocking our radio signals."

"Send somebody up to the summit," Earl suggested.

"I was about to look for someone to do just that when you two showed up. Feel like volunteering?"

"I'll do it," Annabel and Earl said at the same time.

"Only one of you needs to go. I want the other to stay here in case anything else comes up."

"That's you, Earl," Annabel said. Before he could argue, she spun on her heel and ran back toward the Jeep.

The summit of Mount Diablo would be closer to the fire, and she could at least get a good look at it, she thought as she hurried back to the vehicle and climbed behind the wheel. And someone had to warn Captain McPhee of the impending wind shift. If the smoke-jumpers were already on the ground, they might find themselves facing a much more formidable task than they had expected. That wasn't the worst-case scenario, however. If the wind shifted strongly after they jumped but before they were on the ground, they might find themselves parachuting down into the heart of an inferno.

Earl had taken a few steps after her, she saw as she cranked the Jeep's engine and then backed it up. He probably intended to argue with her. Annabel's foot came down hard on the gas pedal, sending the Jeep spurting forward. In the rearview mirror, she saw Earl wave a big paw in frustrated defeat.

The road to the summit twisted and turned up the side of the mountain in a series of dizzying switchbacks. Annabel took them fast but still tried to be careful; she couldn't deliver the warning to her fellow firefighters if she and the Jeep went tumbling down the side of the mountain. Finally the big, old stone building came into view. Every light in the place seemed to be lit. Annabel wasn't sure, but she thought some of the staff probably lived here now, during tourist season. They would have already been evacuated.

She brought the Jeep to a skidding stop in the parking lot, grabbed the radio, and ran toward the observation deck on the far side of the building. From there, she could see all the way down Mitchell Canyon, and she ought to be able to raise Captain McPhee on the radio without any trouble. She stopped on the observation deck and began repeating urgently, "Calling Tango One-Niner," into the radio.

The canyon spread out before her. Normally in the daytime, it was a beautiful vista, the slopes covered with trees and wildflowers and lush grass, and in the background the lower peaks of the Diablo range falling away to the San Joaquin Valley.

Tonight, though, it was a vision straight out of a nightmare.

Flames were spread across the canyon, some of them in pockets, others in long, seemingly solid sheets. The timber on both sides of the canyon was ablaze, the flames leaping high into the sky. The floor of the canyon was also burning in dozens of places.

In the light of the blaze, Annabel saw the figures of the firefighters down below as they worked with bulldozers, chain saws, and Pulaskis to clear a firebreak. More and more in recent years, specialists in the art of fighting forest fires had come to the conclusion that it was better for the ecology and less risky to human life to contain fires, letting them burn themselves out, than to try to extinguish them. Containment was what the dedicated men and women at the head of the canyon were attempting to achieve tonight.

Annabel lifted her head and turned it to the right and then the left, searching for a touch of breeze. She didn't feel anything. The wind had dropped off to nothing. That sudden stillness was a precursor to the wind shift Captain Skinner had warned her about. She lifted the radio to her mouth and keyed it.

"Tango One-Niner, come in please! Captain McPhee, are you out there?" She broke radio protocol by imploring, "Captain, please answer!"

Static was all that came back from the radio.

Annabel hit the transmit button again. "Captain Skinner? I can't raise Captain McPhee. Captain Skinner?"

No response, just the annoying hiss and crackle.

"Blast it!" Annabel said. She tried the radio again. "Earl? Are you there? Can anybody hear me? Anyone at all?"

Something was very wrong. Either her radio had failed or something was jamming the transmission.

A sudden gust of wind blew over the observation deck from behind her, whipping up a small cloud of dust and grit and sending some discarded pieces of paper swirling into the air. The front was passing, Annabel thought, and she had not succeeded in warning her fellow firefighters about the wind shift.

A fire road ran through the canyon, she recalled. Though the floor of the canyon was burning in quite a few places, the fire wasn't solid down there; the worst of it was still up on the slopes. She might be able to take the Jeep and follow the road, might even make it to the other end of the canyon before the wind strengthened enough to pose a real threat.

"Blast it!" she said again as she turned and ran from the observation deck, around the building, and into the parking lot. She tossed the radio into the Jeep and followed it in. A moment later, she sent the vehicle screeching out of the lot and onto a narrow dirt road that curved around the shoulder of the mountain.

What she was doing went against everything she had been taught. She was taking a chance that Earl, Captain

McPhee, and all the other firefighters on the team would have called foolhardy.

But those men and women were her friends, and they were heading into more trouble than they knew. Annabel had to do anything possible to warn them.

The fire road straightened, and Annabel pressed down hard on the gas pedal. She saw state firefighters on both sides of her. Some of them waved frantically, trying to stop her. Annabel didn't even slow down.

If the road proved to be blocked by fire, she would turn around and come back, she told herself. Of course, there was always the chance that the flames would move across the road behind her after she had passed, cutting off her escape.

In that case, she would just have to hope that she could keep going forward.

It was hard to breathe. The flames were sucking oxygen out of the air. Thick clouds of smoke blew across the road, so thick that the Jeep's headlights couldn't penetrate them. Annabel had to slow down until the smoke cleared enough for her to see. She pulled her goggles and mask on to protect her eyes from the smoke and to keep any more of it from reaching her lungs. She had already inhaled enough of the stuff to make her cough.

Hunched forward over the steering wheel, Annabel kept driving. She came to an area that was temporarily clear of smoke and sped up again, holding tightly to the steering wheel as the vehicle slewed around the road's twists and turns. Off to the right, flames were racing across a meadow toward the road.

Annabel shot past the fire just before it reached the road and entered a grove of juniper trees that were burning. She gasped for air.

Suddenly, from the corner of her eye she saw one of the tall junipers toppling toward the road. Punching the gas, she sent the Jeep leaping ahead. The blazing tree crashed across the road right behind the speeding vehicle.

Annabel's heartbeat raced even faster at the narrowness of her escape.

But more trees were falling ahead of her. There was no way she could make it through. She jammed on the brakes to avoid smashing into one of the junipers as it crashed to earth directly in front of her. The Jeep fishtailed madly. Annabel spun the wheel, trying to bring the vehicle under control. She spotted an opening in the trees and tried to point the Jeep toward it. She was going to have to leave the road and try to make her way across country. With any luck, she could rejoin the road farther down the valley.

That was the plan, anyway. The Jeep shot off the road and was airborne for a split second as it hurtled over a ditch at the side of the road. Then it landed with a bounce, slid sideways, and started to tip over. Annabel had been in such a hurry earlier she hadn't fastened her seat belt, and suddenly she felt herself thrown into the air like a rag doll.

She spun crazily, with blackness and flames alternating around her, willing herself to go limp.

Then she hit the ground, and the flames seemed to go away. All Annabel was aware of was the blackness of night, welling up and engulfing her. . . .

Chapter 2

THE COUGHING WOKE her up.

Spasms shook her body so violently that she had no choice except to regain consciousness. With returning awareness came the heat, fierce waves of it breaking over her. Annabel forced her head up and her eyes open.

Flames were all around her, making the burning forest as bright as high noon. Smoke clogged the air and her lungs. The paucity of oxygen made her want to draw deeper breaths, but she knew that to do so would only force more of the smoke into her body. She fought down the impulse.

She looked around and spotted the overturned Jeep about ten yards away. It wasn't going to do her any good. Being thrown clear was the only thing that had saved her life, she realized. If she had been belted into the vehicle it would have landed on top of her, crushing her.

But that freakish bit of luck wasn't going to her any good unless she could somehow get away from the flames. Annabel pushed herself onto her hands and knees, then heaved herself to her feet. She staggered a couple of steps to one side before she was able to catch herself. Her head was spinning. She laid her hand on the trunk of a tree that had not yet caught fire, bracing herself there for a few seconds until things settled down inside her brain. She tried to take stock of herself. There didn't seem to be any broken bones, and she had feeling in all her extremities. No injuries other than minor cuts and bruises.

If she could find a stream, she might be able to use it for refuge from the flames. She tried to remember the details of the park and wished she'd had a chance to study a map of the area before venturing out here.

One thing was certain: If she stayed where she was, she would die. Movement was the key to her survival.

She stumbled away from the tree where she had been leaning. After only a couple of steps, she tripped on something and almost fell. She looked down and saw the portable radio. Moving carefully so as not to lose her balance, she bent over and picked it up. It hadn't been working earlier, but maybe it was now. Maybe she could call for help.

She turned the volume knob all the way up so she could hear over the crackling and roaring of the flames. At first there was only static from the radio, but then Annabel caught a few words in a distorted voice. She pressed the radio against her ear and waited for the voice to speak again.

"Tango One-Niner, come back."

That was Earl's voice, Annabel thought excitedly. He was calling Captain McPhee.

". . . firebreak established . . . under control . . . pretty bad for a few . . . One-Niner . . ."

And that was Captain McPhee himself. The transmission was cutting in and out, but Annabel had heard enough of it to know that the smoke-jumpers were all right. They must have been on the ground before the wind shift hit. They would have found themselves facing a bigger job than they expected, but clearly, they had coped with it just fine.

Earl's voice came again. *". . . can't find . . . Jeep's gone. . . ."*

They were talking about her, Annabel realized. Earl must have gotten up to the summit of Mount Diablo somehow. That was probably where he was now.

She pressed the transmit button and said, "Earl! Earl, I'm here! I'm all right, but I need help!"

". . . could she have gone?"

". . . the canyon, maybe. I'll go . . ."

"Stay where you are, Tabor . . . an order."

Earl wanted to come looking for her, and McPhee was ordering him not to. That was the right thing to do, Annabel suddenly realized. She didn't want Earl or any of the other smoke-jumpers risking their lives because of her recklessness.

She keyed the mike again and said, "Guys, I'm all right. I'll try to make it to the firebreak at the other end of the canyon. Keep an eye out for me."

There was no response. Judging by that, and the exchange she had overheard earlier, her transmissions weren't making it out of the canyon. This unit definitely had a problem, and getting thrown out of the Jeep probably hadn't helped it.

So she was on her own, Annabel told herself. Whether she lived or died depended entirely on her. And she wasn't ready to give up.

She walked forward to the Jeep and retrieved her Pulaski and an asbestos fire blanket, both of which had been tossed out of the vehicle during the crash. She looked around until she thought she had herself oriented, then started trotting briskly toward the mouth of the canyon—at least, she hoped that was where she was headed.

Exhaustion and smoke quickly took their tolls on her. She had to dodge around areas of the fire, which meant she could never go more than fifty yards or so in a straight line. Weaving back and forth as she was, she had a hard time knowing if she was still going in the right direction. She had her mask over her nose and mouth to block out some of the smoke, but it couldn't filter all of the noxious stuff.

Suddenly, there were nothing but flames in front of her. The various patches of fire had finally all joined together in this spot, stretching from one side of the canyon to the other. Annabel came to a stop and stared at the massive blaze, feeling her heart sink as she did so. She knew now she wouldn't be able to make it to the mouth of the canyon. Her only hope would be to find someplace to hide from the flames.

She turned to her left, knowing that the results of whatever she did now were pretty much up to the workings of fate. For several minutes, she ran parallel to the wall of flame. At least the wind was blowing it away from her, she thought. But there were fires in the other direction, too, and they were coming closer to her with each passing second. Eventually they would hem her in, and there would be no place to run.

She realized she was going up a hill; at first she hadn't even noticed the slope. In the light of the fire, she saw that the hillside was covered with wildflowers, flowers whose fragile beauty would soon be consumed by the hungry flames.

It was then she noticed the dark opening in the side of the hill.

Annabel angled toward it, recognizing it for what it was: the mouth of a cave. If it was big enough for her to get inside, and deep enough that the worst of the heat wouldn't penetrate to the far end of it, she might be able to ride out the fire there. That was just about her only chance.

The opening was narrow, less than a yard wide, and only a couple of feet high. Annabel knelt in front of it and thrust the Pulaski inside as far as she could reach. It occurred to her that there might be a bear or some other wild animal denned up in there, in which case the cave's occupant probably wouldn't want to share. But she encountered nothing except empty air with the Pulaski, and when she moved it back and forth she could tell that the cave widened a bit as it went deeper into the hillside.

That was encouraging. Annabel turned around so that she could back into the hole. Pushing herself along with her elbows and toes, she scooted backward into the cave. When she was completely inside, she opened up the fire blanket and spread it over the opening. That would help keep out more of the heat.

The blanket also cut out the light from the flames, leaving Annabel in utter darkness. She fought down the fear that began to well up inside her. Still, she could sense the walls of the cave pressing in all around her, and she experienced a moment of panic.

"Funny," she muttered. "I never knew I was claustrophobic."

With an effort of will, she conquered her fears and kept moving backward in the cave. Checking from side to side with the Pulaski, she discovered that it did indeed grow larger, until it was about five feet wide and the ceiling had risen another foot. Annabel remembered a phrase from her childhood: *snug as a bug in a rug.* She felt no bigger than a bug, surrounded as she was by such tremendous forces of nature.

The air around her grew cooler as she retreated into the cave. It smelled of rich earth rather than acrid smoke, and several deep breaths of it seemed to soothe Annabel's tortured lungs. When the soles of her boots hit the back wall of the cave, she estimated that she was at least twenty feet inside the hill. That might be enough, she told herself hopefully. At least she had a chance to survive now. The worst of the fire would have passed her by in an hour, and she knew there was enough air in the cave to last that long.

She could still hear the roaring of the flames, and it grew louder as the conflagration reached the hillside and swept over it. Annabel squeezed her eyes shut and tried not to cry. Those wildflowers, she knew, were nothing but charred wisps of ash by now. She dug her fingers into the soft earth of the cave floor as the heat grew worse.

It was bad, but not unbearable. Time seemed to stretch

out, and as unbelievable as it would seem to her later, Annabel actually dozed off for a short time.

When she awoke, it was with a jolt, as if something had shifted around her. Her head jerked up and she gasped, blinking in the darkness. Her heart was pounding. She could hear it like a drumbeat in her brain.

It took a moment before she realized that she could hear her pulse so clearly because the sound of the fire was gone. No more roaring, no crackling and popping and trees exploding in the heat. The heat was gone from the cave, too. In fact, the air was cool, almost chilly.

And when Annabel looked toward the mouth of the cave, she could see light seeping around the edges of the fire blanket. Not the reddish glare of flames, but the warm, rich glow of sunlight.

Had she slept until morning? That was hard to believe, but it was the only sensible explanation. That meant her fellow smoke-jumpers were probably out there in the canyon, searching for her. They had probably given up hope that she had survived the blaze, but they wouldn't leave one of their own behind. They would recover her body, no matter how long it took.

They were going to be surprised when she turned up alive, Annabel thought with a tired smile. She started crawling toward the mouth of the cave.

She expected to smell smoke and ashes as she approached the entrance, but instead there was a sweet fragrance in the air. Annabel frowned. She would have sworn that the fire had swept over this hillside, but perhaps it had been spared after all. She had seen some odd things happen in the middle of forest fires, such as little spots that were surrounded by devastation somehow remaining untouched by the flames. Maybe that was what had happened here.

But nothing in her experience had prepared Annabel for the sight that met her eyes when she reached out, took hold of the fire blanket, and pulled it aside.

Brilliant, early morning sunlight flooded in around her.

Annabel flinched from it, squinting her eyes against the brightness. She blinked rapidly as her vision adjusted to the light, then levered herself forward on her elbows so that she could stick her head out of the cave mouth.

Instead of being surrounded by the grayness of ashes and death, everywhere around her was the vividness of life.

The trees were green and tall, the grass thick and lush. Annabel gasped as she looked at the carpet of wildflowers on the hillside. Swaying back and forth in the sweet-smelling breeze that brushed them, they formed a rainbow of colors.

For a moment, as she stared at the verdant beauty all around her, Annabel thought she was hallucinating. Then she thought wildly that she had died, and this was heaven.

But she could feel the dirt under her fingers and the warmth of the sunshine and the breeze on her face. She knew beyond a shadow of a doubt that she was alive.

But . . . but how was it possible? How could she be seeing what she was seeing? The night before, nearly all of Mitchell Canyon had been consumed by fire. It was impossible that the next morning it could be so . . . so pristine, untouched by the flames.

Annabel closed her eyes again, and kept them shut for a long moment. When she opened them, she saw the same things she had earlier. The trees, the grass, the flowers . . . and birds, sitting in the trees and singing, as squirrels darted from branch to branch.

Reaching behind her in the cave, Annabel felt around until her hand fell on the radio. She took it with her as she crawled out of the cave, but left her Pulaski, fire blanket, and mask inside. Shakily, she climbed to her feet and tried the radio.

Nothing, not even static. She tried calling, "Earl? Captain McPhee? Anybody?" but there was no response. It was dead. With a grimace of disgust, Annabel turned and pitched it lightly back into the cave.

Well, she told herself, no matter what the explanation

was for the impossible unburned condition of the terrain around her, one thing was certain. . . . She was going to have to walk out of the canyon. There was no other way. She turned around, surveying her surroundings, and had no trouble locating Mount Diablo. With that landmark to go by, she was able to approximate the direction in which the fire road lay. She started toward it, and she had gone about a hundred yards before she remembered that she had left everything inside the cave. She hesitated, debating whether to go back and retrieve the gear, then decided against it. She was filthy and exhausted. She could always come back for the stuff later.

After a little while, she reached the place where she remembered having crashed the Jeep. From what little she recalled of the chaos from the night before, the spot looked familiar. But the Jeep wasn't there, and there was no sign of a wreck of any sort. Obviously, she had gotten turned around, Annabel told herself. Considering the circumstances, that would have been easy enough to do.

Nor was the fire road where she thought it would be. Frowning, she stopped and peered around. Could she have gotten so mixed up that she didn't know where she was? The general outlines of Mitchell Canyon looked familiar enough, but there was nothing else to go by.

She turned toward Mount Diablo. Surely there would be people at the summit, and with any luck the phones would be working. She could call Earl on his cell phone and let him know where she was.

Walking up the canyon was a lot slower going than driving down had been the night before. After an hour, she didn't seem to be much closer to Mount Diablo than she had been when she started. She didn't see any signs of civilization, and did not encounter anyone who was looking for her. Had they all forgotten about her?

She was being irrational, she told herself. But there was still no evidence of a forest fire's having ravaged its way through the canyon less than twelve hours earlier. Annabel knew that most ecologies could repair themselves after a fire, but not in a matter of hours!

She hiked to the peak of a ridge and almost stumbled in the deep ruts of a road that ran atop it.

She didn't recall this road from any of the maps she had seen of the park, but right now, Annabel didn't care. She was just glad to see something that told her she was still in the real world. As she looked at the ruts, however, she was surprised at how narrow they were. Could a truck or a car have made them?

A loud braying sound made her cry out involuntarily in surprise. She spun around to face the sound as it came again.

A hundred yards away, around a bend in the road, came a wagon being drawn by a team of mules. There were six of the animals, and as they came closer, they continued to bray at each other. The man sitting on the driver's seat popped a short whip over the heads of the mules and shouted at them. Annabel couldn't make out all the words the man was using, but the ones she understood were colorfully obscene.

Suddenly, the man stopped yelling and hauled back on the reins, bringing the mules to an abrupt halt. He sat there, staring straight ahead, and Annabel knew he had spotted her. Clearly, he was surprised to see her there. She started walking quickly toward the wagon.

As she drew nearer, she saw the load of logs stacked in the back of the wagon. There were a lot of them, explaining why the ruts in the road were so deep. What Annabel didn't understand was why the wagon was carrying a load of logs in the first place. Logging wasn't allowed in the park.

Maybe this man was poaching, illegally cutting down trees in some sort of shady deal with one of the timber companies. Maybe she was just asking for trouble by approaching him.

But right now, she was desperate for contact with another human being who could perhaps explain all the strange things going on around her. She broke into a jog.

The man stood up on the wagon seat. He was big and broad-shouldered, wearing a flannel shirt with the sleeves rolled up on his brawny forearms. He had an old hat with a broad, floppy brim crammed on his head. As Annabel approached, the man reached up and tugged the hat off, revealing a shock of blond hair. His eyes were a pale blue, and they were wide with confusion and puzzlement as Annabel came up to the wagon.

"Can you help me?" she asked.

"Uh . . . I reckon I can try, ma'am," he said. He didn't look particularly threatening, despite his size and obvious strength.

"You don't happen to have a cell phone on you, do you?"

The man wiped the back of his hand across his mouth. "I don't think so," he said hesitantly.

"Well, I could sure use a ride out of here, then."

"Yes'm. I can do that." He clapped his hat back on his head and reached down. "Let me give you a hand."

With the man's help, Annabel climbed onto the wagon seat. She sank down on it gratefully. The man sat beside her, shot a glance at her from the corners of his eyes, then picked up the reins and flapped them to get the mules moving again. Stubbornly, they stayed where they were, standing stolidly in the center of the road.

"If you don't mind, ma'am, could you hand me that whip?"

"Sure." Annabel picked it up from the floorboard and handed it to the driver.

He smiled a little and said, "Might want to cover your ears. These jugheads don't respond too well unless you cuss at 'em a while first."

Being in a profession that was still largely male-dominated, Annabel had heard plenty of highly fluent profanity. But she sensed that the driver would be somehow disappointed in her if she didn't do as he asked, so she put her hands over her ears and said, "All right, go ahead."

The driver popped the whip and yelled at the mules until they strained against their harness and sent the wagon lurching into motion. Annabel swayed back and forth on the seat as it rocked over the rugged ruts. Once the mules were moving, the driver stopped shouting.

Annabel lowered her hands and asked, "Where are you headed?"

"Oakland," the man replied. "Got to deliver these logs to the ferry there."

Why ferry the logs across the bay when they could be loaded on a truck and driven over the Bay Bridge? Annabel asked herself. She didn't voice the question, however. Instead, she introduced herself to the burly Good Samaritan beside her. "I'm Annabel Lowell."

"Herman Simmons is my name. Pleased to meet you, Miz Lowell." He was still glancing suspiciously at her from time to time. "Those are, uh, mighty bright overalls you got on."

"It's a fire suit. I'm a smoke-jumper for the Forest Service."

For a moment, Herman was quiet. Then he grunted, "Uh-huh."

He doesn't have a clue what I'm talking about, Annabel told herself. He didn't seem mentally challenged, but she supposed it was possible. Still, if he would take her to Oakland, she didn't much care.

"You don't mind taking me all the way to Oakland, do you?" she asked.

"No, ma'am. You from there?"

"San Francisco."

"Oh. Well, I reckon you can catch the ferry in Oakland, right enough."

"Or call a cab."

Herman said "Uh-huh" again, the same as before.

After a few minutes of silence, Annabel risked saying, "I didn't know there was any logging going on in the park."

"In the canyon, you mean? Yeah, we been workin' it for

a while. This really ain't as good country for timber as up north a ways, though, so I don't 'spect we'll be here long."

"What company are you with?" Annabel felt a little guilty pumping him for information this way. He was helping her, and she might have to turn around and testify against him and his fellow workers if they were charged with illegal logging.

"Amalgamated Timber," Herman replied.

Annabel had never heard of the company. It was probably a pretty small outfit, she supposed, especially considering that it engaged in illicit deals like this one. She supposed she could look the other way about the company's activities, but that would go against the grain for her. It was the job of the Forest Service to help protect the environment.

The wagon continued to rock along. The crude road twisted and turned and finally swung northwest as it left the Diablos and headed toward Oakland. Progress was slow, and around midday, Herman said, "I got some sandwiches in a bag under the seat. I'd be happy to share 'em with you, ma'am."

Just the mention of food made Annabel aware of how long it had been since she had eaten. Suddenly ravenously hungry, she reached under the seat and found the bag of sandwiches. "Thank you, Herman," she said. "Are you sure you don't need all of them yourself?"

"No, ma'am, you go right ahead."

"All right . . . on the condition that you stop calling me ma'am. My name is Annabel."

"Well, uh . . . all right . . . Annabel." He was blushing furiously.

Annabel smiled and took out one of the sandwiches, thick slabs of roast beef between slices of what appeared to be homemade bread. She ate eagerly.

She kept expecting the wagon to reach a highway, but the only roads they crossed were dirt paths much like the one they were following. Tilting her head back, Annabel looked up at the blue sky overhead, searching for airplanes. Now that she thought about it, she hadn't seen a plane all day.

"Herman," she said, "why don't you use a truck to haul these logs?"

"A truck?" he repeated with a frown, then a second later said, "Oh, you mean one o' them newfangled gasoline things. Why, they won't get up in the mountains where we're workin', and besides, they ain't nowhere near as dependable as a good team of mules."

New-fangled gasoline things? Poor old Herman really had spent too much time back in the woods, Annabel thought.

But yet, she asked herself, worry beginning to tickle at the back of her brain, where were the roads? Where were the airplanes? And the power lines and the cell phone towers and all the other reminders of modern life?

What had happened while she was waiting out the forest fire in that cave?

By mid-afternoon, the wagon had reached another road that, while still dirt, was wider and harder-packed. As she and Herman rolled on toward Oakland, Annabel saw several other wagons and a few men on horseback. She still had not seen any sort of motorized vehicle.

A tiny clamor began to sound inside her head. Something was very, very wrong. She had either lost her mind, or . . . or . . . She didn't know what to think.

She looked for the haze of pollution that often hung over Oakland, but the sky was clear as she peered toward the west, toward the ocean. They passed several large farms, a grove of redwood trees, and quite a few clusters of oaks. Nestled in the trees were large, Mediterranean-style villas, most of which appeared to be quite new. Some of them even looked slightly familiar to Annabel. She was beginning to feel dizzy.

Things just got worse as Herman drove the wagon on through town to the waterfront. The streets were paved now, but with cobblestones instead of asphalt. Annabel saw a few cars—black, ugly-looking things with wire wheels and motors that spit and sputtered. *Model A's,* she thought. The only cars on the streets of Oakland were Ford Model A's. Most of the vehicles were still horse-drawn.

Worst of all, when she looked where the Bay Bridge should have been, there was nothing, only the choppy expanse of San Francisco Bay. And when she peered across the bay to San Francisco, she searched in vain for the Transamerica Tower and all the other downtown skyscrapers. The general outlines of the city were the same; she had no trouble spotting Telegraph Hill, Russian Hill, and Nob Hill, but everything else was different.

She really *was* crazy, or . . .

"Herman," she managed to say thickly as he brought the wagon to a stop near a dock where a ferry was berthed, "what's the date today?"

"The date? Lemme see. . . . It's, uh . . . March sixth, I think."

"Of what year?"

"Why, 1906, of course."

With a groan, Annabel did something she'd sworn she'd never do.

She fainted.

Chapter 3

COLE BRADY MADE an effort not to tap his foot impatiently as he stood on the dock and watched the ferry chug its way across the waters of San Francisco Bay. He took his pocket watch from his vest and flipped it open, checking the time. Almost three o'clock. Knowing that just made him more impatient, he realized as he stowed the watch back in his vest pocket. His meeting over here in Oakland had run late, and he would have to hurry to be at the station in time for his shift.

He stretched and then stifled a yawn. He had been on duty last night, of course, and then had come over here on the ferry after only a couple of hours of sleep. It was a good thing he was a relatively young man, he thought, or he wouldn't have been able to stand up to all the demands on his time.

You could give some of it up, Cole told himself. But he knew, even as the thought went through his head, that it would mean giving up what he liked best in his life. The San Francisco Fire Department could get along without him; Brady Enterprises couldn't.

He thumbed back the derby he wore on his thick brown

hair. It would be good to get out of this tweed suit and into his uniform. Of course, the blue woolen uniform wasn't any cooler or more comfortable than the suit; Cole just felt more at home in it. When he got duded up like this, he always felt a little like a boy dressing in his father's clothes and pretending to be something he wasn't. In some ways, he thought, that was exactly the case. Thomas Brady was the businessman who had built a small company into something that could almost be called an empire. Cole had inherited that business, but he wondered sometimes if he would ever feel that it was truly his.

A harsh shout broke into Cole's reverie. He wheeled around and saw a burly man in a flannel shirt standing next to a wagon full of logs. The man was yelling, "Hey, I need some help over here! Somebody fetch a doc!"

Cole wasn't a doctor, but he started striding toward the man anyway. The man was cradling a figure in his arms. The sight had caught Cole's attention right away.

The person being held by the man was an unconscious woman.

A crowd was beginning to gather, so Cole caught only glimpses of the woman through gaps between the hurrying people. He saw the long brown hair that hung down her back, the pale, finely featured face, and the strange-looking garment she wore. It was like a pair of long-sleeved overalls, and it was bright yellow. The legs of it were tucked into high-topped, laced-up brown boots. Cole had never seen a getup like that before, and certainly not on a woman.

He shouldered his way through the crowd until he reached the side of the man who had called for help. "What's going on here?" he asked.

"Your guess is as good as mine, mister," the man replied. "I was just talkin' to this lady, and she up and swooned. Fell right off my wagon, she did."

"Who is she?"

"Told me her name was Annabel, but I never saw her

before today. I run into her over in the Diablos, while I was haulin' out this load of logs."

Cole whipped off his coat, looked around for a fairly clean spot, then bunched up the garment so it could serve as a pillow of sorts. "Let's lay her down," he suggested as he took hold of the woman's right arm.

Carefully, the two men stretched the woman out on the pavement. Cole tucked the folded-up coat under her head. She had black smudges on her face and hands, he saw, and if he had been in a different line of work, he might have mistaken them for streaks of dirt.

But those marks weren't dirt. They were smudges of ash. This woman had been around a fire, and recently, too.

Several members of the crowd were debating about the woman's odd clothing and the question of whether they ought to send for a doctor. Cole looked at them impatiently and snapped, "Give her some air! That's what she needs." He hoped he was right. He picked up her limp right arm and began massaging the wrist.

Suddenly, the woman stirred. Her eyes opened, and Cole found himself looking down into one of the most luminous sets of brown eyes he had ever seen. Even surrounded by that pale, ash-streaked face, there was so much beauty in those eyes that Cole felt himself catching his breath.

"What . . . who . . ."

Cole rested a hand on her shoulder to hold her down as she started to bolt upright. "Take it easy," he told her. "You fainted. You need to rest for a minute."

Her eyes—*those eyes!*—flicked from side to side. Her gaze darted past Cole, and the woman said tentatively, "Herman?"

The burly man in the flannel shirt knelt on her other side. "Right here, Miss Annabel."

"Did . . . did you say it was March sixth?"

"Yes, ma'am."

"March sixth, 1906?"

Herman nodded. "Yes, ma'am, that's what I said."

The woman's head sank back down on the makeshift pillow, and her eyes closed. "That's what I thought you said," she murmured.

Cole ran his gaze down her body, hoping he wasn't being too brazen as he did so. He didn't see any blood on the strange-looking yellow suit, and the woman's arms and legs didn't seem to be twisted at any unusual angles. There were some scratches on her face, along with a couple of bruises, but as far as he could tell, she wasn't badly injured.

"Did she hit her head when she fell off the wagon?" Cole asked Herman.

The burly man shook his head. "Not that I saw. But she could have before I run into her in the woods. She's been talkin' kind of crazy ever since I picked her up."

One of the men in the crowd leaned over and asked, "Do you want me to fetch a sawbones or not?"

Annabel's eyes flew open again. "No!" she cried, and this time she was able to sit up despite Cole's hand on her shoulder. She heaved a deep breath, then said in a calmer tone, "No, I don't need a doctor. I'm all right."

"Looks to me like you've been through the wringer," Cole observed. "Let me give you a hand up, if you feel like standing."

"Th-thank you." Annabel clasped his hand, and he helped her to her feet. She was almost as tall as he was, which was somewhat unusual. He picked up his coat, shook it out, and put it back on.

"Well, I got to deliver these logs," Herman said quickly, with a glance toward the dock, where the ferry had come in unnoticed amidst the commotion. "Since the lady's in good hands and all."

"Wait a minute," Cole started to say, but Herman had already turned away and was climbing onto his wagon. He didn't look back. The crowd was breaking up, too.

Cole didn't have time to be saddled with some strange woman, either, but when he glanced at Annabel and saw how lost and alone she looked, he knew he had no choice in the matter. He couldn't leave her here on the docks by herself when there was a chance she was out of her head, or injured, or both. The least he could do was see her safely home.

"Where do you live, ma'am?"

"Where do I live?" she repeated. Her voice had a hollow sound to it. She closed her eyes, gave a little shake of her head, and then opened them again to say, "San Francisco. I live in San Francisco."

"Well, you're lucky, because that's where I'm going. I'll see that you get home all right." He took her arm and turned her gently toward the dock. "Let's catch that ferry."

He felt her muscles stiffen a little under his touch. He wasn't trying to be forward. Surely she understood that.

"I can get home all right by myself," she said. She wasn't afraid of him at all, Cole sensed.

"I insist. Come on." He could be just as stubborn as she apparently was, especially once he had committed to a course of action.

She held back a second longer, then with a shrug relaxed slightly and went with him. He led her over to the line of people waiting to board the ferry. They drew a lot of curious looks, and he knew it was because of the way she was dressed.

"That's a colorful outfit you've got on," he commented once they were on board and standing next to the railing.

"It's a firefighter's suit," she said without looking at him. She was staring across the waters of the bay at San Francisco as if hoping to see something that wasn't there.

"Really?" The exclamation was jolted out of Cole in surprise. "I'm a fireman."

That got her attention. She turned her head slowly and looked at him, really looked at him for perhaps the first time. "You are?"

He held out his hand to her. "Cole Brady, Engine Company Twenty-one."

She took his hand and said, "Annabel Lowell."

"I'm pleased to meet you, Miss Lowell." The ferry pulled away from the dock, and Cole went on, "If you don't mind my asking, how did you come to be wearing some sort of fireman's suit?"

"Fire*fighter's*—," she began, then stopped abruptly. After a second, she went on, "It's mine."

"Yours?"

"That's right." There was a hint of defiance in her eyes as she looked at him. They were still the prettiest eyes he had ever seen.

Cole smiled. "I'd heard that New York had itself a lady fireman now, but I never figured to run into her out here. I didn't know about that fancy new uniform, either. And I thought you said you live in San Francisco."

"I do," Annabel said. "I'm not from New York."

"Then I'm afraid I don't understand."

"Neither do I," Annabel said. "But I'm afraid I'm beginning to."

All right, Annabel thought as she tightly grasped the ferry's railing and stared out over the water, it was time to pull a Scully and come up with a rational explanation for all this . . . this lunacy. Time travel was *not* possible. Was it?

Of course not. But then how to explain why everyone around her thought it was 1906? And where were the Bay Bridge and the Transamerica Tower and all the other landmarks that she was so used to seeing?

Annabel took a deep breath. Mass hysteria. That had to be it. For some unknown reason, everyone around her had gone delusional, and it was contagious, so she was seeing the same things they all *thought* they were seeing. But it was all hallucination. She was probably in an ambulance right now, not on a ferry—

Cold spray pelted her in the face.

"Whoa!" Cole Brady exclaimed beside her. "Better step back, Miss Lowell. If we keep on standing this close to the rail, we'll be soaked by the time we get across the bay."

He put his hand on her arm, and Annabel fought down the impulse to jerk it away. She knew he was just trying to help her. There was the fact that he claimed to be a member of the SFFD, too, although he wasn't in uniform at the moment. She didn't want to insult a fellow firefighter . . . even if he was crazy enough to think it was 1906.

"All right," she said. "Let's get out of the spray."

She pried her fingers off the railing and allowed him to steer her across the deck toward the superstructure of the ferry. Round metal tables were bolted to the deck in places, and some of the passengers were sitting at them having drinks. Despite the chill that always hung over the bay, the atmosphere was almost festive.

Cole found an empty table. "Let's sit down."

Annabel hesitated, then nodded. She was aware of the discreet stares being directed toward her, no doubt because of the way she was dressed. Maybe, she hoped, her clothes would be less noticeable if she was seated.

Cole held her chair for her—he was a gentleman, of course; what man in 1906 wouldn't be?—and then sat down across from her. He took off his derby and placed it on a chair. The breeze ruffled his brown hair a little.

She looked at him. He was a handsome man, in a rugged way. Not pretty, by any means; the lines and angles of his face were too prominent for that. His eyes were blue and had a few smile lines around their corners. They weren't really deep-set, but his broad forehead made them seem slightly so. The line of his jaw showed strength and determination. There was a tiny dimple in the center of his chin, so small that it was barely visible. And his ears stuck out a little, not enough to be funny-looking, but enough that Annabel noticed them.

She hadn't paid that much attention to the way he was built while he was standing, but now that he was sitting, and all she could see was the upper part of his torso, she noticed that his chest and shoulders filled the tweed suit coat and white shirt quite nicely. His hands lay at rest on the table, the fingers long and strong-looking, as well as rather blunt on the tips. They were hands that could easily wield an ax or control a fire hose, Annabel found herself thinking. And yet they had a certain delicacy about them, too, as if their touch under the right circumstances could be light and caressing. . . .

"Well," Cole asked, "do I pass inspection?"

Suddenly, Annabel felt her face growing warm. True, she probably had been staring at him, but he didn't have to call her on it. She didn't know whether to be angry or embarrassed, and finally settled for a little bit of both. She said, "Hey, don't think I didn't notice *you* checking *me* out earlier."

Instantly, he was contrite. "I meant no offense, Miss Lowell—"

She waved off his apology and said, "That's all right. I'm used to it."

That was true. Ever since she had entered her teens, she had been tall and athletic, with the sort of body that naturally drew men's eyes. In fact, she had been told more than once that she was wasting her looks by being a firefighter.

She summoned up a smile as she went on. "Anyway, you pass inspection just fine, Mr. Brady. You said you're a . . . fireman?" She was careful to use his word this time.

"That's right," he said with a nod. "Engine Company Twenty-one. We call ourselves the Eagle Company. Back in the days when all San Francisco had were volunteer fire companies, they all had names like that."

What he was saying sounded familiar somehow, and it took Annabel only a moment to recall that she had heard similar stories from Earl Tabor. Earl knew everything there was to know about the history of San Francisco, especially concerning the San Francisco Fire Department. If anyone was going to go back in time, Annabel thought, it should have been Earl and not her.

That mental reminder of her circumstances made her stiffen. There was that pesky time travel business again.

She had almost forgotten about it for a second as she talked to Cole Brady. She suddenly wished she had paid more attention to Earl's impromptu history lessons over the years. If she knew more about San Francisco's past, she might be able to tell if her surroundings were accurate. If there were flaws in the illusion, if this was just a distorted version of what she thought San Francisco might have been like, then she would *know* that it was all in her imagination.

Maybe she was back there in the cave, dreaming the whole thing.

The cave! She remembered the wrenching sensation that had woken her from her sleep. That was when it must have happened, she told herself. That was when the very fabric of time and space had shifted around her and thrown her back over ninety years in time. . . .

"Pseudoscientific gibberish," she muttered.

"Beg your pardon?" Cole asked, leaning forward a little and frowning in concern.

Annabel waved a hand again and said, "Nothing. I'm just trying to make sense of everything."

"That's hard to do sometimes, isn't it?"

"Damn right."

The words were barely out of her mouth before she saw his eyes widen a little in surprise. Of course, she told herself. It was 1906. He wasn't used to such blunt talk from a woman. In this day and age, women were supposed to be demure, soft-spoken creatures whose only concerns were frills and lace.

Baby, Cole Brady would have been in for a shock, she mused, if he had found himself in her era instead of the other way around!

That thought brought a laugh bubbling to Annabel's lips, and she said, "I'm really freaking you out, aren't I?"

Cole toyed with the brim of his derby for a minute before he said diplomatically, "I'm not completely sure what you're asking, but I reckon it's safe to say I find you a tad . . . uncommon, Miss Lowell."

"Well, at least you didn't say I was crazy. I suppose I should be thankful for that."

He was looking worried again. "Maybe when we get to the Ferry House, it would be a good idea to take you to see a doctor after all. You could have been hurt—"

"Hit my head and lost my mind, you mean?" Annabel shook her head. "No, I'm fine. I don't have amnesia, and my mental processes are quite clear, thank you."

"Well, if you're sure . . ."

Annabel looked down at the fire suit and said, "What I could really use is a bath and some clean clothes."

Cole started blushing. He was probably thinking about her in a bathtub, Annabel realized. That was sweet.

Clothes were going to be a problem, she suddenly thought. If this was really 1906—and while she wasn't ready to admit that it was, she supposed she had no choice except to proceed as if it were true—then her apartment wouldn't be there. The building might be; she wasn't sure when it had been constructed. But all of her clothes and her other belongings certainly wouldn't be.

Which meant she didn't have any money or other resources, either. What she had on her represented the sum total of her earthly possessions.

That was a sobering realization. How was she going to function in this era with no money, no job, no friends?

That last thought made her glance once more at Cole Brady. He had befriended her—or at least, taken pity on the poor madwoman he no doubt thought her to be. The idea of accepting even more help from him went against the grain for her; she had always taken care of herself. But until she figured out exactly what was going on and what to do about it, she had to have *somebody* on her side. And Cole seemed like a nice enough man. She might feel guilty for taking advantage of his gentlemanly nature, but there was nothing else she could do, Annabel decided.

"I . . . I really hate to impose on your generosity, Mr. Brady," she said, trying to phrase her words carefully so that she wouldn't accidentally slip in any end-of-the-millennium, postmodern brittleness, "but I find myself in a . . . a vexing situation."

"I'll be glad to do whatever I can to help, Miss Lowell."

She took a deep breath. "I said that I live in San Francisco, but the truth is I . . . I really don't have a place to stay. And I only have a little money."

Two twenties tucked inside her billfold, in fact, and they wouldn't do her a bit of good here because they were those blasted newly designed bills that looked like Monopoly money. No one in this day and age would recognize them as the real thing. And her credit cards were now just worthless pieces of plastic.

"So, if you . . . if you could do me the kindness of a small loan," she went on, "I would appreciate it so much. I swear to you, I'm not a . . . a gold digger or anything like that." Was that word in use yet? she asked herself. Or did it date from the Roaring Twenties or some other era? Blast it, she wasn't an expert on words!

"No, I didn't think you were," Cole said with a smile. "Although an outfit like that might help keep you warm in the Yukon."

She didn't bother with correcting him. Instead she continued, "It would just be a loan, just until I get on my feet. But I'll have to find a place to live, and buy some clothes, and get a job. . . ."

Why? she abruptly asked herself. Why would she have to do all those things? She wasn't planning on *staying* here in 1906, was she? Why couldn't she just go back up into the Diablos and find that cave again and crawl inside it? Maybe when she crawled out again, she would be back in her own time. If the cave had worked one way, why not the other?

And if it didn't, so what? Would she be any worse off than she was now?

But she was so tired and dirty. What harm would it do to wait a while before trying that experiment? Then too, there was a chance she would go further back in time, and that wasn't something she wanted to try.

"One thing at a time," Cole was saying as Annabel came out of her brief reverie. He pointed. "There's the Ferry House. Let's go ashore."

Annabel looked and saw a huge building on the shore with docks jutting out from it into the bay and a square clock tower rising above it. She recognized it immediately as the headquarters of the Port Commission—at least, that was what it was in the era she came from. Now, it was obviously the terminus of the ferry line.

The ferry's pilot brought the big boat to a smooth stop next to one of the docks. Annabel and Cole joined the throng of people disembarking. He linked his arm with hers as they were jostled by the crowd, and she didn't pull away. Instead, she found the warmth and strength of his touch comforting.

They made their way through the crowded, high-ceilinged lobby of the Ferry House, and as they emerged from the Market Street side of the building, Annabel caught her breath at the sight of a dozen or more cable cars lined up in bays along the front of the building. Rail lines stretched out and veered this way and that, and Annabel judged that a person could take a cable car to almost anywhere in the city from here. That had been the chief means of public transportation in 1906, she recalled. Even someone not steeped in the history of the city knew that.

"All right," Cole said. "I think the first thing to do is get you some more suitable clothing. I'm, uh, not an expert on women's clothing, you know, but there are some good shops downtown, I'm sure. . . ."

"You're certain you don't mind helping me?"

"How can I refuse?" He held up a hand, palm out. "But I assure you, Miss Lowell, I have no, ah, improper designs."

"Of course not," she agreed. Although she might not have minded if he had.

Now *that* was a strange thought, she told herself. Not like her at all. But then, traveling through time had probably played with her head a bit.

Keeping his arm linked with hers, he led her toward one of the cable cars. It looked remarkably similar to the ones that tourists still rode up and down the hilly streets of the city. As they climbed aboard, the driver reached up and tugged on the brim of his black cap as he said, "Good day to you, Mr. Brady. How are you?"

"Just fine, Seth," Cole replied.

"Headin' downtown to your office?"

"Not just now. Doing a bit of shopping instead."

The driver glanced at Annabel and said, "Uh-huh."

She was beginning to dislike that reaction in people, she thought.

And what was that business about Cole going to his office? Since when did firemen have offices?

She was still pondering that as he sat her down on one of the upholstered benches, then settled himself beside her. He took off his derby and rested it on his knee. "When we get downtown, I'd better call the station and let them know I'm going to be late," he said.

"Oh, no!" Annabel exclaimed. "I'm causing you to miss your work."

Cole shook his head. "Don't worry about that. I was just thinking earlier today that the San Francisco Fire Department could get along without me." He grinned. "Now I'll have a chance to see if that's true."

"Well, if you're sure . . ."

"I'm certain."

A moment later, with a slight jerk, the cable car began moving. Annabel watched out the open sides in fascination as it carried them along Market Street. With a shock, she saw two buildings in the distance that she recognized. One of them was the St. Francis Hotel, the other the Sheraton Palace. Of course, it hadn't been a Sheraton in 1906, Annabel reminded herself. Then—or rather, now, she supposed—it was just the Palace Hotel. And it wasn't exactly the same, she recalled, because it had been destroyed by the earthquake and then rebuilt. . . .

Her eyes opened wide and she froze in her seat as that word, the one word that hadn't even occurred to her until now, echoed ominously in her brain.

Earthquake.

Chapter 4

WHY WAS HE doing this? Cole asked himself. Simply because Annabel Lowell was a pretty girl with the most compelling eyes he had ever seen? Well, that was reason enough, he supposed, but he was convinced that wasn't his only motivation for helping her.

Perhaps it had something to do with her claim that she was a lady fireman. Not that he really believed that for a minute. As he had told her, the only lady fireman he had ever heard of was in New York City. Besides, that scandalous overall-like garment she wore wasn't like any kind of fireman's uniform he had ever seen. But clearly, she was interested in firefighting, and since it was one of his lifelong passions, it was only natural that he would be sympathetic to her.

Besides, she was clearly out of her head, and if he left her alone to wander unattended around San Francisco, there was no telling what sort of trouble she might get into. The city wasn't as wild and rowdy as it had been in the old Barbary Coast days, but there was still plenty of sin in the city by the bay. Why, in Chinatown alone—

Cole stopped that thought with a tiny shake of his head.

He didn't want to dwell on his troubles with Wing Ko and the old man's *boo how doy*. He had enough on his mind right now with the mysterious Miss Annabel Lowell . . .

He felt her stiffen beside him, and when he looked at her, he saw something very much like terror in her eyes. She had gone pale again, too. She was staring out the open side of the cable car, but when he looked where she was looking, he saw nothing that should have provoked such a reaction, only the crowded sidewalks along Market Street. Perhaps she had seen someone she knew, someone of whom she was afraid.

"Miss Lowell?" Cole said, leaning closer to her. "Miss Lowell, are you all right?"

A little shudder went through her, as if his words had broken a spell of some sort. She turned to look at him and said, "March sixth, 1906?"

So she was back to the business of the date again. "That's right," he told her.

She pointed to a building several blocks away. "That's the St. Francis Hotel, isn't it?"

"That's right," he said again, trying to remain patient.

"And it was built . . . how long ago?"

He had to stop and think. "About two years, I'd say."

She pointed to another building. "And that's the Palace Hotel?"

"Yes, it is. It was built in 1875, in case you're interested. I know because that's the year I was born, and my mother used to tell me that she'd rather have me than dance in the Great Court of the Palace Hotel." He smiled at the memory. His mother had died when he was ten years old, but his recollections of her were still quite clear. "Of course, she managed to do both."

Annabel didn't seem too interested in his reminiscing. She leaned closer to the window and started peering around again. "No signs of fire damage," he heard her mutter.

"Of course not," Cole said. "We have the best fire department in the world. We have to, because the city has been almost destroyed several times by blazes. There's nothing San Franciscans fear more." He frowned. "You'd know that if you really lived here, Miss Lowell."

She settled back against the seat and sighed. "I suppose I should tell you the truth, Mr. Brady," she said. "I've never been here before."

That was even more puzzling. "But you seem to know your way around, at least to a certain extent."

"I've been told a great deal about San Francisco and its history. One of my best friends knows everything there is to know about this city."

"Oh. I see." Cole looked around and was glad to see that they were nearly at their destination. This conversation showed every sign of becoming even more odd and awkward than it already was. "Here's Montgomery Street. I know there are good tailor shops along here. Perhaps there'll be some ladies' clothing stores, too."

He stood up as the cable car came to a stop at the corner. Taking Annabel's arm again, he helped her down the step at the rear of the car. They joined the throngs on the sidewalks in the heart of the city.

Cole stopped in front of an impressive building with the name *Halliwell's* engraved across its front. "I sometimes buy suits in here," he said. "Perhaps Edgar might suggest a place we can purchase some suitable clothing for you."

Annabel was still distracted. She nodded without seeming to pay much attention to what he was saying.

Cole led her inside and immediately was struck by how dark and musty the store was. Odd, he hadn't noticed that before. It was as if the introduction of Annabel in her strange, bright yellow clothes pointed to just how drab these surroundings really were.

Edgar, the chief tailor, bustled up to them. Cole could tell the little man was trying not to stare at Annabel as he said, "Mr. Brady! How good to see you again! What can we do for you today?"

"Hello, Edgar. I was wondering if you might be able to

tell me where I could buy some clothes for my, ah, friend here."

"For the . . . young lady?"

"Yes," Cole said firmly. "This is Miss Lowell. She's a visitor to our fair city, and she finds herself in a rather distressing situation."

"So I see." A smirk threatened to play around Edgar's mouth.

Cole felt himself growing angry. His voice hardened as he said, "No, I don't think you do, Edgar. I want the name of the finest shop for ladies in San Francisco, and I want it now."

Edgar practically snapped to attention like a private in the army being dressed down by a general. "Of course, Mr. Brady. Just go right on up the street two blocks to Miss Mellisande's Emporium. She has the finest ladies' clothes in the city, many of them imported straight from Paris."

"Thank you, Edgar."

"Of course, sir. Glad to be of service, anytime."

As they left the building, Annabel leaned over and said quietly, "That man thought I was either a hooker or an escaped lunatic."

"I suppose so," Cole said grimly. "But I trust that I set him straight."

"He seemed very impressed with you."

"San Franciscans value their firemen." His face relaxed into a smile. "That's all it is." He looked at her and went on, "You don't seem quite as upset now. I'm glad."

"Why should I be upset?" Annabel asked with a queer little laugh. "I'm walking arm in arm with a handsome man through the most beautiful city in the world. What could possibly be wrong?"

Only the fact that sooner or later the whole blasted city was going to come shaking down around them, and that which wasn't destroyed by the earthquake would be consumed by fire, Annabel thought silently.

And there wasn't a thing she could do about it.

As soon as the realization had come to her in the cable car, she had looked around for any sign that the famous catastrophe might have already occurred. It had taken only a few minutes for her to be certain that there had been no recent disasters. That meant the quake was still out there, lurking somewhere in the future.

The earthquake *had* happened in 1906, right? she'd asked herself. The year sounded correct to her. But was she remembering it wrong? Could it have been 1907, or even 1908? The past had never been as important to her as the present and the future, which was one reason she'd never paid that much attention to Earl's lectures. Now she wished she had. Then she would have known the precise date of the earthquake, probably right down to the minute it had started.

She'd tried to force that worry out of her mind as she and Cole visited the tailor shop. That fussy little snob Edgar had proved a welcome distraction, and by the time she and Cole had left and headed up Montgomery Street toward Miss Mellisande's, thoughts of the earthquake began to recede. There was nothing she could do about it anyway, no way to look up the date of something that hadn't even happened yet. And if she told Cole about it, he would definitely think she was insane.

She didn't want to be locked up in an asylum. If that happened, she would never get back to her own time.

For now, she was just a strange, down-on-her-luck visitor from out of town—*way* out of town. That was the way she would play it.

Miss Mellisande's turned out to be a small shop with a large front window. Displayed on wooden mannequins in the window were several gowns and hats, and Annabel had to restrain herself to keep from laughing at the quaintness of them. Of course, the clothes weren't quaint now, in 1906; in fact, they were the height of fashion.

A little bell over the door tinkled as Cole and Annabel

went inside. The shop was crowded with more mannequins and shelves upon which hats and scarves and gloves were displayed. From the rear of the store came an attractive, middle-aged woman with graying blond hair. Her intelligent gaze took in both of her visitors, and if she was shocked by Annabel's strange garb, she gave no sign of it. Instead, her gray eyes fastened on Cole, and she said in a husky voice, "Why, it's Cole Brady, isn't it?"

Cole seemed surprised that she recognized him. "Yes, ma'am," he said politely.

"You don't have to 'ma'am' me," the woman said with a smile. "I was a good friend of your mother's. I'm sure you don't remember me, though." She extended her hand. "Mellisande Dupree."

Cole took her hand and . . . Annabel's eyes widened in surprise. Was he really going to . . . ? Yes, he was. He bent over and *kissed* the back of Mellisande Dupree's hand.

Well, Annabel thought, if she'd had any last remaining doubts about being in another time period, they had just been erased. "We're not in Kansas anymore, Toto," she muttered under her breath.

Cole let go of Mellisande Dupree's hand and straightened up as the woman turned to Annabel. "Did you say your name was Toto, my dear?"

"Uh, no," Cole said quickly. "This is Miss Annabel Lowell. She's a newcomer to San Francisco."

Mellisande raised one carefully plucked eyebrow. "So I see. And a very beautiful one, I might add."

"Yes, indeed," Cole said.

Annabel glanced at him. He was agreeing with Mellisande that she was beautiful? Annabel found herself inexplicably flushing with pleasure.

"And she needs some clothes," Cole went on hurriedly. "Several outfits. Her bags were lost, you see, in an accident." He smiled, clearly pleased with himself for the story he had just fabricated.

"Of course," Mellisande murmured. She began walking

slowly around Annabel, eyeing her critically. "You're a rather tall girl, darling. That may present something of a problem. But perhaps not. I have the best seamstresses in the city working for me." She completed her circuit of Annabel, then clapped her hands lightly together. "All right. You, Mr. Brady, may hie yourself off to your club or some such establishment and drink brandy and smoke cigars for the next two hours. When you return, the lovely Miss Lowell will be even lovelier."

Annabel felt a twinge of panic at the thought of being separated from Cole, even though she had only known him for a little over an hour. He didn't appear as if he cared much for the idea of abandoning her, either. They looked at each other worriedly. . . .

"Oh, shoo," Mellisande Dupree said impatiently. "I won't drug the young lady and sell her into white slavery. You have my word on that. Run along now like a good boy, and come back in two hours like I told you."

"I . . . I suppose I should," Cole said. "I need to call the station anyway."

"I assume you will be responsible for the bill, Mr. Brady?"

"Of course," Cole said, at the same moment as Annabel said, "But it's only a loan."

Mellisande smiled and said, "I'll leave that for the two of you to work out." She took Annabel's arm. "Come along, dear. The fitting room awaits."

Annabel was bigger and stronger than the older woman. She could have pulled away easily. But she had decided to try and blend in here in 1906 San Francisco, at least for the time being, and she couldn't do that without the right clothes. She allowed Mellisande to steer her toward the back of the shop, but not without throwing one last glance over her shoulder at Cole.

He stood there, his hat in his hands, looking torn about what he should do.

Then Mellisande swept a curtain aside, marched her

through it, and let it fall closed behind them, hiding Cole from Annabel's vision.

As he walked back down Montgomery Street toward Market, Cole hoped he had done the right thing by leaving Annabel at Miss Mellisande's. Despite what the woman had said, he had no memory of her being a friend of his mother's, but it was certainly possible. No young child knew everything about his or her parents.

It was just that Annabel seemed so . . . lost, somehow. As if she were totally out of place. And it wasn't just the strange clothes she wore. The way she looked around, the questions she asked told Cole that something had happened recently which had disturbed the young woman greatly. So far, though, Annabel hadn't seemed inclined to go into specifics about what the incident had been.

It was none of his business, Cole told himself as he turned and headed a block west to Kearny Street. He went up a short flight of steps to the front entrance of a two-story brick building. A shallow portico over the doorway was supported by a pair of stucco columns. The door itself was mahogany, elaborately carved and elegantly stained. It opened just before Cole reached it, and a man in butler's livery said, "Good evening, Mr. Brady."

"Good evening, Frank," Cole replied as he took off his derby and handed it to the man.

"Will you be dining with us this evening, sir?"

"No, I don't believe so. I would, however, like to use the telephone, and then perhaps I'll have a brandy in the salon."

"As you wish, sir," Frank murmured. He closed the door behind Cole with only the barest whisper of sound.

Quiet permeated the entire Olympia Club, in fact. It was one of San Francisco's oldest and most exclusive clubs for gentlemen, dating from the days of the Comstock Lode and the Silver Kings. Cole's father had been a member, and so Cole was a member, though he didn't come here frequently.

Business deals of national import were conducted almost daily in the salon, the bar, the sitting room, the card room, and the library, but Cole seldom took part in them.

Parquet flooring gleamed in the foyer, its brilliant shine reflecting the glow from a gas chandelier that hung from the ceiling. Cole turned to the left, going into a small, windowless chamber which had once been a cloakroom. Now it contained a comfortable armchair and a small table which held only a lamp and a telephone. Many of the members of the Olympia Club, old-fashioned gentlemen that they were, had resisted for years the very idea of installing a telephone. The club members were businessmen as well as gentlemen, however, and eventually simple expediency had demanded that a telephone be put in. Still, its use was limited to this small, unobtrusive room, and members were expected to close the door and be discreet when placing calls.

As soon as he'd shut the door, Cole sat down and picked up the receiver. He held it to his ear with one hand while using the other to turn the crank on the wooden box that held the rest of the apparatus. When the operator came on the line, he leaned closer to the mouthpiece and asked to speak to Fire Station Number Twenty-one.

He heard a distant ringing, then a broad Irish brogue said, "O'Flaherty's Gardenin' and Undertakin' Parlor. We specialize in all kinds o' diggin'."

With a frown, Cole asked, "Patsy, what if this had been someone reporting a fire?"

"Well, it ain't, now is it? I recognized yer voice, Cole."

"I hadn't even said anything when you—" Cole stopped, took a deep breath, and resumed. "Is everything quiet?"

"Oh, aye, quiet as a wee church mouse. Where are ye, lad? I expected ye in afore now."

"I ran into . . ." How to refer to Annabel Lowell? Cole suddenly found himself wondering. Not as a problem; certainly not that. A delay? That word didn't seem right for such an attractive woman. He settled for, "I ran into something unexpected, and I may not be able to get to the station for a while."

"Sure and it's nothin' to worry yer head about. 'Tis quiet here, and if there is a fire, I expect ye'll hear the alarms, wherever ye might be."

"All right, then. I'll be there when I can."

"Have a good time, lad," Patsy O'Flaherty said. "The Good Lord knows ye deserve one. Sure and I never saw such a serious young fellow, always workin' all the time—"

"Good-bye, Patsy," Cole said, then broke the connection with his thumb. He had listened to the little Irishman's lectures often enough that he knew them by heart.

He was relieved that there had been no fire alarms, but he still felt guilty about not being on duty. As he left the telephone room and walked down the hallway from the foyer to the salon, he checked his watch. After he picked up Annabel, it would be time for dinner, and given the fact that she knew no one else in the city and had no money, he would have to take her somewhere to eat.

Then there was the matter of where she was going to stay. He couldn't invite her to be a guest at his house, despite the fact that there were plenty of empty rooms in the big old house on Russian Hill. He kept no servants other than a cook and a housekeeper who came in during the day, and to have a young, unmarried woman staying with him would be the height of scandal, no matter how proper things really were.

Of course, Annabel was quite lovely. Under the right circumstances, perhaps a little impropriety might be in order. . . .

He gave a little shake of his head. Such musings could only lead to trouble.

Speaking of trouble, Cole thought, a tall, slender man in evening clothes appeared in the doorway of the salon, brandy glass in one hand and cigar in the other. He smiled a greeting at Cole.

"Hello, Brady," he said. "I was just thinking of getting up a game. Care to join us?"

Cole shook his head. "No thanks, Garrett. I'm afraid I won't be staying that long."

"You're certain?" Garrett Ingersoll asked.

"Yes," Cole replied, trying not to be curt. He didn't like Garrett Ingersoll and never had, despite the fact that the man's shipping line did a considerable amount of business with Brady Enterprises. Several of the Brady warehouses along the docks were filled with cargos from Ingersoll vessels.

"Whatever you say, old boy. By the way, how are things going with that Chinaman? Still having trouble with the old yellow devil?"

"Wing Ko and I have an understanding," Cole said stiffly. He didn't like having his business bandied about, but he supposed it was unavoidable. Despite its cosmopolitan airs, San Francisco was still a small town at heart, and gossip traveled fast.

Ingersoll chuckled. "You'd best hope Wing Ko understands the same way you do, or else he's liable to send his hatchet men after you. Human life means nothing to those tong leaders, you know."

Cole wasn't afraid of Wing Ko's soldiers, his *boo how doy* or hatchet men or whatever else anyone wanted to call them. The last time Wing Ko had sent emissaries to call on him, Cole had made it very clear that he did not intend to share control of his holdings along the docks with anyone—not even Wing Ko. The man had made a business proposal, Cole had turned it down, and that was that.

Frank appeared, silently as always, at Cole's elbow. The butler was holding a silver tray with a snifter of brandy balanced on it. "I believe you said you would take your brandy in the salon, sir?" Frank said.

"That's right." Cole nodded to Ingersoll. "Good night, Garrett. Good luck in your game," he added, not really meaning it.

Ingersoll smiled. "Luck usually has very little to do with success, my friend." He put the cigar in his mouth and wandered off down the hall in search of other pigeons to pluck.

"Thank you, Frank," Cole said as he went into the salon, accompanied by the butler. "And not just for the brandy."

"I know exactly what you mean, sir," Frank said.

Cole took the brandy and settled down in one of the comfortable, overstuffed armchairs scattered artfully around the room. On a small table next to the chair was a humidor containing fine cigars from Cuba. Cole considered smoking one of them, then decided he wasn't in the mood. He sipped the brandy instead and listened to the low buzz of conversation going on around him.

His thoughts drifted back to Annabel. He was rapidly discovering that being apart from her only deepened his appreciation of her beauty. It was difficult to believe that this morning, as recently as this afternoon, in fact, he had not known her, had never even seen her. She seemed to have burst on him like a bombshell, filling his mind and occupying his thoughts. From the moment she had opened her eyes and looked up into his, he had thought of her and almost nothing else.

Why? Why should he feel this way about her? It wasn't her beauty alone—he was convinced of that. Nor was it the fact that she was so lost and abandoned. He had a feeling that once she had gotten over whatever event had shaken her so badly, she would be perfectly capable of handling things. There was strength and confidence in the way she carried herself and in the keen intelligence in her eyes.

He took another sip of the brandy and realized what it was about her that was so compelling to him: She was a mystery. He wanted to know more about her. He wanted to know where she was born and where she had grown up and what her family had been like and whether or not she had had any pets. She claimed to be a lady fireman, and he decided he wanted very much to know about *that*, about where she worked and how she had come to be in such a profession.

He wanted to know what her favorite flower was, and whether she liked the taste of wild strawberries, and how her hair would smell if he buried his face in it, and how soft and warm her lips would be if his mouth came down on hers, stroking and exploring. . . .

"Cole?"

He jumped slightly and looked up as a chuckle followed his name. He saw a tall, angular, white-haired man with a neatly trimmed beard sitting down in a nearby chair. The man pointed with the cigar in his hand and went on, "You looked like you were about to snap the stem of that brandy snifter, my boy. Thought I'd better bring you out of whatever daze you were in."

Cole set the snifter on the table next to his chair and said, "Thank you, Commodore. My thoughts had certainly wandered off."

The Commodore chuckled again. "They wandered far afield, from the looks of your face. I take it there was a young woman involved?"

Cole smiled faintly. There was no hiding things from the Commodore. He hadn't gotten to be the third-richest man west of the Mississippi by being slow on the uptake.

"Perhaps." That was all Cole would allow for the moment.

"I'm glad to hear it. Your father was always worried that you'd never produce an heir. Too busy with that firefighting foolishness of yours. His words, not mine. I'm glad the fire department has such dedicated men in its ranks."

"My father never understood anything except business," Cole said.

The Commodore inclined his head. "Thomas Brady was my friend for forty years, but I have to agree with you there. Ah, well, at least you weren't sitting here brooding about Wing Ko."

Cole sighed in exasperation and said, "Does *everyone* in

San Francisco know that he sent his men to see me?"

"Quite possibly," the Commodore drawled. "What are you going to do about him?"

"I sent him a message making it very clear that I wasn't interested in doing business with him. I was very respectful about it."

The Commodore put the cigar in his mouth and nodded. "Good lad," he said around the Havana. "So, who's the young woman who has you so starry-eyed?"

"I wasn't starry-eyed," Cole said, though he was afraid that he might well have been. "But her name is Miss Annabel Lowell."

"Lowell, Lowell," the Commodore repeated. "Old New England name, isn't it?"

"I don't know, but she just arrived in the city today."

"And you've already taken her under your wing? Fast work, my boy."

"It's not like that," Cole insisted. "She needed some assistance, and I happened to be on hand. . . ."

"Fortuitous, indeed. And where is the young lady now?"

"At Miss Mellisande's Emporium. She, ah, was in need of some clothes, since all her baggage was lost in an accident."

"I see." The Commodore took the cigar out of his mouth and leaned forward. In a quieter tone, he said, "I don't have to tell you to be careful, do I, lad? Sometimes people are not what they seem, and that applies to young women, too, unfortunately."

"That's just it," Cole heard himself saying. "I don't know what Miss Annabel is, and I want to find out."

The Commodore's shrewd eyes regarded Cole intently for a long moment, then the old man gave another bark of laughter. "You're lost, lad," he said. "Once a man finds himself actually curious about a woman, it's too late."

"I'm just trying to help her."

The Commodore hauled his bony form upright and grinned. "Think whatever you want. I know." He started to turn away, then glanced back and said, "If you need someone to intercede with Wing Ko for you, let me know. I might not be able to help, but I'd be glad to try."

Cole nodded. "Thank you. But I'm sure it's settled."

The Commodore stuck his Havana back in his mouth, shook his head, and walked away.

Cole sat back and frowned. His sojourn at the Olympia Club, intended to simply pass the time, had turned out to be rather disturbing. From the encounter with Garrett Ingersoll to the completely improper thoughts he had been having about Annabel to the Commodore's totally unwarranted conclusions concerning how he felt about her, it was all just too much.

Cole took his watch out and checked the time. Only an hour had passed. Well, perhaps he would leave the club anyway and spend the other hour walking the streets until he was supposed to return to Miss Mellisande's. Right now, he needed something to clear his head, and some fresh air might just do the trick.

He stood up, drained the last of his brandy, and left the salon.

Chapter 5

ANNABEL HADN'T REALIZED that fitting into this era was going to be quite so painful.

"Come on, darling, you can take a deeper breath than that," Mellisande Dupree said.

Annabel felt like telling the woman that she could take a deep enough breath to stay underwater for a good three minutes. However, Mellisande wasn't interested in lung capacity. At the moment, she was concentrating on waist measurement.

Hauling in the biggest breath of air she could, Annabel grunted as the Chinese seamstress tugged hard on the laces of the corset and then quickly fastened them. Mellisande, who was standing to one side observing, clapped her hands lightly in satisfaction. "Much better," she said. "Just look at yourself now, dear."

Annabel studied herself in the gilt-edged, full-length mirror standing nearby on a couple of clawed feet. After a moment, she came to the undeniable conclusion that she looked like a freak. The corset shrunk her waist to unnaturally tiny dimensions and made her boobs stick out like she was some sort of pouter pigeon. On top of that, she could barely breathe. Thinly, she said, "I don't care for the corset."

"Oh, but it's absolutely necessary if the gown is going to fit properly," Mellisande insisted. "At least try it on, dear. I promise you, young Mr. Brady will think you look stunning."

Mellisande claimed she had been a friend of Cole's mother, so Annabel didn't want to offend the woman. Breathing shallowly—the only way she *could* breathe with that blasted corset on—she bent awkwardly so that the seamstress could slip the gown over her head. The Chinese woman went around behind her to fasten the buttons that ran up the back of the garment.

The first thing Mellisande had done was to pile Annabel's hair on top of her head and pin it there in an elaborate arrangement of curls. That made her look even taller. So did the long, tight-waisted gown, Annabel saw as she glanced again at the mirror. Mellisande had called this a walking dress. It had a white, frilly, high-necked bodice, sleeves that were puffy from the shoulder to the elbow and tight from the elbow to the wrist, and a small bustle in the back. The skirt flared slightly as it fell from Annabel's hips to her ankles. The sleeves and skirt were a rich, dark gold color.

"Lovely," Mellisande declared. "Stay right there, dear. I have just the thing to complete the outfit."

She hurried into the front of the shop and came back carrying a large brown hat with a silk flower attached to it. She had to pull over a stool and stand on it in order to reach up and settle the hat on Annabel's now upswept hair.

"Perfect," Mellisande said as she stepped down from the stool. "Your beau won't even recognize you."

"He's not my beau," Annabel said. "Just . . . a friend." Even that was stretching things, she thought. Cole was nothing more than an acquaintance, and a very recent one at that.

But why, she asked herself, would an acquaintance go to

all the trouble that Cole had gone to for her?

"Well, he's still going to be very impressed," Mellisande insisted. "You look every bit the height of fashion, my dear. And in your case, I do mean height."

There she went again, talking about how tall Annabel was. Annabel knew that people's average height had steadily gotten taller over the years, but even here in 1906, it wasn't like she was ready for the WNBA. Not that there was a Women's National Basketball Association yet. . . .

"So everybody wears getups like this?"

"Those who want to be fashionable do," Mellisande said. "It's called the Gibson look."

Annabel vaguely remembered hearing references to Gibson Girls, and now she knew what they meant. She'd always been the jeans-and-sweatshirt type herself.

She turned, looking over her shoulder at the mirror for the rear view. The sight of the bustle made her want to laugh. She finished the turn.

"Excellent. Now, you'll want another walking dress, and a dinner gown, and a theater gown—"

"Let's not get carried away," Annabel interrupted Mellisande's enthusiasm. "I don't want to get so far in debt to Mr. Brady that I can never pay him back."

Mellisande waved an elegantly manicured hand. "Oh, I wouldn't worry about that if I were you, dear. I can't imagine a gentleman such as Cole pressing a young lady for money. He's hardly the type. In fact, you won't find a more stalwart young man in San Francisco." Mellisande laughed lightly and added, "Besides, a beautiful young woman such as yourself can always trade in a different sort of currency, shall we say."

"No," Annabel snapped. "We shall not say."

"Of course not," Mellisande murmured, a little taken aback by the sharpness of Annabel's reaction. "I didn't mean to imply anything, my dear. It's just that you don't have to worry about Mr. Brady's finances. He's quite well-to-do. Although I'm sure you know that about him already."

"On a fireman's salary?"

"Oh, my dear." Mellisande looked at her in surprise. "Do you mean to tell me you *don't* know about Brady Enterprises?"

Annabel shook her head. "I'd never met Mr. Brady before this afternoon." To tell the truth, there was a great deal she didn't know about him . . . but she suddenly realized, to her surprise, that she *wanted* to know more.

"Well, then, I shall simply have to inform you that you have been befriended by one of the wealthiest young men in San Francisco. Brady Enterprises owns some of the most valuable real estate in the city, including many of the warehouses along the docks."

That news made Annabel suck in her breath, sort of like the corset had done. She had already seen enough to know that Cole was known and respected around town, but he had told her that was because San Franciscans valued their firemen so highly. That might be part of the reason people treated him as they did, she thought, but money was a more logical explanation.

"You honestly didn't know, did you?" Mellisande asked.

Annabel shook her head. "No, I didn't. Why in the world . . . If he's so rich, why does he work as a fireman?"

Mellisande rolled her eyes, shook her head, and said, "Because, for some completely unfathomable reason, he *likes* being a fireman."

The hour's walk had made Cole feel better. He had nodded to a dozen or more acquaintances as he strolled along the hilly streets. Once he had even found himself near Chinatown, but he had stopped before venturing into that quarter. It wasn't that he was afraid of Wing Ko's men; he just didn't believe in asking for trouble.

Now, as he approached Miss Mellisande's Emporium, he found himself looking forward to seeing Annabel again. He had missed her—difficult to believe given he'd been totally unaware of her existence until today, but true. Something had seemed to be missing the entire time he was apart from her.

The little bell above the door chimed again as he went inside. Mellisande Dupree bustled out through the curtain that closed off the rear of the shop. "Cole!" she exclaimed. "I'm so glad you're back. Are you prepared?"

He frowned a little. "Prepared for what?"

"To be dazzled," Mellisande said with a smile. She laughed and turned, clapped her hands together twice, then swept the curtain aside.

Annabel walked into the front room and stood there rather stiffly, as if she were unaccustomed to posing. Cole's eyes grew larger as he looked at her, taking in everything from the brown hat on her head to the high-topped, pearl-buttoned shoes on her feet. The strange yellow overalls and the work boots were gone. Her long brown hair, which had hung thick and luxurious down her back, was now carefully arranged atop her head. She was still beautiful, but she looked so different that he might not have recognized her had he not known it was her. He could have passed her on the street without taking any more notice of her than he did of the thousands of other pretty girls in San Francisco.

That is, he could have if it hadn't been for her eyes. *Those* had not changed. They were still rich and brown and sensuous, still intelligent and alert and challenging. Cole met their gaze squarely and murmured, "My God, it *is* you, isn't it?"

"Do you like it?" Annabel asked. Her tone told him that she cared what his answer was going to be.

"Of course he likes it," Mellisande said without giving Cole a chance to open his mouth. "What man wouldn't like a dress such as this on such a lovely young woman? She *is* lovely, isn't she, Mr. Brady?"

"Very much so," Cole said. "The belle of the ball."

Mellisande shook her head. "Oh, no. This isn't the ball

gown. This is just a simple walking dress." She fluttered a hand toward the back room. "We have all the ballroom accoutrements boxed up and ready to be delivered, however, as well as an excellent selection of other evening wear and everyday clothing. I knew you wouldn't wish to skimp on anything."

"No," Cole said. "I wouldn't want to do that."

"Listen," Annabel said quickly, "I'll pay you back. I've said all along this is only a loan—"

"Don't worry about it right now." Cole was still looking intently at her, wondering at the miracle Mellisande had wrought in only a couple of hours. Annabel had gone from a beautiful but definitely odd visitor to a young woman who was the very picture of genteel grace and loveliness.

Annabel took hold of the corset through the dress and tugged on it, trying in vain to make it more comfortable and keep the whalebone stays from biting into her flesh. "I still don't know how anybody stands to wear these things for very long," she said.

Cole swallowed. Annabel would always have eccentricities, he supposed. He strode across the room and offered her his arm. "Shall we go?" he asked.

"Where?"

The blunt question took him by surprise. "Well . . . I thought we might have some dinner."

Annabel nodded and said, "That would be fine."

"Have all the other clothes delivered to my house," Cole told Mellisande. That wouldn't be their ultimate destination, of course, but for the time being, there was nothing else he could do.

"Wait just a minute," Annabel said sharply. "Your house?"

Cole felt himself flushing with embarrassment. "I meant the St. Francis Hotel, of course," he lied. Renting a room for her there would be the simplest thing to do, he supposed, though such a course of action might still expose Annabel to some ugly gossip.

He was surprised to see Annabel shake her head. "What about a nice, inexpensive boardinghouse? Aren't there any of those in this city?"

"Well, yes, I suppose there are," Cole said. "I can make some inquiries."

"You do that," Mellisande said as she came over to stand beside him. She patted his arm and whispered, "In the meantime, I'll have the clothes sent to Russian Hill."

To his house, she meant. Dear Lord, Mellisande thought that Annabel was his mistress!

But then, what else could she have thought under the circumstances?

Cole squared his shoulders. Appearances be hanged! He was just trying to help Annabel, and he would do as he saw fit.

"That would be fine," he told Mellisande.

Smiling happily and keeping one hand on Cole's arm, Mellisande led him over to Annabel and took her arm with her other hand. She steered both of them toward the front door of the shop. "Go on now and enjoy your dinner," she said. "And please come back to see me sometime, Miss Lowell . . . Annabel. I find you a delightful young woman."

"Thank you," Annabel said. "And thank you for the clothes. They're . . . they're lovely."

"Oh, don't thank me. Thank your gallant rescuer, Mr. Brady."

Cole felt the full power of Annabel's eyes at close range as she turned her gaze on him. "I intend to," she murmured.

Feeling disconcerted by the way she was looking at him, Cole rather awkwardly linked his arm with hers and cleared his throat. "We should be going," he said. "It's already late, and we may have to wait a bit for a table at a decent restaurant."

"I don't mind waiting," Annabel said.

Behind them, Mellisande watched them go, a satisfied smile on her face. Nothing made her happier than matchmaking. . . . Well, unless it was an unusually lucrative sale, such as the pile of boxes in the back room of the shop represented. But she had to admit that, despite Annabel Lowell's oddities, the girl truly was beautiful, and she and Cole Brady made a lovely couple. Mellisande wished them nothing but happiness.

She was already toting up the cost of a trousseau in her head.

She should have been ashamed of herself, Annabel thought. She hadn't meant to embarrass Cole. And after all he had done to help her!

At the same time, when he had said something about having the new clothes delivered to his house, she hadn't been able to keep from wondering about what he had in mind. Did he expect her to be his mistress now? If so, he was going to be disappointed. She was intrigued by him, true enough. Anyone with the sort of money that Mellisande claimed he had who continued to work as a fireman because he enjoyed it . . . Well, that was the sort of man in whom Annabel was going to take a keen interest. Nearly every firefighter she had ever known had chosen that career because of a sincere desire to help people and a love for the work. But how many of them would have kept at it if a fortune had dropped in their laps? She wasn't sure even she had that dedication.

Those thoughts were going through her mind as she walked arm in arm down Montgomery Street with Cole. Suddenly, he broke into them by asking, "What are you thinking?"

"About firemen," she said, and then, abruptly, she stopped in her tracks. Her hand went to her mouth. "Oh, no!"

Cole frowned worriedly. "What's wrong?"

"I have to go back," Annabel said. She slipped her arm out of his and turned quickly. She wanted to break into a run, but in the corset and long dress, that was impossible.

The best she could manage was a fast walk back toward Miss Mellisande's Emporium.

Cole hustled along beside her. "Did you forget something?" he asked.

She nodded. "Something important."

A few moments later, they reached the shop. Annabel didn't wait for Cole to open the door for her. She grabbed the knob herself and tried to turn it. The knob wouldn't budge; the door was locked.

Annabel let out a groan of dismay. In the short time since they had left, Mellisande had closed for the evening.

"I have to get in there," she said.

"Maybe Miss Mellisande is in the back." Cole rapped sharply on the glass pane in the door. He raised his voice and called, "Miss Mellisande!" then cupped his hands around his eyes and leaned closer to the window.

Annabel tried to fight down the feeling of panic that was welling up inside her. After everything that had happened in the past eighteen hours, she didn't think she could stand it if she lost her most tangible link to her own time.

"Wait a minute," Cole said. "I see someone. . . . Yes, there she is, coming out of the back room."

Annabel felt a surge of relief, but it was tempered by worry. Just because Mellisande Dupree was still here didn't mean that Annabel would recover the thing that was so precious to her.

Mellisande appeared on the other side of the glass and thrust a long key into the lock. She twisted it and opened the door. "My, I didn't expect to see you two back so soon," she said. "Did you forget something?"

"My clothes—," Annabel began rather breathlessly.

"Oh, don't worry, dear, I told you I'd see to it that they were delivered safely."

"Not the new clothes," Annabel said. "The old ones."

Mellisande's nose wrinkled slightly. "Those . . . things . . . you were wearing when you arrived? Whyever would you want them? To be honest, Miss Lowell, they're not fashionable at all, and they have a distinct odor of smoke about them."

Annabel suppressed the impulse to grab the older woman by the shoulders and shake her. "What have you done with them?" she demanded.

"Nothing. They're in a box in the back room. I was going to have Ling put them out for the rubbish collector."

Annabel stepped into the shop so determinedly that Mellisande had no choice except to retreat. Mellisande sent a look of alarm at Cole, but he just spread his hands and shrugged. He had no more idea what was going on here than she did.

Striding into the back room, Annabel looked around quickly and spotted one of the sleeves of her yellow fire suit draped over the edge of a cardboard box. She practically sprang on it and pawed the fire suit aside. Underneath it were the T-shirt, jeans, bra, panties, and socks she had been wearing under the fire suit when she left her apartment the night before to head for Mount Diablo State Park. She plucked the T-shirt out of the box and clenched her hand around the small gold pin that was attached to it. Her eyes closed in relief. She couldn't believe that she had almost lost the pin.

"Did you find what you were looking for?" Cole asked from the doorway dividing the two rooms.

Annabel jerked a little. She opened her eyes and looked down at the shirt in her hands. Her fingers worked swiftly and deftly, unfastening the pin. She slipped it into a pocket of her dress as she turned.

"Yes, I just didn't want to lose these clothes," she lied. The fire suit was important to her, the other things less so. But it was the pin she had really come back for. She didn't know why she was instinctively keeping that from Cole, unless it was because the pin's meaning had always been intensely personal to her.

He stepped into the room, and Mellisande followed him. "If you want those old things, I suppose I can have them delivered, too," Mellisande said. "But would it be all right if I had them laundered first?"

"Of course," Annabel said. "Thank you."

Clearly, they both thought she was crazy. But she was getting used to that. In fact, she had spent a large part of the day trying to convince *herself* that she wasn't insane.

"Well, I guess we should be going," Cole said. He offered Annabel his arm again. She took it and let him lead her out of the shop. At the front door, he tipped his hat to Mellisande and said, "Sorry for the disturbance."

"No need to apologize, dear boy," she assured him. "Perhaps we should become accustomed to the idea that there will always be the potential for excitement as long as Miss Lowell is around."

Annabel wasn't sure if she meant that as a compliment or an insult. Her only reaction was a weak smile as she started walking down the street next to Cole.

The closest place to eat was the Richelieu Cafe, with its usual pile of beer barrels on the sidewalk beside the front window. Cole was worried that it might be too crude an establishment for Annabel, but when he suggested it, she asked only, "Is the food good?"

"Excellent, but not fancy."

"I don't care about fancy," she said with a shake of her head. "As long as there's plenty of it. All I've had since last night is a sandwich packed by that logger."

Cole steered her past the pile of barrels and through the door of the cafe. "How in the world did you ever come to be lost in the Diablos?" he asked.

"It's a long story," she said. "It would take much too long to tell." Under her breath, she added, "More than ninety years."

"What?"

"Nothing," Annabel said. She smiled brightly. "The food smells good."

Cole supposed it did, but at the moment he was less

concerned with that than he was with the fact that she was obviously hiding something from him. Ever since he had met her, he had felt that she was dodging his questions and supplying answers that were no better than half-truths. He was going to have to extract the truth from her slowly and carefully, he sensed.

With that realization came another one: He had passed the point of courtesy, of being merely a gentleman helping out a lady in distress. He couldn't simply send her on her way and forget about her, and it had nothing to do with the fact that he had already missed a day's work and spent a considerable amount of money on her. Finding out the truth mattered because *it was the truth about Annabel.* He had to know everything he could about her.

"We're in luck," he said as he gripped her arm just above the elbow and pointed with his other hand. "There's an empty table over there. You don't find that often in Richelieu's, especially at this time of day."

They made their way across the crowded room and reached the table in question, which sat in one of the cafe's rear corners. Next to the table was a potted palm which separated the dining area from the entrance to the kitchen. Not the most elegant location, Cole thought, but clearly Annabel didn't care.

He held her chair for her and then sat down across from her. A young, redheaded waitress in a long gray dress and starched white apron came over and greeted them. "Mr. Brady, isn't it? Haven't seen you in here for a while. How's Patsy?"

"Just fine," Cole replied with a smile. "We'd like two steak dinners, please."

"Comin' up. Schooners of beer with those?"

Cole looked across the table at Annabel, who said, "Sure."

The waitress said to her, "That's a lovely gown, ma'am. Dressed like that, you ought to be dining in the Palace, not in a place like this."

"Not at all," Annabel said. She looked across at Cole. "I've heard good things about Richelieu's."

"Well, we'll try to live up to our reputation, ma'am." The waitress grinned at Cole. "Say hello to Patsy for me, will you, Mr. Brady?"

"I'd be glad to," Cole assured her.

When the waitress had left, Annabel asked, "Who's Patsy?"

A certain tightness in her tone took Cole by surprise. Was she . . . could she actually be jealous? He couldn't stop himself from laughing.

"Did I say something amusing?" Annabel asked, and now there was a hint of coolness in her voice.

"Not at all," Cole quickly told her. "I was just thinking about Patsy. Patsy—or actually, Patrick—O'Flaherty. He's the stoker on our crew. A bandy-legged little Irishman, barely five feet tall, but he seems to think he's John L. Sullivan. Considering the swath he cuts all over town with young ladies like that waitress, I suppose he might as well be."

"Oh." She seemed relieved. "Who's John L. Sullivan?"

That question brought a real look of surprise to his face. "Just the former heavyweight champion of the world. I don't imagine you keep up with prizefighting, though. I suppose it really is a barbaric sport."

"The sort of thing where one fighter might bite another fighter's ear off?"

"Well, I doubt if any pugilist would ever go *that* far." Cole laughed and shook his head. "How in the world did we wind up talking about such things?"

"I don't know. I have a feeling I could talk to you about almost anything."

Cole's expression became more solemn. Suddenly things seemed much more serious. Annabel looked as if she wished she could take those words back, but Cole was glad she couldn't. They meant that she was beginning to trust him. He leaned forward and said, "Annabel . . ."

Nervousness flickered in her eyes, but she said, "Yes?"

Before he could say anything else, the waitress reappeared beside the table and placed two huge mugs of beer in front of them. "There you go," she announced. "Be back with those steaks in just a minute."

Cole sat back. The moment was lost. He picked up his beer and said, "What shall we drink to?"

"How about San Francisco?" Annabel suggested. She picked up her schooner. "And new beginnings."

"To San Francisco," Cole agreed. "And to new beginnings . . ."

Chapter 6

"THAT WAS A wonderful dinner," Annabel said later. She found herself sleepy, wanting to stretch like a contented cat. There was nothing quite so satisfying as a good meal.

Well, maybe one thing . . .

She banished that thought from her mind as Cole said, "Yes, it was, wasn't it? Are you ready to go?"

He stood up and came around the table to hold her chair as she got to her feet. She had taken off the large brown hat during dinner, not really caring that doing so had drawn some curious looks from the other diners in the Richelieu. What she really wanted to do was unpin her hair, shake down that elaborate arrangement of curls, and slip her shoes off. But that would have to wait, she supposed with a sigh.

"Are you all right?" Cole asked solicitously.

"I'm fine," she assured him quickly. "Just a bit tired."

"Of course. You've had a long day." At least he supposed that was true. He didn't know for certain how or where her day had really started.

Annabel read that thought on his face. She wished she could tell him that she was from the future. If he understood, it would certainly simplify things.

Having him believe her, that was the trick. No one in his right mind would.

She put the hat on carefully while he retrieved his derby from a hat rack and settled it on his head at a rakish angle. He wasn't really the rakish type, she decided, but he was capable of it at times, and this was one of those moments. With a grin, he dropped some bills on the table and then offered her his arm.

"Shall we go?"

"We shall," she said, linking her arm with his.

They strolled out of the restaurant and toward the cable car line on Market Street. The sun had set while they were dining, and when it left it had taken the warmth of the day with it. A familiar chilly dampness was descending over the city. Some things never changed, Annabel thought. The fog rolling in felt just the same in 1906 as it did in her own era.

Cole helped her up into one of the cable cars, then said as he sat down beside her, "We're going to my house, and I won't have any argument about it. I'll be going down to the fire station anyway, so there won't be anything the least bit improper about it."

"All right," Annabel said, and she could tell that he was a bit surprised by her ready agreement. The arrangement was really the only thing that made sense. She added, "As long as you don't mind having a strange woman staying at your place overnight."

"Mind?" he asked, genuinely surprised now. "Why should I mind?"

"Well, I might be a thief. You might come home to find everything in the house gone."

Cole laughed quietly. "You don't really look like the brigand type, Miss Lowell."

"Annabel," she said.

He hesitated, then nodded. "Annabel. At any rate, I trust you."

"Good. I trust you, too."

And instinctively, she did. So far, he had done nothing to suggest there was any reason not to.

They changed cable cars at Market and Powell and rode north past Union Square and Chinatown. Annabel noticed Cole looking rather intently at Chinatown, with its splashes of gaudy light in the midst of the darkness. "Is something wrong?" she asked.

He gave a little shake of his head. "Not at all. What could be wrong on such a lovely evening?"

"Lovely evening?" she repeated. "The fog is rolling in."

"What do you expect in San Francisco?"

"True," she agreed. She glanced down at his hand and wondered how he would react if she slipped her fingers around his. She decided to stop thinking about it and act instead.

She laid her hand on his, lightly.

Cole didn't jerk away, but he did turn his head and look at her for a second. Then he turned his hand over and twined his fingers with hers, closing them in a grip that was warm and strong, yet at the same time gentle. Annabel smiled tentatively.

When the cable car reached the stop at Green and Powell, Cole said, "This is where we get off." He got to his feet without letting go of her hand.

Annabel stood, too, and followed him off the car. He let go of her hand as she was stepping down to the street, but only so that he could rest both hands lightly on her waist to steady her. When her feet were on the ground, she turned to face him. As she did so, she realized that his hands were still touching her. They had slid down a little, so that they rested just below her waist, where the swell of her hips began. They stood like that for a moment, before she reached up and rested her hand on the front of his vest. "Cole . . . ," she breathed.

His hands jerked away from her body as if she were on fire. He stepped back and looked flustered in the glow of a nearby streetlight. "I . . . I'm sorry," he said. "I didn't mean to be so bold, Miss Lowell."

"You agreed to call me Annabel," she reminded him.

"Yes, so I did." He offered her his arm. "We'd best be going. The steps get a bit tricky after the fog comes in."

"All right," she murmured. He thought she had wanted him to stop touching her, she realized. Just the opposite was true. She wouldn't have minded at all if he had pulled her even closer to him and kissed her.

What in the world was she thinking? Annabel asked herself. *Twenty-four hours ago, you were shooting down that new guy in your building before he even got around to asking you out. Now you're practically panting over this perfect stranger.*

This was different, Annabel tried to tell herself as she continued the inner debate. This was truly a different time, a different place. Levelheaded Annabel Lowell, who only indulged her daredevil side in her work, could afford to take some chances here. After all, none of this was permanent. Sooner or later, she would return to her own time. Surely she would.

"Careful here," Cole said as he turned to the left. "The steps get pretty slippery."

Annabel saw a set of steep, narrow wooden steps leading up the side of the hill into the darkness. There was a handrail, but only along one side of the steps. Cole switched places with her so that she would be on the side with the railing as they climbed the steps.

These steps were vaguely familiar to her, Annabel realized, just as many things here in 1906 San Francisco had struck a chord of memory within her. She thought the steps were probably still there in her own time, though the surroundings would be considerably different. They weren't really far from her home in North Beach; Columbus Avenue was just a few blocks down the other side of the hill.

As she looked around during the climb, however, she didn't see the brilliantly lit skyline of San Francisco that was so familiar to her, or the lights of the Bay Bridge, or Oakland's sprawl of fluorescence across the water. A lot of the lights in this era were fueled by gas, and the electric ones that were already in use were rather primitive. Their illumination didn't penetrate the murk of the fog like the neon and sodium lights from her time. So the glows that she saw floating in the darkness were softer to start with and were softened even more by the moisture in the air.

The lights were gorgeous, she realized, warm yellow reminders of a quieter, gentler time.

Somewhere out on the bay, the blast of a foghorn rolled out, sounding for all the world like the plaintive cry of some gigantic prehistoric beast wandering the night calling for its lost mate. Such sounds could still be heard in the San Francisco Annabel knew, but they had to be filtered out from the steady background rumble of traffic and the whining roar of airplanes taking off and landing at San Francisco International Airport.

There were three landings before the steps reached a lane that extended a couple of blocks in each direction. "You live up here?" Annabel asked as they finally reached the top of the steps.

"That's right," Cole said. The lane was lined with elegant, relatively small mansions. He turned right and led her toward one of them. In the darkness, she couldn't tell much about it other than the fact that it was three stories tall and had several gables and cupolas adorning it. A tall, wrought-iron fence with a gate divided the sidewalk from the small, terraced front yard. Annabel found herself looking forward to seeing the place in the daylight.

He pointed to the east as he stopped in front of the gate. "The lane runs in switchbacks down to Taylor Street at that end so wagons can get up here. But I thought you might enjoy taking the stairs."

"I did," Annabel said. "I imagine the view is magnificent during the day."

"It certainly is. There's an excellent view of the bay and Alcatraz and Angel Island."

Was Alcatraz already being used as a prison in 1906? Annabel wondered. Just another bit of history that she couldn't quite recall.

"Well," Cole continued after a slightly awkward pause, "I suppose I'd better take you in and show you around, so you can get settled for the night."

He opened the gate and led her up the walk to the house. Only one light seemed to be burning inside, and Annabel remembered that Cole was supposed to be on duty at the station of Engine Company Twenty-one right now.

"Do you have servants?" she asked.

"Just a cook and a housekeeper, and they've gone home for the day by now. I'm afraid we'll be here unchaperoned, but it won't be for long."

"I'm not worried. You're a gentleman, aren't you, Mr. Brady?" she teased.

"I . . . try to be."

There was just enough roughness in his voice to excite her. Annabel sensed that if she gave him enough encouragement, he might throw caution to the winds.

Forget it, she told herself sternly. She had gone through too much in the past twenty-four hours, experienced too many shocks, to even be considering something as . . . as unlike herself as trying to seduce Cole Brady. Being a little reckless and flirtatious was one thing; completely losing her mind was another.

But there was every possibility that she would wake up in the morning and discover that the whole thing had been a dream. So what harm could a little romp do?

Plenty, she realized, if it *wasn't* a dream and it meant hurting Cole. He had been kind to her, so kind that she could probably never repay him for it. She wasn't going to take advantage of his generous nature by playing fast and loose with his feelings.

He led her onto the porch and unlocked the front door,

then took her inside. The interior of the house had the same understated elegance that she had glimpsed in its exterior. Ahead of them, a staircase curved toward the second floor, its banister polished to a high gleam, a brass knob shining atop the newel post. A gilt-edged mirror hung on the wall, and a gaslight burned in a sconce next to it. Despite its size, the house seemed warm, friendly, and cozy.

"I'll take you on a tour of the place if you'd like," Cole offered when he had hung his hat on a brass hat stand just inside the door.

Annabel found herself stifling a yawn. The heavy meal, plus the long day, had left her tired. "If you don't mind, I'd rather postpone that until tomorrow."

"Of course," Cole said quickly. "You'd like to retire. I'll take you up to one of the guest rooms." He hesitated, then said, "I'm not sure what we have in the way of nightclothes. . . ."

"Oh, don't worry about that," Annabel said without thinking. "I don't mind sleeping in the buff."

Cole's eyes widened. "Well, ah," he said after a moment, "however you're comfortable is fine with me." He took her arm again. "The guest rooms are on the second floor."

He led her up the stairs, pausing to light another lamp on the second-floor landing. Then they went down a hallway, their steps almost soundless on a thick carpet runner. Cole stopped in front of a door and opened it. "I'll just light the lamp," he said.

The glow revealed a small but lovely bedroom with a four-poster bed, a dressing table with a mirror above it, and a mahogany wardrobe. The spread on the bed was a rose print, which matched the ornate tracery in the wallpaper.

"It's beautiful," Annabel said in a hushed voice.

"My mother decorated the house before she passed away," Cole said, "and my father was careful not to change anything. Neither have I."

"Oh." She realized he hadn't spoken much about his parents. What little she knew about them came from Mellisande Dupree, in fact. She asked hesitantly, "How old were you when you lost your mother?"

"I was ten," he said quietly.

"That must have been very difficult for you."

He nodded. "My father tried, but . . . he was hurting over her loss, too, of course, and he . . . he never quite understood me the way Mother had. . . ."

"I'm sorry, Cole," Annabel said quickly. "I shouldn't have asked you—"

He shook his head and smiled faintly. "No, that's all right. I don't mind talking about it. My father passed away four years ago. We loved each other, I suppose, but things were never the same after my mother died."

"And you've been . . . alone . . . since then?"

"Pretty much," he shrugged. He glanced around the room. "Well, will this be all right?"

"More than all right," Annabel assured him. "It's a lovely room. Thank you for letting me stay here. But tomorrow I'll start looking for a place of my own."

Assuming I'm still here tomorrow and haven't been whisked back to my own time by whatever forces brought me here in the first place.

Annabel realized with a shock that she wasn't in as much of a hurry to get back now.

"I noticed the boxes from Miss Mellisande's downstairs," Cole said. "I'll just leave them there for the night, if that's all right, until you decide what you want to do."

"That's fine," Annabel told him.

"Well, then . . . good night."

"Good night." She looked up at him, not knowing what she expected of him, not even knowing what she wanted.

He hesitated, took half a step toward her, and lifted a hand as if to reach out and touch her. Annabel waited.

Suddenly, he leaned forward and kissed her on the forehead like she was nine years old, then practically leaped backward. "Good night," he said again, hurriedly, and turned to almost run out of the room. The door closed firmly behind him.

Annabel stared after him for a moment, taken by surprise, and then she started to giggle. She was still laughing when she threw herself backward across the bed and sank down into the soft mattress and thick covers.

As he walked down the hill ten minutes later, Cole wore the dark blue uniform and the black cap with the short, stiff brim that he should have donned earlier in the evening. His duty time at the firehouse was more than half over, but he was going to report anyway. It was quite possible that Lieutenant Driscoll would hand him his head for being so late. Whatever lectures or punishment the lieutenant handed out, Cole intended to accept them with equanimity. He deserved them, after all, he told himself. He had no suitable explanation for why he had been so negligent in his duty.

No explanation except for the fact that he had been utterly bewitched by a woman who might be mad, a woman with the most beautiful eyes he had ever seen.

He had wanted so badly to kiss her as they stood there in the guest room, saying their awkward good nights. He could sense that she wouldn't have minded if he kissed her, either. Not that she was a . . . a loose woman; even knowing her less than a day, he wouldn't have believed that of Annabel Lowell in a million years. It was just that there was some sort of mysterious connection between them, a bond of some kind.

A common interest in firefighting, he told himself. That was all it could be.

Of course, he had never been the least bit tempted to plant a big kiss on Patsy O'Flaherty.

Cole was no stranger to the charms of young women. He was known throughout San Francisco as a wealthy, though eccentric, young man, which made him a very eligible bachelor in the eyes of many young women—and their mothers. They looked at the properties he owned and were more than willing to overlook his oddities. So there had been no shortage of dalliances and flirtations in his life, especially a decade earlier when he had been in his early twenties and anxious to outrage his staid, conservative father in any way he could.

He supposed that as the years had rolled on, he had become the staid, conservative one. A lot of the ambitious young women had given up on ever being able to hook him. As it stood right now, it had been over a year since there had been a woman in his life.

The firehouse was only a few blocks away on Lombard Street, within easy walking distance of the hillside lane where Cole lived. It was nearly nine o'clock when he arrived. His shift would have normally been over at midnight, but he planned to work an extra shift to make up for the time he had missed.

Besides, that would keep him out of the house so that Annabel could sleep without having to worry about having her reputation compromised. And he wouldn't be tortured by the thought of her sleeping "in the buff" only a few rooms away.

"Well, look who's decided to honor us with his presence," a voice said sharply as Cole walked into the two-story brick building. The three steam-powered Amoskeag pumpers were kept on the first floor, along with the extra hoses, axes and other firefighting equipment, and the long coats and helmets worn by the crew when they went out on an alarm. In one corner of the first floor was a small kitchen and mess hall, and upstairs were sleeping quarters and offices.

Cole saw Lieutenant John Driscoll coming out of the mess hall with a steaming cup of coffee in his hand. Driscoll was a tall, lantern-jawed man, slender almost to the point of gauntness. His cap was off, revealing fair, nearly colorless hair.

Patsy O'Flaherty followed the lieutenant out of the mess hall. The little Irishman was a head shorter than Driscoll, with a cap of tight red curls on his head and freckles scattered across his broad, pleasantly ugly face. He had always reminded Cole of a redheaded bulldog. He said, "Didn't expect to see you here tonight, lad. The lass throw you over already, did she?"

"What's that?" Driscoll asked sharply. "You're late because of a girl, Brady? And you didn't even have the consideration to call?"

Cole glanced at Patsy, who suddenly looked embarrassed. "Sure and it slipped me mind to tell ye, Lieutenant. Cole called all right, and explained that he had some personal business t' take care of."

"I'm sorry, Lieutenant," Cole said. "It won't happen again."

Driscoll snorted. "See that it doesn't." He took a sip of the coffee, made a face, and looked around at Patsy. "Are you *ever* going to change the grounds in that coffeepot, O'Flaherty?"

"First thing in the mornin', sir. And that's a promise."

Driscoll nodded and went upstairs. With a grin, Patsy scurried over to Cole and asked in a low voice, "How was she, lad?"

"It's not like that at all," Cole said.

"Then how is it?" Patsy asked. "Ye tell me."

"I met a young woman who was in need of assistance. She's a stranger here in San Francisco, and she'd lost all her bags. . . ." He might have to stop falling back on that lie eventually, he thought, but for now it was coming in handy.

He fell silent when he saw the way Patsy rolled his eyes. "Lad, lad," Patsy said with a shake of his head, "ye didn't fall for that old yarn, did ye?"

"It's true," Cole insisted. "Miss Lowell was quite upset, and if I hadn't helped her, I don't know what she would have done."

"Found herself another pigeon, that's what she'd have

done. 'Tis a bunco artist she is, m'boy. Did ye give her money?"

Cole shook his head. "No, I just bought her some clothes and something to eat. And gave a place to stay for the night."

"At yer house?"

"Well . . . yes."

Patsy rolled his eyes again. "Ye'll go back there in the mornin' and find everything of value gone, along with the lass. Mark my words."

"Absolutely not," Cole said emphatically. "Annabel joked about that same possibility, and she'd have hardly done that if she really intended to rob me."

"Annabel, is it?" Patsy's smile was shrewd and knowing. "Sure and she's wormed her way in good an' proper, hasn't she?"

"Do I interfere in your romances?" Cole snapped, and as soon as the words were out of his mouth, he wished he could call them back. But it was too late for that, of course.

"Oh, ho!" Patsy chortled. "So ye admit ye've fallen head over heels for the lass!"

"I'm admitting no such thing!" Cole snatched his cap off his head in frustration. "I just . . . I'm fond of her, I suppose, but I only met her today. . . . You can't seriously think that I would be so foolish . . ."

Patsy folded his arms across his chest and said smugly, "For every man in the world, there's a woman who doesn't have t' do a blessed thing except look at him to make him lose his senses. All ye have to do is be around her, even for a minute, and ye can't think straight anymore. You're lost, lad. 'Tis hopeless."

"That's insane. What about you? You're usually courting a dozen women at the same time. Are you saying that you're immune to this mysterious power you seem to think females have?"

Patsy laughed. "Immune? Saints above, lad, I'm an Irishman! I'm the most vulnerable of all."

Cole stared at his friend and fellow fireman. "You mean you're genuinely in love with all those women you've got on your string?"

"Of course I am! How do ye think I was able to recognize the symptoms so easy in you?"

Cole took a step back, thunderstruck. In love with Annabel Lowell? He couldn't be! He had known her less than twelve hours. In order to accept what Patsy O'Flaherty was saying, he would have to believe in something as nebulous and improbable as love at first sight. Such things simply didn't happen.

Did they?

Cole was saved from having to answer that question by the sudden, shrill sound of the fire bell going off. Without even thinking, he and Patsy dropped everything and turned to grab their gear.

Chapter 7

ANNABEL STRETCHED LUXURIOUSLY. She knew she ought to get up, but it felt so good to simply lie here on her belly and feel the smooth, clean sheets sliding over her bare skin. She usually slept in a nightshirt or pajamas, but this morning she was nude. She couldn't quite remember why she didn't have any clothes on, but it felt so good she didn't care. She would stay here for a while longer before getting up and going to work. . . .

Wait a minute. Something was wrong. She rolled over onto her back and opened her eyes.

What she saw wasn't at all what she'd been expecting.

Instead of the tile ceiling of her apartment, she saw wallpaper above her, and in the center of it wasn't a regular light fixture but some sort of chandelier. Catching her breath, Annabel bolted upright and cast a wild-eyed gaze around the room. At first glance, nothing was familiar about it, not the four-poster bed or the dressing table or the old-fashioned wardrobe or the rug on the floor.

Then memories of the night before came flooding back. So it hadn't all been a crazy dream after all. She was still in 1906, staying in a house belonging to a man named Cole Brady.

Unless . . . she was still dreaming. . . .

"Ow!"

When she pinched herself, it hurt just as it should have. She rubbed at the sore spot on her arm.

She had dozed off the night before not knowing what to hope for. A part of her expected that she would wake up back in her own time. It was difficult to believe that anybody could travel ninety-odd years back into the past; it seemed just as far-fetched that they would stay there.

But she had felt an instinctive liking for Cole Brady. She had liked him a lot, in fact, and it was more than just physical attraction, although that was a definite factor. She wanted to get to know him better.

But what about the earthquake?

With a shake of her head, Annabel pushed that thought out of her brain. There was nothing she could do about that, no way to stop it from occurring. And unless she racked her brain to remember Earl's historical lectures, she couldn't even be sure when it was going to happen. In a way, she realized, she was just like every other Californian: She knew a big earthquake was coming, she just didn't know when.

So for now, she wasn't going to worry about it. She had more important things to be concerned with, such as figuring out how she was going to fit into this time period, for as long as she was here.

She heard a heavy thump from downstairs.

Annabel caught her breath at the sound. Her gaze darted to the window. Enough light was coming in through the gauzy curtains that she knew it was morning. Exactly how late she had slept she couldn't tell, and there was no clock in the room.

But someone was definitely downstairs, because she heard another thump a few seconds after the first one.

Cole was back. That was the most reasonable explanation, she told herself. He had said the evening before that he was going to stay at the fire station overnight. He had probably come home when the sun came up. Either that, or the noise could have come from the cook or the housekeeper, if either or both of them had already reported for work.

Someone groaned, as if in pain.

Annabel swung her legs out of the bed. She had to find out what was going on. She gathered the covers as she stood up, wrapping them around her like a giant toga.

The bedroom door was locked. While she was undressing the night before, she had found a big, old-fashioned key on the dressing table and used it to lock the door. She hadn't done so out of any fear of Cole Brady; chances were, he had another key just like the one she'd found. But it had made her feel better anyway, semiparanoid modern-day urban dweller that she was.

Now she snatched up the key from the table and fitted it carefully into the lock. She turned it, then grasped the knob. Easing the door open, she peered through the gap into the hallway.

The hall was empty. She stepped out of the room, listening intently for more sounds. None came, so she started toward the stairs. The moan she had heard had definitely been one of pain. Someone was hurt downstairs. Even if it was a burglar, Annabel couldn't stand by and not investigate. Old habits died hard, and she was in the habit of helping people.

On the other hand, she didn't want to be foolhardy. She looked around the upstairs hallway for something that could be used as a weapon. Nothing. With a grimace, she wished she had the pepper spray that was back in her apartment.

She kept moving, her barefooted steps silent on the carpet runner. When she reached the stairs, she lifted the bedspread and sheet she had wrapped around her, so that she wouldn't trip over them, and started down.

Another sound came from below. Somebody had dropped something. Annabel froze halfway down the stairs and listened. Silence descended once more on the house.

She started moving again, one careful step after another. When she made it to the bottom of the curving staircase, she glanced to her left and saw a door that led into a parlor. Inside was a fireplace, and next to it a gilt-covered stand with a couple of pokers. She stole quickly into the room, grasped one of the pokers, and lifted it out of its holder. It was heavy, but the weight was reassuring in her hand. To someone who could swing a Pulaski for hours on end, wielding one little fireplace poker didn't pose much of a challenge.

She thought the sounds she'd heard had come from the rear of the house. She went back to the main hall and turned in that direction. Ahead of her was a door that no doubt led to a kitchen.

The door had no knob; it was the type that swung back and forth. Annabel tightened her grip on the poker with her right hand and used her left to clutch the bedcovers closer around her. Then she lifted her right foot and kicked open the door. She lunged through, the poker raised high, and let out a yell.

Cole yelled, too, jerking back so that the chair in which he was sitting overturned and dumped him hard on the linoleum floor.

Annabel stood there, the poker still poised over her head, paralyzed by surprise. All she was able to do was say quietly, "Oh, my God."

"Annabel?" Cole said, his voice stunned.

Slowly, she lowered the poker and tried to make sense of what she was seeing. His feet, clad only in socks, were pointing toward her, and beside the table stood a pair of high-topped, heavy boots. Nearby, lying on its side, was a leather fireman's helmet, with its high crown, short front brim, and long, down-curving rear brim. Cole must have dropped the helmet accidentally, Annabel realized, and that had produced the clattering sound. He was still wearing a long leather coat and was covered with soot and grime. His thick brown hair was askew and his face was streaked with ashes. He looked like a man who had just spent a long, exhausting night fighting a fire.

"Oh, Cole," she said as the poker slipped from her fingers and thumped onto the floor, just missing her bare toes, "I'm so sorry." She took a step toward him, but her foot got tangled in the dangling covers and she tripped, nearly falling.

Cole scuttled backward against the stove. "Annabel, it's all right," he said hurriedly. "Don't worry."

"But I could have killed you. I thought you might be a burglar."

"Nope, just me. Ah . . . do you think maybe you'd better go back upstairs and get dressed?"

She looked down at herself, remembering that she was naked under the bedspread and sheet she had clutched so haphazardly around her. She started backing up and nearly tripped again. "Just . . . just stay there," she said. "I'll be right back!" She turned and practically ran out of the room. The covers flapped behind her, and a sudden chill on her bottom told her that the sheets were not wrapped as tightly around her as they could have been. In fact, it was likely she'd just given Cole quite a view.

"Can I get up off the floor?" he called after her, his tone mocking.

"Oh!" She didn't know whether to be embarrassed, angry, or just sorry.

She fled up the stairs and down the hall, clutching what little was left of her dignity—and the bedcovers.

Well, *that* certainly hadn't been what he was expecting when he got home, he thought as he pushed himself off the floor and picked up the overturned chair. He lit the stove, used the pump handle at the sink to fill a coffeepot, and put the water on to boil.

She had come through that door like some sort of . . . of Valkyrie or avenging angel, he thought. And she had been as beautiful as one of those legendary creatures, with her hair tousled from sleep and her smooth shoulders and long brown legs flashing as the bedcovers swirled around them. He had never before seen anyone quite so strikingly lovely.

He was just lucky she hadn't clouted him with that poker, he told himself. She had been ready to do battle on his behalf, to defend his home, and any intruder unlucky enough to find himself there would have been facing a female fury.

As if he needed more evidence, Cole thought, this morning had provided even more proof that he had never before met anyone like Annabel Lowell.

He went to the back porch, took off his long coat, and hung it on a hook. Then his uniform jacket and helmet went up beside it. He unbuttoned his shirt collar and his sleeves, rolling them up a couple of turns. Everything smelled strongly of smoke.

He thought about the fire at the warehouse and frowned.

Rarely did a fireman get called out to a blaze in one of his own businesses, he mused. The fire the night before had been at a dockside warehouse owned by Brady Enterprises. Luckily, it had been empty; one cargo had left on a ship the day before, and the next wasn't due until tomorrow. So while the building itself had been gutted, a bad enough loss, it would have been much worse had it been full of goods. Cole's insurance would have covered that, as it did the loss of the building, but losing a cargo would have been a severe blow to his pride, as well as to his clients' confidence in Brady Enterprises.

Was it merely coincidence that he had turned down Wing Ko, leader of the biggest tong in Chinatown, when approached only a few days earlier about a business "arrangement"? Cole didn't want to believe that Wing Ko set the fire. The tongs might use murder and arson as weapons among themselves in their wars, but such tactics were seldom if ever applied in their dealings with legitimate businesses.

Then again, perhaps Wing Ko was getting more daring.

"Cole . . . ?"

He turned to see Annabel hurrying into the kitchen. She had put on the walking dress she'd worn after leaving Miss Mellisande's the day before, only without the hat this time. Her hair was still loose, and Cole liked it that way, rich brown waves that tumbled around her shoulders and on down her back.

"Cole, I'm sorry," she said quickly. "You must think I've completely lost my mind."

"Not at all," he assured her.

"But the way I came bursting in here, yelling and waving that poker around—"

He held up both hands, palms out. "It's all right, Annabel, I understand. You were still sleeping, and you heard strange noises down here. Of course you'd come to see what was going on."

"Actually, I had just woken up," she said with a smile, "but it was taking me a while to remember where I was."

"You must have slept well, then."

"Yes, very well, thank you, but—"

"Coffee?"

She sighed. "That sounds wonderful." As he turned toward the stove, she moved deftly past him. "Why don't you let me make it. You should sit down and rest. You must have had a hard night."

"How can you tell?" he asked with a chuckle.

"Oh, the smoke, the soot, the way you groaned when you took your boots off. I've been there."

"Yes, that's right," he said as he sat down at the table. "You're a lady fireman."

She paused as she was reaching for a bag of coffee on the counter next to the stove and shot a sharp glance at him. "I really am a firefighter, you know."

"That's what you said."

"It's the truth."

He nodded and decided not to press her on the issue. She was obviously sensitive about it. And for all he knew, she was telling the truth. Back where she came from—wherever that was—maybe women really did work as firemen. Cole supposed it was possible. He had caught enough glimpses of her body while she was wrapped up in those bedcovers to know that she was rather athletic.

Those glimpses had also been enough to start his heart pounding a little faster and to expose an emptiness inside him.

Or maybe that was just hunger. After all, he'd worked hard all night, and he couldn't remember the last time he'd slept. He wanted to eat something, take a bath, then fall into bed for a few hours.

"Why don't I fix you an omelette," Annabel suggested. "Do you have any eggs?"

"In the icebox," Cole said. "Which reminds me, the iceman will be around later today. I need to buy a new block."

Annabel opened the icebox, looking at it with great interest, as if she had never seen such a thing before. It *was* a pretty modern contraption, Cole thought; he'd had it for only a little over a year. Maybe Annabel had never seen one before.

In short order, she was cooking eggs, cheese, and potatoes in a frying pan, working quickly and efficiently. The coffee began to boil, filling the kitchen with a delicious aroma. Sally Higgins, the cook, would be arriving soon, Cole thought, and she would probably be outraged to find another woman puttering around in her kitchen. But at the moment he didn't really care. He enjoyed watching Annabel move around the room.

A man could get used to that, he found himself thinking.

When the coffee was ready, Annabel poured cups for both of them, adding milk from the icebox and sugar from the sugar bowl to hers. Cole took his black. She divided the omelette in half and slid it from the pan onto a couple of plates she took from a cupboard after Cole told her where to find them. If she stayed around here a while, he thought, she would soon know where everything was.

She put the food on the table and sat down on the other side. They dug in, eating without much conversation.

When they were almost finished with the food, Annabel said, "I have to find a place to stay today."

"What's wrong with right here?" Cole heard himself saying.

She gave him a stern look. "That's not going to work, and you know it. I'm already in your debt enough, Cole Brady."

"I wouldn't say that. . . ." He shrugged. "But I suppose you're right. It wouldn't be proper."

"I don't care about what's proper. I'm used to having a place of my own."

He tried not to look shocked. She was certainly more plainspoken than any of the young women he had known before.

"All right," he said. "I know of several decent boardinghouses. I'm sure we can find a room for you in one of them."

"That's fine. And I'll start paying you back as soon as I find a job."

"A job?" he repeated with a frown. "What would you like to do?"

There was a mischievous twinkle in her eye as she looked across the table at him and said, "I was thinking about trying to get hired by the San Francisco Fire Department."

Cole's jaw tightened. He didn't want her even joking about such a thing. The idea of working alongside any woman, even one as obviously capable as Annabel, was disturbing.

But of course, he didn't have to worry about that, he told himself. Chief Sullivan would never hire her.

"I think you should consider some other line of work," Cole said as diplomatically as possible.

It wasn't diplomatic enough, he discovered as Annabel

frowned and said, "Why? Don't you think I could handle being a firefighter?"

"We're called fire*men*," Cole pointed out. "There's a reason for that."

"They have women firefighters back in New York. You said so yourself."

"That's New York," Cole said. "And they only have one woman in their department, as far as I know. It's different out here."

"Why?" Annabel asked.

Cole felt himself growing impatient. "It just is. We're . . . we're not accustomed to having women in the fire department."

"And you never will get used to it unless you hire some of them. That day is coming, you know. Sooner or later, women will work in almost every profession there is."

Cole couldn't stop himself from snorting in disbelief. "The next thing you know, you'll be telling me that women will vote and run for political office."

Annabel's eyes narrowed, and he knew he had perhaps pushed this too far. "It could happen," she said coldly. "There might even be a woman president someday."

Cole couldn't imagine a woman in the White House in any capacity other than First Lady, but he didn't say that. He had already begun to realize that perhaps it would not be wise to have this argument.

"You may be right," he said, "but that doesn't change things right now. I don't think it would be a good idea for you to apply for a position in the fire department. You'd just be disappointed when you were refused."

"Just how fragile do you think I am?" she shot back at him.

He held up his hands, palms out. "That's not what I'm saying. Perhaps you're strong enough to handle the job—"

"But I'm *emotionally* fragile, is that it?"

"No, I just—" He broke off with a sigh. "For now, why

don't we just concentrate on finding a room for you in a nice boardinghouse?"

"A room that *you'll* pay for." She drained the last of her coffee and set the empty cup back in its saucer with a rattle of china. "I want you to keep track of every cent you spend on me, Mr. Brady. I intend to pay you back—with interest."

"That's not necessary."

"I say it is." Those magnificent eyes of hers bored into him, challenging, defiant.

All he could do was sigh in defeat. "All right. If that's the way you want it, that's what we'll do."

Annabel nodded and said, "It is."

Cole put his hands on the table and pushed himself to his feet. "I'm going upstairs to clean up. After that I'll sleep a while, and then this afternoon we'll go out and find a place for you. Does that meet with your approval, Miss Lowell?"

She nodded again. "It does."

He started to turn away, then paused and gestured at the empty plates. "Thank you for breakfast," he said. "It was excellent." An idea occurred to him, and he added, "Perhaps you could get a job as a cook."

As soon as the words were out of his mouth, he regretted them. Annabel's lips tightened, and her eyes began to blaze.

"There's nothing wrong with being a servant, you know," Cole said quickly. He didn't believe she was a snob, so maybe if he appealed to her sense of egalitarianism, he could head off some of her anger.

"Of course not," she said. "I just happen to have talents I can put to better use elsewhere."

Again he held up his hands in a conciliatory gesture. "We'll talk about this later."

"I'm certain we will," Annabel replied coolly.

Cole had the sense not to say anything else. He got out of the kitchen while the getting was good.

Chapter 8

ANNABEL SAT AT the kitchen table fuming for quite a while after Cole went upstairs. How dare he act so superior! She was just as good a firefighter as he was. Probably better, since she'd had the advantages of modern-day training and technology.

But this was a different time, she reminded herself. All the gains women had made during the twentieth century were still to come. Many of the things Cole found to be so far-fetched *would* come about, Annabel knew . . . but not for some time.

Well, she told herself, maybe she would just have to hurry progress along a little.

But she had to be careful. She didn't want to wind up in an asylum, and that might well be the result if she started talking too much about what was going to happen in the future.

She heard water running in a bathtub upstairs and imagined Cole lowering his tired, aching body into the tub.

Even though she was still a little angry at him, she let herself slide into a fantasy of stepping into the tub with him, settling down into the warm, soapy water, and reaching out to explore his strong, muscular body.

Her eyes snapped open and she realized she was tightly clutching the edge of the table—so tightly, in fact, that she had pulled the tablecloth several inches toward her, bunching it up in her hands. It was the rattle of china and silverware as the cloth slid over the table that had broken the erotic spell. She took a deep breath and blew it out. "Whoa."

Maybe it would be better not to think about such things, she told herself. He had been really kind and generous to her so far, but unless he was going to treat her as an equal, there was no point in fantasizing about him.

Besides, what kind of future could they have together? They were from different eras. Sooner or later, she would have to try to find a way back to her own time. And if she couldn't, she would always be a misfit here, not the sort of woman that a man like Cole Brady would want for a long-term relationship.

"Give it up, girlfriend," she muttered. "It's not going to happen."

Now, if only her mind could convince her heart of that.

"There's a good rooming house on Vallejo Street, over in Pacific Heights," Cole said as they left the house that afternoon.

He had slept for several hours and awoken to find an excellent lunch waiting for him. Sally Higgins, his stout, gray-haired cook, had been distinctly frosty to him, however, and he knew it was because of Annabel. More specifically, because Annabel had cooked breakfast. Sally referred to her as "that young lady" in a tone dripping with scorn. Upon finding Annabel in the house when she arrived, Sally clearly thought she was some loose woman Cole had picked up. Cole had subtly tried to set her straight about that, but he didn't know if he had succeeded or not.

For her part, Annabel was just as chilly toward Sally. All of it made Cole uncomfortable. The last thing he wanted was to be in the middle of a couple of feuding women.

So the best thing for all concerned, he had decided, was to find Annabel her own place as soon as possible.

"Isn't Pacific Heights an awfully expensive neighborhood for a boardinghouse?" Annabel asked during the cable car ride.

There it was again, Cole thought, her uncanny knowledge of San Francisco. He said, "Many of the people who live there are very well-to-do, that's true. They've inherited fortunes from the Comstock Lode and things like that. But fortunes get away from people sometimes, and I'm told that one silver widow who lives over there has begun taking in boarders."

"Where did you hear about that?"

"Patsy told me at the firehouse last night." Cole chuckled. "Patsy knows just about everything that's going on in the city. He's an invaluable resource."

"I'll have to meet Mr. O'Flaherty sometime."

"I don't know about that," Cole said with a shake of his head. "With his eye for a pretty girl, he'd swoop down on you right away."

"Is that so?" Annabel asked. "You believe I'm pretty?"

Cole cleared his throat. "Only a blind man could ever think otherwise. And even he would change his mind once he heard you speak."

"Why, Mr. Brady. I believe that was a compliment."

Cole found himself smiling. "I meant every word of it."

"Thank you."

Cole relaxed slightly. He would have been willing to bet that Annabel hadn't forgotten about the argument they'd had that morning, but if she was willing to pretend that it hadn't happened, so was he. In fact, he was quite grateful. In the future, he told himself, he would have to be more careful of her feelings.

They changed cable cars, and the second one carried them up the side of the long ridge that marked the location of Pacific Heights. They got off at Vallejo Street, Cole helping Annabel down from the car as he had the day before. He didn't allow his hands to linger on her this time, however. He thought he saw a flicker of disappointment in her eyes, but told himself he must have imagined it.

"The place is right along here," he told her as he took her arm and led her along the sidewalk between two rows of beautiful mansions. The houses all rose two, three, or four stories and were built in a variety of architectural styles, but what they had in commom was sheer opulence—and in their tiny yards. Space was at a premium here on the Heights.

After a couple of minutes, Cole paused in front of the wrought-iron fence that bordered one of the minuscule yards. The house on the other side of the fence was painted a sedate gray. It was three stories tall, and the upper floor was topped with gables and a widow's walk, giving it a New England look. Instead of facing the sea, however, the house faced San Francisco Bay. There was a wonderful view from up here of Russian, Nob, and Telegraph Hills, with the dock area and the blue-gray waters of the bay beyond. To the north, one could see all the way to the Presidio, and hazy in the distance loomed the headlands of Marin County.

A small sign on the fence read *Rooms to Let.* Cole opened the gate beside the sign and led Annabel up the short walk to the porch. A pearl button that activated an electric bell was beside the door. Cole leaned his thumb on it and heard the shrill ringing inside.

A moment later, the door swung open as a short, bald black man in butler's livery answered the summons. He looked out at Cole and Annabel and asked in a deep, cultured voice, "Yes? May I help you?"

"We came to inquire about renting a room," Cole said.

"For both of you?" The man's voice was like the purr of a large cat.

Cole shook his head. "No, just for Miss Lowell here."

The man's lip curled slightly. "This is not a seraglio, sir. You shall have to seek elsewhere for accommodations for the . . . young lady."

Cole felt Annabel stiffen beside him, and anger flooded through him. "Now see here—," he began.

At the same time, Annabel blustered, "Why do people keep on thinking I'm some sort of . . . of tramp!"

The man murmured, "If you'll excuse me," and the door started to swing shut.

Cole's palm thudded against the door, stopping it short. His foot thrust forward into the gap, assuring that it wouldn't close. "Listen to me," he said hotly. "Miss Lowell is a lady, and I'll not have anyone talking as if she's not!"

His voice was rising with fury, and he didn't care. Obviously, it could be heard deeper in the house, because a woman's voice suddenly shouted, "Lucius! Who is it?"

The servant turned his head and called, "No one, madam. Don't trouble yourself."

"Oh, it's no trouble." The woman's voice was closer now. "Step back and let me speak with our visitors."

Grudgingly, the man called Lucius moved back in the foyer. Cole pushed the door open and saw an elderly woman in a wheelchair rolling toward him. He took his hat off and said, "Mrs. Noone?"

"Yes, I'm Frances Noone," the woman said. "And who might you be, young man?"

"My name is Cole Brady."

The woman's eyes lit up. "Not Thomas Brady's little boy?"

"Well, I hope I've grown up a little," Cole said with a smile, "but Thomas Brady was my father, yes."

"Why, my dear, I haven't seen you since you were a child. Come in, come in."

Cole hadn't been aware that his father had known this woman. He had no memory of her himself. However, he wasn't going to overlook any sort of advantage. Trying not to cast a glance of triumph at the protective butler, he led Annabel into the house.

"Come into the parlor," Frances Noone said. "Lucius, bring us some tea."

"Yes, ma'am," the butler said.

Mrs. Noone wheeled herself into a parlor that was filled with fragile-looking furniture. Lace doilies covered every free surface. She turned her chair so that she was facing a divan and said to her guests, "Please sit down."

Cole and Annabel had no choice except to sit beside each other on the divan. Not that Cole minded. He rather enjoyed the feel of Annabel so close to him.

Mrs. Noone's head leaned forward, birdlike. Her hair was white and well-groomed, and she was wearing a Japanese dressing gown. She smiled at Cole and Annabel and said, "This lovely young woman is your wife, I take it?"

"Ah, no," Cole said. "This is Miss Annabel Lowell. She's a good friend, and it's on her behalf that we've come here today. I understand that you rent rooms?"

Mrs. Noone nodded. "That is correct. I'm afraid my late husband did not leave me as well-off as everyone supposed. As a matter of fact, he frittered away most of the fortune he made from his silver mines on cheap rotgut whiskey and even cheaper women."

Cole and Annabel exchanged a glance, and Cole said, "I'm . . . ah . . . sorry to hear that."

Mrs. Noone fluttered a gnarled hand as she said, "It was my own fault for allowing it. Several people tried to warn me that he was a wastrel, including your own father. Thomas was just trying to be kind, but I didn't believe him at the time." She sighed. "I'm afraid it ruined our friendship. And a fine friendship it was. Did you know that he kissed me one day?"

"My . . . my father? You're speaking of Thomas Brady?"

"Yes, and you must forgive me for speaking so bluntly. When one reaches my advanced age, one knows that there is nothing to be gained by obfuscation. Plain speaking is best." Mrs. Noone turned to look at Annabel. "Are you young Mr. Brady's mistress, my dear?"

"Blast it!" Annabel burst out before Cole could stop her. "Why does everybody think that? Do I have a sign on my back that says *Slut*?"

Cole caught hold of her hand and squeezed it hard, trying to calm her down. "I'm sure no one thinks any such thing—," he began.

He realized that Frances Noone was laughing. "Oh, my dear," the elderly woman said. "You are a feisty one, aren't you? I can see now that you would never be any man's plaything. Good for you!"

Annabel nodded and muttered, "That's right."

Cole sat there and wondered exactly when it was that all control of the situation had slipped away from him.

"You see, I'm new here in San Francisco," Annabel said as she leaned forward on the divan, "and Mr. Brady has been kind enough to help me out after I found myself stranded with no money and no baggage. But I intend to pay him back for every cent that he spends on my behalf."

"Good for you, dear," Mrs. Noone said again. "I've been making my own way in the world for fifteen years now, ever since my late husband passed on, and I can tell you that there's not a thing wrong with a woman doing for herself."

Annabel cast a triumphant glance at Cole. He didn't rise to the bait. Instead he settled back on the divan and let Annabel do the talking, since she was hitting it off so well with Mrs. Noone.

"I need a place to stay and a job," she said, "and Cole thought this might take care of the problem of a room. You have a lovely house."

"Thank you. Good luck and the Comstock Lode built it."

"You've kept it up splendidly."

"With the help of my good friend Lucius."

As if hearing his name, the butler came sweeping into the parlor carrying a silver tea set. He put the tray on a sideboard and began filling the delicate china cups from a silver teapot. He brought the cups to Cole, Annabel, and Mrs. Noone, then stepped back and asked, "Will there be anything else, madam?"

"Not at the moment, thank you, Lucius."

He bowed from the waist and then backed out of the parlor, disappearing into the hall.

"He's so devoted," Mrs. Noone said. "He was a slave, you know. My late husband owned him, back in Louisiana before he came west after the war."

"And he still works for you?" Annabel sounded as if she found that difficult to believe.

"Of course. Why wouldn't he?"

Annabel just shook her head and changed the subject by asking, "Do you have a room for rent right now, Mrs. Noone?"

"As a matter of fact, I do. Would you care to see it?"

"I'd like that very much," Annabel said with a smile.

"I'll have Lucius show you." Mrs. Noone picked up a small silver bell from a table beside her chair and rang it. No more than two seconds later, the butler reappeared in the doorway.

"Show Miss Lowell the vacant room on the third floor," Mrs. Noone said, and Lucius nodded.

Cole started to get up, but Mrs. Noone motioned for him to sit down. Annabel said to him, "I'll be right back," then followed the butler out of the parlor.

Cole frowned as he listened to Annabel and Lucius climbing the stairs toward the upper floors. He was all too aware of the intense gaze Frances Noone turned on him as he sipped his tea.

"Your father was a good man," she said. "A bit stiff, but still a good man. He would never have taken advantage of a young girl." Mrs. Noone sighed a little. "Even when she perhaps wouldn't have minded . . . but that's neither here nor there. What I want to know, Mr. Brady, is what your intentions are toward Miss Lowell."

"Why, I . . . I don't have any," Cole said. "I only met her yesterday. I'm just trying to be a gentleman and help her."

"Are you certain that's all it is?"

"Yes, of course," he answered without hesitation, but the words sounded a little hollow even to himself.

"But you're already quite fond of her, aren't you?" Mrs. Noone pressed.

"Well . . . Miss Lowell is a . . . a very nice young woman."

"She's beautiful, and you know it," Mrs. Noone snapped.

"Yes," Cole agreed. "She is beautiful."

"And intelligent, and not the sort to be made a fool of."

Cole couldn't argue with either of those statements. "That's true."

"But she *can* be hurt, and probably quite easily." Mrs. Noone's eyes narrowed. "I would be very upset with anyone who hurt one of my boarders."

"Then you're going to rent the room to her?"

"If she wants it, yes. I pride myself on being a good judge of character, Mr. Brady, and I like her. I like her a great deal, and I want to have her here in this house."

"That's what I want, too," Cole said. "If Annabel is agreeable to the arrangement."

Mrs. Noone nodded and leaned back in her chair. "Very well. You'll find the rent quite reasonable." She named a figure, and Cole did find it reasonable, especially for a neighborhood as fashionable as Pacific Heights.

"That's fine," he said, then gave in to his curiosity. "Now that that's settled, perhaps you could tell me some more about my father. . . ."

Mrs. Noone might well have done so, but footsteps sounded outside the parlor just then, and Annabel entered, followed by Lucius. "The room is lovely," Annabel said. "I'll take it, if that's all right with you, Mrs. Noone."

"Certainly, my dear. Mr. Brady and I have already discussed the rent and come to an agreement."

Annabel seemed to bristle a bit at being left out of that

discussion, so Cole said quickly, "It's really a very reasonable rate, Miss Lowell. I know that's important to you, since you intend to pay me back."

"I sure do," Annabel said.

"I believe that concludes our business," Mrs. Noone said briskly. "Supper is promptly at six-thirty, my dear, and breakfast is at seven. You'll find that Lucius is an excellent cook."

The butler smiled thinly, and Cole supposed that was as much of an expression of pleasure as anyone ever got from the man.

"Now, if you'll excuse me," Mrs. Noone continued, "I'm rather tired, and my afternoon nap beckons. Lucius, show our guests out, and then you can take me upstairs."

"Very good, madam," Lucius murmured. He held out a hand for Cole and Annabel to precede him.

The front door closed softly behind them as they left the house, and Cole took Annabel's arm again. "I'll have your things brought over here," he said. "It shouldn't be much trouble. Did you really like the room?"

"It was very nice," Annabel said. She didn't sound quite as enthusiastic about the move as she had a few minutes earlier, though.

"Is something wrong?" Cole asked as they walked down Vallejo Street toward the cable car stop.

"No, of course not. I have a place of my own now, so that problem's taken care of. What could be wrong?"

Cole could think of only one possible answer.

Could she possibly be upset because she was moving out of his house?

Why wasn't she happy? Annabel asked herself. She had a place of her own, just like she had wanted. Was it the fact that she was still beholden to Cole Brady for it, and for everything else she had, including the clothes on her back? Was it because the only thing that was truly hers was the pin attached to the shift under her dress?

She had insisted on riding the cable car back to Pacific Heights by herself. She wasn't going to get lost, she had assured Cole. In truth, the streets were very similar to the ones in her own time period, and her years as a member of the SFFD had left her with an almost encyclopedic knowledge of San Francisco's streets.

"I have to be on my own eventually," she had told Cole. "I don't need a mother hen following me around."

"Well," he'd replied, a little offended, "if that's the way you want it . . ."

"It is," Annabel had declared.

Only now she wasn't so sure. She had made it back to Mrs. Noone's house just fine, and the boxes full of her new clothes had arrived shortly after her. As she sat in her room, though, the realization of just how alone she really was came crashing in on her.

On all the earth, she mused, there was surely no one else like her, no one else who came from a world ninety-odd years in the future. Even in her own time, first as a female firefighter and then as a smoke-jumper, she had been a little unusual . . . but this was much different.

She looked around the rented room and tried to get her mind off Cole Brady and all her other problems by concentrating on her surroundings.

The bed frame was solid oak, polished to a high gleam. The headboard was tall and arching, like a cathedral. There were no posts on the corners of this bed, but it was still solid and imposing. The mattress was covered with crisp cotton sheets, a quilt with a wedding ring design, and a bright yellow spread. The rug on the floor next to the bed was also yellow.

There was a built-in wardrobe on the wall opposite the bed. Annabel unpacked the clothes from the boxes and hung them. She had no idea who had lived in this room originally—one of Mrs. Noone's daughters, maybe, if the Noones had any daughters—but there was certainly plenty of room for clothes. There was also a dressing table with an even larger mirror than the one in the room at Cole's house.

Beside one of the two windows was a rocking chair with embroidered cushions tied on its seat and back. This room was in the front of the house, so when Annabel sat down in the rocking chair and looked out the window through the gauzy yellow curtains, she could see Russian Hill in the distance. She searched for Cole's house, thinking that she might be able to see the roof, but it was no use. The house was too far down on the other side of the hill.

Annabel sat there and watched the sunlight fade. Her second day in 1906 was coming to a close. For some reason, she felt sadder now than she had the night before, even though her mind had grown more used to the idea that she was really in the past—or what was the past to her, anyway. To everybody else in San Francisco, today was just the present.

Maybe she would be better off if she started thinking of it that way herself, she decided.

There was no telling when she might be able to get back out to the Diablos and find that cave. And no guarantee that when she did, it would take her back to her own time. She might be stuck here for the rest of her life, and if that was the case, all she could do was make the best of it. She would miss her friends from her own time, of course . . . Earl and Vickie and even Captain McPhee. She knew they would wonder what had happened to her, would probably think she was dead and might even blame themselves for her death. She wished she could reach out to them in some way and let them know that she was all right. She wished she could hear their voices and see their friendly faces again.

A bell rang downstairs. That would be Lucius, summoning the boarders to supper. With a wistful smile, Annabel got to her feet. She might as well go down and eat, she told herself. It wouldn't do any good for her to go hungry.

She gave the back of the chair a little push and left it rocking slightly as she exited the room.

Chapter 9

IT WAS HARD to believe that a week had passed since she had crawled out of that cave and found herself in the past, Annabel thought. So much had happened since then. She sat in the parlor, an open notebook propped on her lap. The pencil in her hand fairly flew as she took notes, trying to keep up with Mrs. Noone's words.

In the old days—which was still forty or fifty years in the future—a lot of women would be going to secretarial school and learning to take shorthand. Annabel could have used that education right now. Still, it hadn't stopped her from accepting the job when Mrs. Noone offered it.

"Are you interested in literature, my dear?" the elderly woman had asked at breakfast on Annabel's first morning in Pacific Heights.

"Well, I've read a lot of poetry," Annabel had replied. "And some novels—" She stopped herself before mentioning Kerouac and Burroughs and Kesey. She didn't think any of them had even been born yet.

"I've long wanted to write my memoirs, you know," Mrs. Noone said, not having paid much attention to Annabel's answer. "But I'm afraid I've waited too late. I couldn't possibly do it by myself now, and poor Lucius has too much to do just keeping the household going. To do a proper job of it, I would require the services of a full-time assistant."

"Are you . . . offering me a job, Mrs. Noone?" Annabel had asked, surprised by this development. She had already started worrying about what sort of employment she might be able to obtain in this day and age. In the back of her mind, she hadn't given up on the idea of joining the fire department, but she had to be practical and admit that it was unlikely she would be hired there. About the only thing she had come up with was working as a clerk in a store of some sort, and that didn't appeal to her at all.

"I would not be able to pay very much in the way of wages," Mrs. Noone said, "but I could include the cost of your room and board in your compensation."

A tingle of excitement went through Annabel. If Cole didn't have to pay for her room, she wouldn't become any further indebted to him. And if Mrs. Noone could afford to pay her anything at all, she could devote nearly all of her salary to paying back what he had already spent on her.

"What would you want me to do?" she asked.

"Oh, just listen to me while I ramble on about the past," Mrs. Noone said with a wave of her hand. "Take some notes, then organize them into a coherent volume. Do you think you could do that?"

It was a job for which she was totally unsuited, Annabel had told herself. But it was also a better situation than she could have hoped for. She heard herself saying, "I'll give it a try."

Now, five days later, she found herself wishing—for at least the thousandth time—that she had a microcassette recorder and a good computer. Better yet, some state-of-the-art voice recognition software and a recordable CD drive . . .

Might as well wish for the moon, she told herself wryly. Come to think of it, astronauts had in fact gone to the moon—or *would* go to the moon—way before any of that other stuff became available.

It's 1906, she told herself. *For now, just remember that and nothing else.*

She became aware that Mrs. Noone had fallen silent. Looking up, she saw the woman staring intently at her.

"I-I'm sorry," Annabel stammered. "I'm afraid my mind wandered. What were you saying, Mrs. Noone?"

"Are you all right, my dear?"

"Yes, I'm fine, really. I'm sorry I got distracted."

Mrs. Noone laughed. "How could your mind not wander, a vital young woman such as yourself having to sit here all day in a dusty parlor listening to the maudlin reminiscences of an old woman?"

"Madam," Lucius said indignantly from the foyer, where he happened to be passing by, "the parlor is *not* dusty."

"I didn't mean it literally. All I meant is that young people need to get out and enjoy the fresh air. Don't you have some shopping you need to do?"

"There are a few things I need to pick up at the market," Lucius admitted grudgingly.

"Then why don't you have Annabel go and get them for you," Mrs. Noone suggested. "I'm sure she wouldn't mind."

"Not at all," Annabel said quickly, as she placed the notebook and pencil on the low table in front of the divan where she was sitting.

Lucius sniffed. "Very well. Come out to the kitchen with me, Miss Lowell, and I shall give you a list, along with a note for that Italian bandit at the market, so that he will know you are my representative and not attempt to overcharge you."

Annabel looked at Mrs. Noone and said, "We'll get back to the work later."

"Certainly, my dear. Go along now."

Annabel followed Lucius to the kitchen, where he wrote out the shopping list and the note for the grocer in a neat, precise hand. Annabel took them and headed upstairs to fetch a hat before she went out.

Maybe she was getting into the spirit of the period, she thought. In her own time, the only hat she ever wore was her firefighter's helmet. In 1906, though, women always wore hats when they went out in public. Miss Mellisande Dupree had included several when she'd packed up the clothes and accessories and had them delivered to Cole's house. Annabel chose a straw boater with a bright blue ribbon that formed a band around it, hanging down in twin tails from the knot in the back. The hat went perfectly, she thought, with the blue walking dress she had put on that morning—without the corset. She had spent some of her time in the past week letting out the seams of the garments so that she could fit into them without resorting to that infernal whalebone contraption that was practically impossible to put on by oneself.

The morning fog had already burned off, leaving an absolutely gorgeous spring day in San Francisco. The air was so clear and the bay seemed so close that Annabel felt as if she could pick up a pebble from the sidewalk in front of the boardinghouse and throw it all the way into the blue-green water. She took a deep breath, relishing the fact that there was no pollution to drift over from Oakland.

She walked down the street to the cable car stop and had to wait only a few minutes before one of the cars came along. Lucius had given her detailed instructions on how to find the market on Columbus Avenue, never realizing it was only a few blocks away from where Annabel had lived for the past few years. She knew the area well and wasn't going to be in the least surprised if the building which housed the market was one that still existed in her time.

She swung up into the car and settled herself onto one of the empty seats for the steeply slanting ride down from Pacific Heights. As she did so, she thought about the last time she had ridden one of the cable cars.

Cole had been with her then.

She felt a pang of regret go through her. She had thought that they had parted on friendly enough terms, but since he'd left her at Mrs. Noone's house five days earlier, Annabel hadn't seen him or heard from him. It was as if he had washed his hands of her completely.

She knew Mrs. Noone had talked to him. The same day Annabel had agreed to help her with her memoirs, the elderly woman had called Cole on the telephone to let him know that he would not need to pay Annabel's room and board, at least for the time being. But he hadn't asked to speak to her. She had asked Mrs. Noone if he had, and the landlady had said, "No, I'm afraid not, dear."

She knew, too, that it wasn't a matter of his being too busy with his work. There hadn't been any fires, either major or minor, in San Francisco during the past five days. She was certain of that, because she had checked the newspaper every day. Fires were big news around here and always made the *Chronicle*.

Well, if that was the way Cole wanted to be, there was nothing she could do about it, Annabel supposed. Maybe, in fact, she should be saying good riddance. He never would have understood her, not with his old-fashioned attitudes toward women—old-fashioned as far as she was concerned, anyway.

But still, as she thought about how it had felt to share a cable car seat with him . . . about the warmth and strength of his thigh as it pressed against hers . . . she couldn't help but feel a sense of loss.

It wasn't, however, like mourning a lost love. . . .

It was more like mourning a love that might have been.

"Wake up, lad. You're dreamin' again."

Cole jerked in his chair, and his hand nearly knocked over one of the rooks on the chessboard in front of him. "I'm not asleep," he said.

"Maybe not," Patsy O'Flaherty said, "but you're dreamin', right enough." His pleasantly ugly little bulldog face creased into an even wider grin. "About a gal, I'd wager. Ah, lad, I've been there meself, so many times."

Cole tried to force his attention back on the game. He and Patsy had been dueling for well over an hour. As usual, the chess match had been a fiercely fought battle of move and countermove, gambit and ploy.

It didn't make things any easier for Cole that instead of rooks and knights and bishops and pawns, he often found himself seeing a queen instead, a queen who looked just like Miss Annabel Lowell . . .

He felt terrible for having practically abandoned her at Mrs. Noone's house. He knew he should have gone back to see her and make sure that she was all right, but after Mrs. Noone had told him that Annabel was going to be working for her, there hadn't seemed to be any real need—or excuse—to return. Annabel had a good place to live, a job—at least for the time being—and pleasant companions.

So, when you came right down to it, Annabel didn't need him around at all anymore.

And that was such a painful thought that he'd done his best to banish it—and her—from his mind.

He'd failed miserably, of course.

"Och, there ye go again already!" Patsy exclaimed. "Sure and that lass ye found wanderin' on the ferry dock has taken over yer brain completely, lad."

"Nonsense," Cole declared. He reached for his only remaining bishop and moved it. "I'll prove it. Check."

Patsy sighed, slid a rook over and took the bishop, leaned back in his chair, and said, "Check—and mate."

Cole stared at the board for a moment, then rolled his eyes and blew his breath out in disgust with himself. He put a fingertip on his king and tipped it over. "Good game."

"Not necessarily." Patsy sat up again and clasped his hands together on the table in front of him. "Why don't ye go see her? If ye really want to get her out o' yer system—and I seriously doubt that ye do—the only way t' do it is with a clean break. Take it from me, boyo: I'm speakin' from experience."

Cole shook his head. "No, there's no need for that. I'm sure Miss Lowell is doing fine. If there was any problem, Mrs. Noone would have let me know."

"The problem is ye're pinin' away for that gal."

Patsy had a point, Cole supposed. But what would bother him more: the guilt he felt for not going to see Annabel, or the disappointment he would feel when he saw that she was getting along just fine without him?

Cole scraped his chair back and stood up. "Think I'll get a cup of coffee," he said, deliberately changing the subject. "You want some?"

"Irish coffee?" Patsy waggled his bushy eyebrows.

"Not while we're on duty," Cole said sternly. He headed for the potbellied stove in the corner of the firehouse crew's living quarters, where a pot of coffee was always warming.

Before he got there, a heavy weight landed on his left shoulder, staggering him. Thick, soft fur brushed his ear, and sharp claws dug through the uniform jacket and into his shoulder. He was grateful for the thick wool garment. The cat was able to hang on without inflicting too much pain or damage.

Not that it would have mattered to the huge black-and-white cat if he did. Fulton went where he pleased and did what he wanted, deeming it a perfectly legitimate right in return for his services as the firehouse mouser.

Cole reached up, pried Fulton off his shoulder, and tucked the cat under his arm as he continued on his way to the stove. When he got there, he dropped the animal carefully to the floor. "Go find a mouse." Fulton just stared at him for a second, then commenced washing his long, silky fur.

Cole filled cups for himself and Patsy and then carried them back to the table. The two of them were the only ones awake in the headquarters of Engine Company Twenty-one, even though it was mid-morning. Their crew had changed shifts only a few days earlier, and most of the men were still having trouble adjusting to the new schedule. Loud snoring came from several of the bunks along the wall.

Lieutenant Driscoll came into the room from downstairs as Cole sat down again at the table and slid Patsy's cup across to him. The lieutenant said, "All's quiet, I suppose?"

"That's right," Cole said. "What did Chief Sullivan have to say?" He knew that Driscoll, along with all the other lieutenants in the department, had been summoned downtown for a meeting with the chief engineer this morning.

"He gave us a schedule for a test of the new alarm system," Driscoll replied. "Also, he was letting us know that a photographer will be traveling around the city for the next few weeks, making official group photographs of all the engine companies."

Cole grimaced. "Why is he going to do that?"

"Because good publicity is good for the department," Driscoll explained patiently, with the air of a man who had gone over this issue before. "We always want the fire department to appear in the best light possible, so the city fathers won't even consider cutting our funds when it comes time to establish a budget."

"They'd never do that," Patsy declared without hesitation. "Not as long as they're afraid that the whole city might someday burn down around their blessed ears."

"Well, at any rate, it's going to be done, so you'd better get used to the idea. I'll let you know later when the photographer will be here."

Patsy licked his fingers and slicked down a little of his rumpled thatch of hair. It didn't improve his appearance much, but he grinned and said, "I'll be sure to make meself beautiful."

Annabel Lowell, Cole thought. Now, there was someone who didn't have to make herself beautiful. She was just naturally that way. He remembered the way she had looked in the soft light of the street lamps, her hair dark and luxurious, and the way the sun had seemed to lighten it several shades the next day when it shone so brightly on her. He would never forget her. . . .

"There ye go again!" Patsy said as his fist thumped the table. "Lieutenant, ye might as well send this boy home. He's worthless to us now. His head's full o' moonbeams an' fairy dust. He's in *looooove.*"

Cole leaned over the table and took a halfhearted swipe at Patsy's head, which the genial Irishman ducked easily. "That's a lie!" Cole said.

"I hate to quote an Englishman, but methinks thou doth protest too much, boyo."

Lieutenant Driscoll said sharply, "That's enough of that. I'm not going to send you home, Cole, but we could use some more coffee." He lifted the lid of the pot on the stove, took a sniff of the contents, and wrinkled his nose. "These grounds are going to get up and walk away by themselves if someone doesn't replace them soon."

"All right," Cole said as he got to his feet. "I'd be glad to go to the market, Lieutenant." He glared across the table at Patsy. "At least that'll get me away from this blasted leprechaun for a while."

"Aye, run away," Patsy said. "Ye're just afraid I'll ask ye for a rematch on the chess game."

"Not likely," Cole muttered.

Not while his thoughts were still taken up by the lovely, haunting memory of Annabel Lowell.

It was like going home again. Actually, she *was* going home again, Annabel thought as she walked along Columbus Avenue. Only this area of the city wouldn't actually be her home for another eight decades.

A lot of the buildings were different, but some of them were recognizable enough that Annabel had no trouble figuring out where she was. Her apartment building wasn't there, but another was located in its place. This was strictly an Italian neighborhood now; the Beats wouldn't move in for another forty years. The air was full of familiar, delicious smells. Many of the buildings Annabel passed were either markets or restaurants, much as in her own time.

Up ahead she saw the shop where Lucius bought groceries and produce. It was on one of the small triangles of real estate formed by side streets' cutting across Columbus Avenue at sharp angles. A single-story building, it had large, open doors leading into a shadowy interior, and on the sidewalk in front of the place were bins of fruits and vegetables. A sign over the main entrance proudly proclaimed *Avallone's Market.*

A slender man with a mustache stood on the sidewalk exchanging greetings with nearly everyone who went past. He was wearing a white apron over work clothes but managed to look dapper in spite of it. He had a friendly smile on his face, and Annabel didn't think he looked the least bit like the bandit Lucius had referred to him as. As Annabel approached, he grinned at her and said, "Hello, lady. Beautiful day today. You need to buy something?"

"As a matter of fact, I do," Annabel replied. "I'm here on behalf of Mrs. Frances Noone—"

"Mrs. Noone!" the man exclaimed. "One of my favorite customers! I don't see her nearly often enough. How is she?"

"She's fine," Annabel said, a little distracted by the man's ebullience. "Her servant, Lucius, gave me a list of what we need and a note for you—"

Again the man interrupted, but he didn't sound as enthused this time as he said, "Lucius!" He rolled his eyes. "All the time trying to cheat a poor merchant out of an honest profit. The man's so tightfisted you can't pry his fingers open with a crowbar!"

Annabel tried not to smile. She had a feeling that watching Lucius and this man haggle would be a sight to behold. And that the two of them would probably enjoy every minute of it.

She handed over the list and the note, which the store owner—Annabel supposed he was Mr. Avallone—scanned quickly and then crumpled with a grimace and tossed in the gutter. He waved the list and said, "You come with me, Miss Lowell. I'll take good care of you."

Annabel followed him into the market and watched while he began gathering the items on the list and placing them in a cardboard box. Since she didn't have anything to do, she looked around the shop. The front of it was filled with cluttered shelves, and in the rear was a butcher's counter with long strings of salamis, pepperonis, and franks hanging from the ceiling behind it. Annabel had never seen the inside of such a market except in pictures.

Square beams supported the ceiling in places, and tacked to them were signs and notices of all sorts. Evidently, Avallone's Market served as a sort of neighborhood bulletin board. The words *Fire Department* on one of the signs caught Annabel's eye, and she moved over closer to see what it said.

Her eyes widened as she read the notice. It was an announcement of an annual competition between the San Francisco Fire Department and the Oakland Fire Department, to be held in Golden Gate Park on March 17. That was four days from now, Annabel realized. According to the sign, the competition would be in all sorts of firefighting skills and would be the highlight of a daylong celebration also featuring games for children, concerts by the respective fire department bands, and rides on the horse-drawn fire wagons. The finale would be a race between fire wagons from both departments.

Cole will probably be there. That was Annabel's first thought when she had finished reading the sign. But so what if he was? she asked herself. It didn't matter to her what Mr. Cole Brady did. He'd certainly made it clear that *she* didn't matter to *him.*

"Mr. Avallone?" she heard herself saying.

The grocer turned toward her with a smile. "Yes, Miss Lowell?"

Annabel pointed to the sign announcing the contest. "Is

this new, or has it been up here since last year?"

"Oh, it's new, all right. Big doings in Golden Gate Park. The missus and the kids and I always go. You should, too."

Annabel nodded slowly. "Perhaps I will."

The shopkeeper placed the full carton on the rear counter. "I'll have one of my boys deliver this to Mrs. Noone's right away, and I'll put the charge on her bill. Is there anything else I can do for you?"

"No, I believe that's everything." Annabel turned and started for the door.

She had taken only a couple of steps when she stopped short and stared at the familiar silhouette of the man standing in the doorway.

It was her.

And she was coming toward him like an angel in a blue dress, emerging from shadows into light.

Then she stopped, the surprised look on her face swiftly turning into one of cool anger, and Cole felt a twinge in his chest.

"Annabel," he said, his voice sounding strange even to his own ears.

"Cole," she replied. She didn't really sound angry, he thought, just noncommittal. That was all right. He could stand that, maybe. He knew he couldn't bear it if she were angry with him.

He cleared his throat and took off his uniform cap. "How have you been?"

"Just fine," she said. "You heard that I'm working for Mrs. Noone, I take it."

"Yes, of course. She spoke to me. She . . . she's very fond of you already."

And so am I, he thought. *I just hadn't realized how much.*

"I'm fond of her," Annabel said. Her attitude softened slightly. "I'm happy there. Thank you, Cole."

"What for?"

"For finding a place for me."

"I was happy to help."

Lord, but he sounded stiff and formal! If that was another legacy from his father, it was one he could do without right now, Cole thought. Annabel looked so lovely it was all he could do not to lean forward and kiss the soft, smooth curve of her cheek.

But he knew that if he got that close to those magnificent eyes, he would want to kiss them, too, and then her lips, those sweet, red, inviting lips. . . .

She turned half-around and pointed to something behind her. "I saw the sign announcing the competition between the San Francisco Fire Department and the Oakland Fire Department. Are you going to be there?"

"The competition?" he repeated. "Oh. Yes, I'll be there, I suppose."

"Good." She smiled. "I will, too."

"I'm sure you'll enjoy watching all the contests. The whole day is quite a spectacle."

Annabel shook her head. "No, Cole, I don't think you understand. I won't be going there to observe. I plan to participate."

Chapter 10

ANNABEL WATCHED THE look of utter shock appear on Cole's face and regarded it as partial payment for the way he had ignored her for the past five days. Clearly, he had no idea how much she had missed him.

As he practically gaped at her, she said, "Perhaps you didn't understand what I said—"

"I understood perfectly," he cut in. "But it's impossible, absolutely impossible. Those contests are only open to members of the fire department."

"If you'll remember," she said, "I told you that I'd like to join the fire department."

Cole shook his head. "You can't. You're—"

He was about to say *a woman*. Annabel knew that, and so did he. The look on her face stopped him short. He hesitated, then continued lamely, "You just can't." He brightened abruptly and went on, "Anyway, you already have a job, working for Mrs. Noone."

"That won't last forever."

"The contest is in four days," Cole pointed out with a smug smile.

He could be such an infuriating man, Annabel thought.

But she kept a tight rein on her temper as she continued putting into words the idea that had come to her when she saw the poster concerning the fire department competition.

"If I enter those contests and do well in them, that ought to prove to you or anyone else that I'm qualified to be a member of the fire department."

"Well, maybe, but you'd still be—" Again, he stopped himself short.

"This *is* the twentieth century," Annabel said. "It's time for new ideas, new possibilities."

Cole rubbed his jaw, and grimaced. "I don't know . . . ," he said slowly.

"Who's in charge of your engine company?"

"That would be Lieutenant Driscoll," Cole replied, then looked as if he wished he hadn't answered the question.

"Ask him," Annabel challenged. "I'll compete for the San Francisco Fire Department, and if I do well enough, I'll become an official member of the department."

Cole shook his head. "The lieutenant will never agree to that."

"You'll never know what he would agree to . . . unless you ask him."

Annabel watched the conflicting emotions at play on Cole's face. She saw surprise, confusion, maybe even a little outrage.

Then, finally, a look of resignation came over his features. "You're not going to let go of this, are you?" he asked.

"I think it's a reasonable request," Annabel said.

He nodded. "All right. I'll ask the lieutenant. But that's all I can do. If he says no, that's the way it'll have to be."

"Fair enough," Annabel agreed, although she really didn't think it was the least bit fair. "There's only one more condition."

"What's that?"

"That you put the question to him without any bias. Don't go into the firehouse and say, *There's this crazy woman who wants to enter the competition but she really can't, can she, Lieutenant?*"

Cole frowned and said, "That idea never occurred to me. I told you I'd ask him, and I will. Straight out, no bias one way or the other."

"All right, then." Annabel felt a small twinge of regret. Judging from Cole's reaction, he really hadn't intended to sabotage the request he'd be relaying on her behalf. She realized belatedly that he would have regarded such sabotage as being dishonorable. She changed the subject by saying, "What are you doing here? Are you on duty?"

He nodded. "The lieutenant sent me to buy some fresh coffee."

"Oh." A part of her had entertained the crazy notion that maybe he had gone to Mrs. Noone's house and found out where she was. That he was actually looking for her. Hiding her disappointment, she said as casually as she could, "Well, I'd better be going."

Cole didn't budge as she took a half-step toward him. He was blocking the doorway, so unless he moved she couldn't leave the market without retreating back into the building and going out through one of the other doors.

His intransigence lasted only a second; then he stepped aside. Annabel walked past him, gave him what she hoped was a pleasant nod, and turned away.

"Annabel."

She turned her head so that she could look back over her shoulder at him.

"You look . . . very lovely today," he said.

She couldn't stop the bright smile that broke out on her face. All the friction, all the disagreements between them were forgotten, at least for the moment, as she smiled at him and said, "Thank you."

Then she walked away.

Well, that had gone almost as badly as it could have, Cole told himself as he watched Annabel's easy stride carry her along the sidewalk and into the crowds. He had acted like a stubborn mule. Only at the end had he done a fragment of the right thing.

But the suggestion that she enter the firemen's competition was ridiculous! The lieutenant would never agree to such a thing. Having a woman compete for the department would make them laughingstocks. And if the Oakland department defeated them because of that—! Cole knew that he would never hear the end of it.

Still, he had told her that he would ask the lieutenant, and that he would pose the question fairly. His word was his bond. Always had been, always would be.

Somehow he knew that when Lieutenant Driscoll said no, Annabel was still going to find some way to blame him for it.

"Good morning, Mr. Brady!" an enthusiastic voice said from behind him. "What can I do for you this fine day?"

Cole turned to see the dapper little grocer standing there with a grin on his face. "I, uh, came to buy some coffee."

"I saw you talking to Miss Lowell. She's a very pretty girl, don't you think?"

"Yeah. Very pretty."

"You're acquainted with her?"

"We've met before," Cole said. He didn't feel like explaining the brief but complicated history that existed between him and Annabel. Instead, he stuck his hands in his pockets and followed Avallone into the market to get the coffee.

Across the street, a few feet back from the mouth of a narrow alley, a dim figure moved through the shadows, retreating stealthily. The watcher did not know if what he had just seen was important. Making such judgments was up to someone else; his job was simply to report what he had observed.

A network of alleys led the watcher out of North Beach and into Chinatown. Through a rear entrance, he went into a ramshackle building that fronted on Grant Avenue. The windows of the building were boarded up, and the doors hung crookedly from broken hinges. Inside, the corridor in which the watcher found himself was dim and dusty and littered with trash. At the far end of the hallway was a door which looked just a little too solid for such a dilapidated structure.

The watcher, who wore the pajama-like garb and conical hat of a coolie, rapped on the door in a prearranged sequence. A tiny panel in the door opened, a dark eye peered out at him for a second, and then the panel was snapped shut. The door itself swung soundlessly open a moment later.

The watcher stepped through into another world, a world of colorful silk tapestries and jade carvings and opulent trappings. And this was just the foyer. The room beyond, into which the door guard led him, was ten times as luxurious.

Eyes downcast, the watcher went to his knees in front of the huge chair of carved teak in which his lord and master lounged. In sharp, almost contemptuous tones, the master told him to speak, and the watcher did so. A torrent of rapid Chinese poured out of his mouth.

Though the watcher had not dared to look directly at either of the room's occupants, he had caught a glimpse of a white man in one of the other chairs. The master had a visitor, and so the watcher was not surprised when the master turned his head and spoke to the man in the tongue of the whites.

"He says that Brady met a beautiful woman in North Beach at one of the markets."

"Well, well, well. That's very interesting, Wing Ko. I wasn't aware that Brady was involved with any women at present. We'll have to look into this and find out who she is. You never know when something like that will turn out to be valuable."

The watcher understood more of the white man's tongue

than he let on. He was only a lowly spy, not *boo how doy,* but he aspired to be more someday. He would gladly wield a hatchet for his master and would be honored if he was ever called upon to give his life for the glory of his tong.

But for now, the master spoke to him and told him to return to his home. Another of the master's legion of followers would keep an eye on the white fireman. The watcher bowed until his head touched the brilliantly polished parquet floor, then backed out of the room to show the proper respect.

Annabel had a hard time concentrating on what Mrs. Noone was saying that afternoon. She struggled to take accurate notes, but her mind was elsewhere.

She had missed Cole so badly and wanted to see him so much, but then when she finally did, she had fouled up the whole thing.

It was just that it all made such perfect sense. The competition between the San Francisco and Oakland Fire Departments would be the perfect opportunity to demonstrate to Cole that she was capable of handling a fireman's job. She had thought that surely even he would be able to see that.

But no, he had been a typical bullheaded male, the same sort of man she had run into time and time again during her career as a firefighter. Only Cole was worse, because he'd never even been exposed to the idea that a woman could do a job just as well as a man.

She had managed to extract his promise to ask his lieutenant about her competing in the contest, and Annabel supposed that under the circumstances that was the best she could do. She knew that Cole would keep his word. She wasn't sure *how* she knew that, but she did.

And then . . . and then . . .

You look very lovely today.

He'd had to go and say that, and something inside her had melted. It was just a simple little compliment, nothing very creative or romantic at all. But it didn't matter. She'd heard it, and this dopey grin had appeared on her face, and she knew she must have looked like an absolutely simpering fool, all because of a few little words from a man.

Not just any man, of course. Cole Brady could never be just any man.

"Annabel, darling, are you feeling all right?"

She blinked and looked up from the notebook in her lap. The pencil in her hands had stopped moving, and she wondered how long ago she had lost track of what Mrs. Noone was saying.

"I'm sorry, Mrs. Noone," Annabel said quickly. "I'm afraid I'm just not the right person for this job. I've always worked out-of-doors."

"Oh? Doing what, dear?"

Annabel hesitated before replying. She couldn't keep everything bottled up inside, she realized; she really would go crazy if she did. And if anyone in San Francisco might understand, it would probably be Frances Noone, who had been making her own way in the world for quite some time now.

"I was a firefighter," Annabel said quietly. "A lady fireman, I guess you would say."

Mrs. Noone's pale blue eyes widened. "My word!" she exclaimed. "Really?" Annabel couldn't detect any hint of disbelief on her face or in her voice, just surprise.

"That's right."

"Then it's no wonder you and young Mr. Brady get along so well. You have that in common."

Annabel smiled ruefully. "I'm not so sure about that. The getting along part, I mean."

"But I know he's very fond of you. He sounded so solicitous about you when he telephoned here a few days ago."

"Cole is a very . . . kind and generous man. But I'm afraid that's as far as it goes."

Mrs. Noone leaned back in her wheelchair and shook her

head. "I think you're wrong, my dear. I may be an old woman now, but I was young once, you know. I can still remember what passion looks like in a man's eyes. And I saw it in Cole's eyes when he looked at you."

Annabel felt her heart begin to beat a little faster. "Do you really think so?"

"I'm certain of it."

"Well, I saw him again today," Annabel admitted, "and the only thing he seemed passionate about was the fact that he regards me as an idiot."

"My stars, I can't believe that! Why would he think such a thing?"

Since she'd started baring her soul, she might as well go on, Annabel thought. "Because I told him I want to enter the competition that's coming up between the San Francisco Fire Department and the Oakland Fire Department."

To Annabel's dismay, Mrs. Noone looked so flabbergasted by that pronouncement that for a second Annabel thought the elderly lady was going to take Cole's side in the argument. But then, Mrs. Noone inclined her head in thought for a moment and said, "Well, it's a bit unorthodox, I suppose, but why not?"

"For one thing, I'm not a member of the fire department. But I'd like to be. I told Cole that I would compete for the San Francisco department, and if I did well enough, they could hire me."

Mrs. Noone nodded. "An eminently sensible idea. It might take some bending of the rules, but I don't see anything wrong with that, do you?"

Annabel smiled. "I've been bending them all my life."

The elderly woman clapped her hands together in delight and said, "You know, I can believe that, my dear. You remind me a great deal of an old friend of mine, darling Lillie Hitchcock. She used to dress as a man, you know, and run after the fire wagons when they went racing through the town."

Suddenly, Annabel sat up straighter. "What did you say?"

"That you remind me of Lillie Hitchcock."

"No, the part about how she dressed like a man."

Mrs. Noone laughed. "Oh, it was scandalous, I suppose, but San Francisco has a long history of harboring eccentrics, you know. I was acquainted with the Emperor Norton. A very sweet man, but mad as a hatter, of course."

Annabel tried to get her landlady back on track. "This Lillie Hitchcock went to fires dressed as a man?"

"She's Lillie Coit now, since she's married. And yes, sometimes she dressed in masculine attire. She became a sort of unofficial mascot of the fire department, almost an honorary member."

Annabel knew the story of Lillie Coit, having seen Coit Tower atop Telegraph Hill nearly every day of her life until the past week. She hadn't recalled that the woman's maiden name was Hitchcock.

Being like Lillie Coit wasn't what Annabel wanted. She wanted to be a full-fledged fireman, not some sort of mascot. But the story had given her an idea. A plan began forming in her mind, a plan she might be able to fall back on if the lieutenant of Cole's engine company reacted to Annabel's challenge the way Cole expected him to.

"Why, my dear," Mrs. Noone said, "if I didn't know better, I'd say that you suddenly have a gleam in your eye which is positively devilish!"

"Absolutely not!" Lieutenant Driscoll exclaimed. "Have you lost your mind, Cole?"

From across the room, Patsy O'Flaherty said, "I told ye he's gone daft, Lieutenant."

"Wait just a doggone minute," Cole snapped. "Did I say I thought it would be a good idea for Miss Lowell to take part in the competition?"

"You didn't say it was a *bad* idea," Driscoll pointed out. "And it most certainly is."

Patiently, Cole explained, "She wanted me to ask you in a fair and unbiased manner, so that's what I did."

"So you think this . . . this woman *should* be in the contests?"

Cole suppressed the impulse to throw his hands in the air in disgust. Lieutenant Driscoll was his superior officer, after all. "No, I don't," he said. "But you don't know Miss Lowell, Lieutenant. She's a very . . . determined woman."

"But she's still a woman, and that's all that need be said." Driscoll turned back to the paperwork that was spread out in front of him on his desk. "Is that all?"

"Yes, sir," Cole said.

"I trust that you'll relay my decision to the young lady?"

"Yes, sir," Cole said grimly. He knew Annabel wasn't going to like it.

Still, he had kept his promise, so she couldn't be too angry with him, could she?

Hoping that would be the case, he left the corner of the room that served as Lieutenant Driscoll's office and went back over to join Patsy, who was polishing the brasswork on one of the Amoskeag steam pumpers parked inside the cavernous first floor of the firehouse.

The little Irishman began, "Lad, I'm tellin' ye—"

"I don't want to hear it," Cole stopped him. "Whatever it is, I don't want to hear it."

Patsy gave a dramatic sigh. "Ah, well, then, if ye don't want t' take advantage of me long years of experience with the fairer sex, sure and I can't force ye to listen."

Cole gritted his teeth together for a few seconds, then said, "All right, what is it?"

Patsy stopped polishing the brasswork and shook the rag at Cole. "Do ye like this young woman?"

"What? Of course I like her. If I didn't like her, I wouldn't have helped her when I saw her passed out on the ferry dock."

"Now, that's not true, and ye know it," Patsy said. "I've seen ye help some of the sorriest folks on God's green earth in the course o' doin' yer job. I've seen ye risk yer life for 'em."

"That's my job," Cole pointed out patiently, as if he were trying to explain something to a particularly dense child.

"No, 'tis the way ye are. If ye want proof o' that, just go look at yer bank account. Ye don't *have* to be a fireman, Cole. Ye do it because there's a part o' ye that naturally likes to help people."

Cole wasn't sure where this argument was going, but he was tired of it already. "All right," he said. "I'm the original Good Samaritan. What does that have to do with anything?"

"Just this." Patsy waggled a finger at him. "If Miss Annabel Lowell didn't mean anything to ye, ye could have helped her get on her feet and then walked away without ever lookin' back. That ain't the way it is, though, is it?"

"Well," Cole admitted, "no, I don't suppose it is."

"Ye've thought about her nearly ever' minute of ever' day since ye left her there at Missus Noone's. Am I right?"

Cole didn't want to, but his truthfulness compelled him to nod.

"Lad, I was raggin' ye earlier about bein' in love," Patsy said in a quiet, earnest voice, "but really and truly, ye have all the symptoms. So there's only one thing ye can do now."

"What's that?" Cole asked, interested in spite of himself.

"Ye have t' find out whether or not 'tis real."

"How do I do that?"

Patsy prodded Cole in the chest with a blunt finger for emphasis as he said, "The next time ye see the lass, take her in yer arms and give her the biggest kiss ye possibly can."

Cole snorted and said, "If I did that, she'd probably slap my face."

Patsy's bushy eyebrows danced up and down. "Ah, but what if she didn't?"

Cole frowned. His friend's suggestion sounded insane to

him, but he had to admit that Patsy was known far and wide as a ladies' man despite his less-than-handsome looks. "Is that what you do when you're not sure how you feel about a girl?" Cole asked.

"Aye," Patsy answered solemnly. "When I see a lass who catches me eye, I talk to her a bit, get to know her, an' then I lay the biggest, wettest smacker on her that I can."

"And they don't slap you?"

"Oh, sure, I'd say nine out o' ten do. Or worse." Patsy gestured toward his groin and grimaced slightly. "I've learned t' turn to the side quick-like after I buss 'em."

Cole shook his head. "I just don't understand. If it doesn't work nine out of ten times, then why should I try something so insane?"

"Because of *the tenth time.*"

For a long moment, Cole didn't speak as he digested that. Then he said, "Oh."

"Some o' the best nights of me life have come after those tenth times," Patsy said. "I'm tellin' ye, it works."

"But we were talking about love, not . . . lust."

Patsy shrugged. "Sure and ye got t' start somewheres, don't ye?"

Cole just shook his head, picked up another rag, and walked around to the other side of the Amoskeag. The brasswork over here needed polishing, too, so he went to it, rubbing the smooth shiny surface probably a bit harder than was actually required to do the job properly.

Patsy was wrong, Cole was certain of that. Annabel would not respond favorably if he just up and grabbed her and gave her a kiss. She would never be what Patsy called a tenth time.

But what if he courted her properly? After the upcoming competition was over, he could call on her at Mrs. Noone's house, and they could sit in the parlor and sip tea and talk about . . . well, about something, even though Cole didn't know what. And he could take her for a cable car ride, and they could go out to eat again, and maybe when spring was further along, he could take her to Golden Gate Park and they could go rowing on one of the lakes. He would enjoy that, Cole decided as he thought about how Annabel would look sitting in one of the boats, wearing a white dress with little yellow flowers on it and a white hat with a yellow band. He would row the boat and she would laugh, and the sun would shine on both of them, and then when they got back to shore he would step out first, of course, and reach out to take her hands and help her, and her fingers would twine with his and their palms would press together, and when she took the long step out of the rowboat it would bring her close to him, so that he could lean toward her and brush his lips over hers in a kiss that was supposed to be quick but lingered instead, their lips stroking and tasting and exploring the magical warmth that had sprung up between them. . . .

"You're going to rub a hole in that bell if you're not careful," Lieutenant Driscoll said as he walked past the steam pumper.

Cole jerked and looked around, instantly transported back to the drab confines of the firehouse.

The lieutenant looked over his shoulder and frowned. "Are you all right, Cole?" he asked. "You're not still thinking about that confounded woman, are you?"

Cole managed to shake his head. "Ah, no, sir. I guess I just got a little . . . carried away with my polishing."

Still frowning, Driscoll went on about his business.

Cole heard a tiny whistle and looked over the top of the boiler. Patsy had climbed up on the other side of the pumper and was grinning knowingly at him.

Cole balled the rag in his hand and threw it at the ugly face. With a cackle of laughter, Patsy dropped back down out of sight and the rag sailed harmlessly over his head.

"The tenth time, laddybuck," he called softly. "Never ye forget. The tenth time makes it all worthwhile."

Chapter 11

"ARE YOU ABSOLUTELY certain about this, my dear?" Mrs. Noone asked worriedly.

"It's true that wearing your hair down as you do is far from the height of fashion," Mellisande Dupree added. "But it's absolutely lovely when you put it up."

Lucius said in his deep voice, "For God's sake, it's the young woman's head. Let her do with it what she will."

Annabel smiled at the figures hovering around her. "Thank you, Lucius," she said. "And I *am* certain this is what I want."

"Very well, then." Mrs. Noone nodded to the portly, mustachioed man who stood waiting, wearing a waistcoat, a silk vest, and an elegant cravat with a diamond stickpin. "You may proceed, Luigi."

"As you wish, madam," the man murmured. He moved closer to Annabel and lifted the pair of scissors that he held in one pudgy hand.

Annabel closed her eyes as the snipping started. She didn't want to watch the expressions on the faces of Mrs. Noone, Mellisande, and Lucius as they observed the haircutting. Despite the positive tone of her voice, it had been a difficult decision to make. However, it was necessary if she was going to be able to proceed with her plan.

And it wasn't as if she had hair all the way down her back to her waist or had been growing it for years or anything like that. Hair that long would have been a definite impediment in her work as a firefighter. She'd always kept it short enough so that it could be pinned up and tucked under a helmet.

That wasn't good enough now. If her masquerade was going to work, she couldn't risk having her hair come loose and start tumbling down at an inopportune moment.

Maybe she should have waited until she knew for sure that Cole's lieutenant had refused to give his permission, she thought as Luigi worked his way around her, humming softly to himself, the scissors *click-clacking* around her ears. She might be sacrificing her hair for nothing.

Once she made a decision, though, she generally just plunged right ahead with it. And the more she thought about it, the more she knew that Cole's passing along her request to the lieutenant was just an empty formality. She was *not* going to be given permission to compete openly.

Which just meant she would have to compete secretly.

When she had gotten up this morning and asked Mrs. Noone about having someone come in to cut her hair, Mrs. Noone had called Mellisande first in order to consult about the matter. Mellisande and Mrs. Noone had been acquainted for years, as it turned out, which was not surprising since both of them had also known Cole's parents.

The two older women had agreed that if Annabel was determined to have her hair cut, the best man for the job would be Luigi. As she sat there with her eyes closed, listening to the *snip-snip* of the scissors, Annabel hoped they were right.

Luigi stopped cutting. Annabel heard him step back and say, "Hmmm." As she opened her eyes to see if anything was wrong, he swooped in again, the scissors darting out. A snip here, a cut there. Again Luigi stepped back and pondered. Again he moved in and cut some more. Finally, when he stepped back yet again, a broad smile broke out on his cherubic face. He turned to Mrs. Noone and Mellisande and asked, "The hair, she is beautiful, no?"

"Exquisite," Mellisande declared.

Mrs. Noone rolled forward and held out the large hand mirror she had been holding in her lap. "Why don't you take a look for yourself, my dear," she said to Annabel.

Annabel drew in a deep breath, then took the mirror from Mrs. Noone. She lifted it, holding it a good distance in front of her so that she could see a full view of her head and shoulders. Her head already felt lighter, and she could understand why when she looked in the mirror. Her brown hair was still thick and lustrous—there was just a whole lot less of it. It curled behind her ears now and barely reached the back of her neck. She had bangs for the first time in years, and she thought they made her look younger. The look was so different from what she was used to that for a moment, she had to struggle not to let out a cry of dismay.

Judging it objectively, however, she had to admit that it wasn't bad. And it would certainly serve the purpose for which it was intended. If she slicked it back, she could easily hide it under a San Francisco Fire Department helmet.

"Well?" Mellisande said. "What do you think?"

"It's fine," Annabel said. She summoned up a smile for Luigi. "Thank you."

He held the scissors over his heart and bowed deeply to her. "It is I who should thank you, lady, for allowing me to work my magic on such beautiful hair."

Lucius had left the room a few minutes earlier. He came back in now, carrying a broom and a dustpan. Annabel stood up quickly, being careful not to look down. She wasn't sure she could stand seeing all her hair scattered on the floor around her chair. She was certain she didn't want to be there while Lucius was sweeping it up and carrying it out to the rubbish bin.

Mellisande took Annabel's arm and led her over to another mirror that was hung on the wall of the parlor. "Take a look at yourself. You're lovely, my dear. But then, surely you knew that already."

Annabel studied her reflection, cocking her head first one way and then the other, and she had to admit that the hairstyle really didn't look bad at all. In fact, she was beginning to like it.

She wondered, suddenly, how Cole would feel about it.

His reaction didn't matter in the slightest, she told herself sternly. What she was doing certainly wasn't being done to please him, not by a long shot.

Luigi came up behind her and looked over her shoulder into the mirror. "You are pleased?" he asked.

"Very much so."

"*Grazia.* I must go now." He gathered up a floppy-brimmed hat and a long black cloak with a red silk lining. He donned them, then swept out of the house dramatically, the same way he cut hair. Annabel had a feeling he did just about everything with dramatic flourishes.

As Annabel turned away from the mirror, Mrs. Noone commented, "You haven't really explained why you were so determined to do this, Annabel. I realize it's none of my business, but I do wish you'd indulge an old woman's curiosity. It has something to do with that fireman's contest, doesn't it?"

"The competition in Golden Gate Park?" Mellisande asked before Annabel could reply. "What in the world could that have to do with you, my dear?"

Annabel was glad to see that Lucius had finished sweeping up her hair and had already left the room with it. She smiled at the two older women and said, "It has to do with the competition, all right. You see, I plan to enter it whether Cole's lieutenant says it's all right or not."

"But how could you possibly—," Mellisande began before abruptly stopping in mid-question. Mrs. Noone was already beginning to smile.

"I think I know," Mrs. Noone said. "You're going to pose as one of the young men and take part secretly."

"That's right," Annabel told her.

Mrs. Noone clapped her gnarled hands together. "What a wonderful idea! I'm sure you'll show those pigheaded men what sort of stuff you're made of."

Mellisande understood now, though she was clearly having trouble accepting the idea. "But . . . it may be dangerous," she pointed out. "And you'll . . . you'll get dirty."

"It won't be the first time," Annabel said, "for either of those things. A little danger and dirt never worried me."

And if they had seen some of the harrowing situations in which she had found herself as a firefighter, they would have known she was telling the truth. Running risks had never bothered her. She had risked life and limb dozens of times over the years, first battling blazes as a member of the SFFD and later parachuting into some of the worst forest fires in the country as a smoke-jumper.

But then, suddenly, she thought once again about Cole Brady, and she realized she might be risking more than life and limb this time.

She might be risking her heart.

Cole knew he couldn't put this off any longer. He had stopped by the Olympia Club on the way home and had a drink with the Commodore. The old tycoon had sensed immediately that something was bothering him.

"Bull by the horns," the Commodore had advised without prying into the details of whatever had Cole worried. "Face it head-on. That's the best way."

Cole knew the Commodore was right. Still, he had gone home, taken a bath, shaved, and put on fresh clothes. Then and only then, after there were no more mundane chores to be taken care of, had he telephoned Mrs. Noone's house.

Lucius answered, as Cole had known he would. "Hello, Lucius," he said quickly. "This is Cole Brady. Is Miss Annabel there?"

"Yes, she is, sir, if you'd care to wait just a moment—"

"No," Cole broke in. "That's all right. Just give her a message for me if you would."

"Certainly, sir," Lucius murmured.

"Tell her . . ." Cole took a deep breath. "Tell her that I would like to call on her this evening."

"Of course, sir."

"Thank you, Lucius. I'll see you later." Cole hung up.

A second later, he grimaced. He hadn't given Lucius a time at which Annabel could expect him. He hadn't even waited to make sure that she didn't already have plans for the evening. That was what came of being raised by a businessman and then spending most of his adult life around a bunch of rough-and-tumble firemen. He had missed out on some of the social graces.

Well, he would just have to hope that Annabel would be there to receive him when he arrived. Now that he had girded up his courage, he wasn't about to delay any longer than necessary. He put on his hat and left the house on Russian Hill, striding purposefully toward the nearest cable car stop.

Twenty minutes later, he was approaching the house in Pacific Heights. The three-story mansion was brightly lit. The March evening was cool, almost chilly, and the usual fingers of fog were creeping along the streets and folding around the hills. Cole opened the gate and went up the short walk to the porch. He leaned his thumb on the pearl button beside the door and heard the bell ring inside.

Lucius opened the door almost immediately. A hint of a smile tugged at the corners of the butler's mouth, slightly relieving his usually grim expression. He bowed Cole into the foyer, murmuring, "Won't you come in, sir?" As he straightened, he added, "May I take your hat?"

Cole snatched his hat off and thrust it into Lucius's hands. "Thanks," he said. "Is Miss Annabel . . . ?"

"In the parlor, sir. She is expecting you."

"Very good," Cole said hollowly. He turned toward the

parlor as Lucius moved off with silent steps.

Cole ran a hand over his hair. Even though he had brushed it earlier, it sometimes tended to stick up at strange angles. He squared his shoulders a couple of times, tugged on the lapels of his coat to straighten it, looked down at the toes of his shoes and hurriedly buffed the dust off them by rubbing each one against the back of his trousers on the opposite leg. That done, he hurriedly checked his cuff links and the stickpin on his tie. Everything seemed to be in place.

With his heart hammering, Cole stepped forward through the arched entrance, turning so that he could see the rest of the parlor. Annabel was sitting in an armchair near the fireplace, her hands folded in her lap. She came smoothly to her feet and smiled at him as he entered the room.

He was vaguely aware that she was wearing a dark green dress with a high neck and sleeves that buttoned tightly at the cuffs. Around her throat was a choker of black silk with a tiny gemstone set in its center, but Cole paid only scant attention to the necklace. Instead he looked in surprise at her hair—what was left of it.

Cole had never been overly concerned with the way women wore their hair. As a matter of fact, he had never been concerned with such things at all. But even he realized that it was odd for a woman to have her hair cut so short. He wasn't really surprised, he realized. Ever since he had met her, Annabel had been surprising him, so that by now he was growing accustomed to her doing things that were out of the ordinary.

"You don't have to stare," she said sharply.

Cole gave a little shake of his head. He hadn't realized he was staring. "Sorry," he muttered.

"If you don't like it, all you have to do is say so. I won't be offended."

Despite that claim, he was certain she *would* be offended if he said he didn't like it. But the longer he looked at her, the more he realized he *did* like the way her hair was cut.

He liked the way she looked, liked it very much.

"You're lovely," he said quietly. "Graceful and elegant and very, very beautiful."

He had never spoken more truthful words, and Annabel must have known that. For an instant joy leaped into her eyes in response to the compliment. Then the look of pleasure was replaced by her usual expression of wariness.

"Lucius said you wanted to see me," she said. "Do you have something to tell me, Cole?"

Blast it, that certainly threw cold water on things! He wouldn't have minded standing there and basking in the glow of her beauty for a few more minutes before he got down to the unpleasant business that had brought him here tonight. He took another deep breath and suggested, "Why don't you sit down, Annabel."

"All right," she said. He expected her to sink back down into the armchair where she had been waiting for him, but instead, she crossed the room to the divan and gracefully lowered herself onto it. There was plenty of room beside her, and she patted the cushion to indicate that he should join her.

Cole wasn't sure that was such a good idea, but he didn't want to upset her any more than he had to. He moved over to the divan and gingerly sat down on the front edge of it, making sure there was some distance between his leg and Annabel's.

He recalled suddenly that they had both sat on this divan the first day he brought her to Mrs. Noone's house. On that occasion, he had sat much closer to her, close enough, in fact, for him to feel the warmth of her body. He missed that warmth now and wished that he could move over beside her and slide his arm around her. But under the circumstances, he knew, that would be a bad idea.

He realized he was only postponing the inevitable, but he felt a sudden urge to make small talk. "Your hair looks lovely," he said. "What made you decide to have it cut that way?"

She shrugged delicately. "It was time for a change. Everything has to change sooner or later, doesn't it, Cole?"

"I suppose so," he admitted grudgingly.

She was determined to bring the conversation back to the subject that had brought him here tonight. And she did just that by asking bluntly, "Is this visit about the fire department competition in Golden Gate Park?"

He nodded, hoping his face didn't look as grim as he felt. "It is."

"You told your lieutenant that I want to compete?"

"That's right."

"You explained to him that I would do so unofficially, so that I could prove to you and him and everyone else that I deserve a chance to be part of the San Francisco Fire Department?"

"I put the proposal to him just as you asked me to," Cole said, "without any bias one way or the other."

Annabel leaned forward impatiently. "Are you going to make me drag it out of you? What did he say?"

"He said no," Cole replied quietly.

"What!" Annabel exclaimed. Even though she had expected that answer, she still didn't like it.

"I'm sorry, Annabel."

Her face was tight with anger. She snapped, "No you're not. You thought it was a crazy idea to start with."

"I told you I would ask Lieutenant Driscoll, and I did." He shook his head. "I don't see what else I could have done."

She came to her feet and began pacing briskly up and down in front of the divan. "This is not fair," she said. "You know it's not. You know I can do anything any of you firemen can do."

"Actually," Cole said, "I don't know that, Annabel. How could I? I never even met you until a little over a week ago."

She didn't stop pacing. "I don't care. It's still not right. There must be something you can do."

"There's not." His own voice hardened as he added, "And even if there was, I'm not sure I would."

She stopped short and turned to glare at him. "Why not? You don't believe in giving a woman a chance to show what she can do, is that it?"

He stood up and said, "I just don't want to see you risking your life for something so . . . so silly."

"Is it silly for your department to compete against Oakland's?"

"No, of course not."

"But it's silly for a woman to take part in the competition."

He was not going to win this argument, Cole told himself; it would be foolish for him to even try.

Besides, when he looked at Annabel, he didn't want to be arguing with her. Those magnificent eyes of hers were bright—though with anger, admittedly, not passion. But the results were similar. Annabel was lovelier than he had ever seen her, though before tonight he wouldn't have thought that was possible.

Patsy O'Flaherty's words came back to him, ringing inside his head. *The tenth time, laddybuck. The tenth time makes it all worthwhile.*

If he took Annabel in his arms and kissed her right now, it wouldn't be the tenth time he had ever done something like that in his life. Actually, it would only be the third or fourth. And it would *certainly* be the first time he had done such a thing with Annabel Lowell.

But he had to make her see somehow that this obsession of hers with the fire department competition was unwise. If he could distract her in some manner . . . if he could make her understand how important she was becoming to him . . .

Oh, blast it, he thought, he wanted to kiss her now because she was beautiful and because he had wanted to kiss her almost from the very first moment he had laid eyes on her. And because, in his entire life, he could count the emotional impulses he had given in to on the fingers of one hand.

So, without wasting one more second worrying about the why of it, he stepped closer to her, put his arms around her, and brought his mouth down on hers in a kiss.

Annabel was so shocked that for a long moment, she couldn't move, couldn't even breathe. Cole's lips pressed warmly to hers, not rough and demanding, but not overly gentle, either. There was a firmness to the kiss, an insistence.

And slowly, ever so slowly, she began to respond.

His arms were around her waist, his hands on her back. He held them still, the fingers slightly spread as they pressed against the fabric of the green dress. Annabel felt her arms lifting. Her left hand rested on the broad, muscular sweep of his shoulders, while her right lightly touched the back of his neck, feeling the bristle of his closely cropped hair. Their bodies barely touched, their thighs brushing, her breasts tentatively encountering his chest. Most of Annabel's attention was concentrated on her mouth and his, and the wonderfully natural way in which they came together.

His lips had the faint roughness that spoke of frequent exposure to wind and weather. They were full, strong, and warm—oh so warm, the kind of warmth that made Annabel think of cool mornings wrapped up in a soft quilt.

The way Cole's arms were wrapped around her now.

Without Annabel's even being aware of it, she moved closer to him. Their bodies were beginning to mold together. His hands pressed harder against her back, and her arms tightened around his neck. Her right hand cupped the back of his head, holding him so that he couldn't get away, even if he'd wanted to. Her lips parted slightly as Cole's lips caressed them, the kiss becoming gradually more insistent and urgent. They stroked and tasted and explored, and Annabel felt excitement growing within her.

She had wondered more than once what it would be like

to kiss Cole Brady, and now she was discovering that it was good. It was very good indeed.

Which was why it surprised her almost as much as it obviously shocked him when she brought her hands from his neck down to his chest and shoved hard, making him break the kiss and take a stumbling step backward. "Stop it!" Annabel said in a low, trembling voice. "Just stop it."

"But . . . but why . . . ?" Cole swallowed hard. "I'm sorry, Annabel. I meant no offense."

"No?" she flung back at him defiantly. "Then what *did* you mean? Why did you kiss me, Cole?"

"I wanted to," he said.

"So that you could distract me from what you think of as my foolishness."

She could tell from the brief flare of guilt she saw in his eyes that she was at least partially right. He said, "That's not all of it, and you know it. Ever since the day we met—" Abruptly, he fell silent.

Annabel waited for a space of several heartbeats, and when he didn't say anything else, she prodded, "Ever since the day we met *what,* Cole? What have you felt?" She was going to make him put it into words, all of it.

"I've wanted to kiss you," he said, his voice rough with emotion. "I was hoping that you felt the same way."

"Why? Why should you care how I feel about you? You don't care about what I want. This business about the competition is enough proof of that."

His hands clenched into fists of frustration. "Blast it, I asked the lieutenant, just like you wanted me to. You can ask Patsy whether or not I was fair about it. He was there. He heard the whole thing."

"And he probably thinks I'm crazy, too."

Cole frowned. "Actually, he didn't say one way or the other. But he didn't seem to think your idea was so strange."

"Then perhaps I should meet Mr. O'Flaherty, since it sounds like he's more open-minded than you are."

"That's not the way it was," Cole growled. He said again, "I did what you asked."

Annabel's head was spinning, and she controlled herself only with great effort. It was hard to believe that only moments ago, they had been in each other's arms, sharing one of the sweetest, tenderest kisses she had ever experienced. A part of her wished desperately that she could go back in time yet again, so that she could erase the past few moments. It would be easy, so easy, just to forget all about her plans and ambitions and to settle for being in Cole's arms, with his warm lips pressed to hers. . . .

But if she did that, she knew, she would never forgive herself.

"I think you'd better go," she said hollowly.

"I think you're right." Cole started toward the foyer, then stopped short and faced her again. "For what it's worth, I never meant to hurt you, Annabel."

"I know that," she said softly, her eyes downcast. She was afraid to lift her gaze to meet his. All the danger she had faced in her life, she thought, and now she was afraid to do this one simple thing.

She stayed like that, staring down at the rug on the floor of the parlor, until she heard the front door close firmly a few minutes later, and she knew that Cole was gone.

Chapter 12

FOR THE NEXT few days, Cole had a tremendously difficult time keeping Annabel out of his thoughts. He tried to concentrate on his work, and on the practices for the upcoming competition with the Oakland Fire Department, but every time he relaxed his vigilance, even in the slightest, her image appeared again in his mind, filling his head with her beauty and taunting him with the memory of how her lips had tasted as he feasted on her mouth. . . .

The kiss had almost worked. That was what was so frustrating. When Cole had acted on Patsy O'Flaherty's suggestion, as outrageous as he had thought it was, he had almost succeeded in driving all thoughts of the competition out of Annabel's head. He had sensed that she was close to abandoning the idea and turning to him instead.

For the most part, Cole wished she would do just that. But another part of him stubbornly insisted that he would have been disappointed in her if she had given up that easily.

He was behind the firehouse with Patsy and several other members of the crew the day before the competition in Golden Gate Park. Several bales of hay had been stacked up, and wooden targets with large bull's-eyes were attached to them. Cole stood about forty feet from the targets, hefting a double-bladed fire ax in his hand, trying to judge its weight and balance. He lifted the ax above his head, poised it there for a second, then whipped his arm forward. The ax flew through the air, turning end over end, until the head smacked into the target, just below the bull's-eye, and stuck there. Patsy and the other firemen let out whoops and whistles of admiration.

"What a throw!" Patsy exclaimed. "Sure and I'd like t' see any of those scurvy lads from Oakland beat that!"

"It was a little low," Cole pointed out.

"Pshaw! I've never seen a better one."

The other men took their turns, aiming at the other targets, and while all of them were around the bull's-eye, none came as close as Cole had. He knew that if he performed that well in the competition, there was a very good chance none of the Oakland firemen would best him in the ax throw.

"How are the horses?" Patsy asked one of the other men.

"Rested and ready for the race," he replied with a grin. "We're going to beat Oakland this year."

The competition was always close. The previous year, it had come down to the race between fire wagons at the conclusion of the contest. The Oakland department had won, but only narrowly, breaking a string of three years in a row in which the San Francisco firemen had emerged victorious. Everyone in Cole's department was anxious to win this year's competition and reclaim bragging rights.

Cole retrieved his ax and was about to set up another target when the alarm bells inside the firehouse began to ring. Along with Patsy and the others, he dashed inside. Lieutenant Driscoll came sliding down the pole in the center of the building and called out to them, "Fire on the waterfront! One of the Ingersoll warehouses!"

Cole felt a flicker of relief, but it didn't last long. When the lieutenant had mentioned the waterfront, the fear that it was another of his company's warehouses had flashed through Cole's mind. When he heard that the place belonged to Garrett Ingersoll, it eased his worries—but not by much. The fire could still spread, and Ingersoll's buildings were close to his.

He hurriedly yanked on high boots and a long leather coat as the other firemen did the same. He grabbed his red leather helmet with its gold badge on the front that gave the number of the engine company and clapped it on his head. Two of the other men were already bringing out the horses and hitching teams to the pumpers and hook-and-ladder wagons. Lieutenant Driscoll didn't have to shout orders; the men of Engine Company Twenty-one all knew their jobs and performed them smoothly and efficiently.

Cole swung up onto one of the pumpers. Patsy had already mounted the driver's seat and taken the reins. Several more men clambered onto the narrow ledge that ran around the outside of the pumper. They held on tightly to brass grab bars as Patsy whipped the team into motion and sent the pumper lurching forward. It rolled out through the big open doors of the firehouse and swung toward the waterfront, picking up speed.

The smell of the smoke was probably the thing he hated worst. Cole would have thought that he'd be used to it after all this time, but he wasn't. The sharp, acrid stench still bothered him and probably always would. He coughed wearily as he rolled up one of the fire hoses.

The flames had been extinguished, but not before they had completely consumed one of Garrett Ingersoll's warehouses and a couple of smaller neighboring buildings that had housed an office and a shop. At least the blaze hadn't been too widespread; there was that to be thankful for, Cole told himself.

Unfortunately, at the moment Ingersoll wasn't very thankful for anything, not even the fact that no one had been killed or seriously injured in the fire. The slender businessman was dashing around and cursing at the rubble of the burned-out warehouse. His clothes were disheveled and stained with soot, his hair was askew, and there were streaks of ash on his face. He didn't look much like the dapper clubman that he usually did.

Ingersoll turned to Chief Sullivan, who had come to watch his men at work. "It was arson, I tell you!" Ingersoll exploded. "What are you going to do about this, Chief?"

"We're already investigating to see if we can determine the cause of the fire," Sullivan told him patiently. "We always do that, Mr. Ingersoll. You know that."

Ingersoll ran his fingers through his hair, making it even wilder. "Do you realize how much money this blaze is going to cost me?" he demanded.

"At least it didn't cost anyone's life," Sullivan replied. Cole could tell that the chief was making an effort to hold on to his temper. He could understand that; Garrett Ingersoll's arrogance was enough to get on anyone's nerves, even under the best of circumstances.

Cole hung the hose on the pumper and then drifted over to join Ingersoll and Sullivan. Ingersoll glanced at him and curled his lip in a sneer. "Well, there's the millionaire fireman," he said. "I suppose you're glad this wasn't one of your warehouses that burned down, Brady."

"I lost one last week," Cole said quietly. "You can go look at what's left of it two blocks up the waterfront if you want to, Garrett."

Ingersoll shook his head. "I remember. But that building was empty, wasn't it? Mine was full. Packed to the rafters with merchandise, in fact." He scrubbed a hand over his face tiredly. "My insurance premiums are going to be astronomical after this."

"I'm sorry," Cole said.

Ingersoll looked at him shrewdly. "Mighty lucky for you that your warehouse was empty when it burned down. Mighty lucky."

Cole frowned and said sharply, "What do you mean by—"

He was interrupted by Lieutenant Driscoll, who came hurrying up to Sullivan carrying a charred, misshapen lump of metal. "Look at this, Chief," the lieutenant said. "We found it around back, in the alley next to the building."

Sullivan held out his gloved hands and took the lump of metal. He turned it over and studied it for a moment before saying, "It's a tin kerosene can—or what's left of one."

"That's right," Driscoll said. "There are a couple more back there just like it."

Ingersoll pointed a finger at the melted can. "I told you this fire was deliberately set!" he said. "What more proof do you need?"

Sullivan frowned. "I admit that finding evidence of an accelerant looks suspicious, but it doesn't really prove anything, Mr. Ingersoll. We don't know that someone emptied these cans around your warehouse and then set it afire."

"Then why else would they be there?" Ingersoll asked angrily.

The chief just shook his head. He couldn't answer that.

Ingersoll had a point, Cole thought. Of course, the cans could have been empty to start with and could have simply been discarded in the alley. They couldn't be considered absolute proof of anything.

"Chief Sullivan, I think ye'd better take a listen to this feller."

Cole turned and saw that Patsy O'Flaherty had led an elderly Chinese gentleman up to the group. The man's face was smooth despite his obvious age. He wore a round cap and a long queue down his back. His hands were tucked into the sleeves of his cheap cotton jacket.

"What is it, O'Flaherty?" Chief Sullivan asked.

Patsy jerked a thumb at the Chinese man. "This gent came up to me and told me he seen somebody pourin' somethin' out around the walls o' the buildin' that burned down."

"I told you!" Ingersoll practically howled.

Sullivan shut him up with a hard-eyed glance, then turned to the Chinese man. "Now, what's all this about?" he asked. "Do you speak English?"

"Speakee little Englis'," the old man said, bobbing his head. "See man back in alley, him have can like that." He withdrew one of his hands from his sleeves and pointed a finger at the melted kerosene container. "Him pour out what inside can, then strike match and throw down." The old man made an eloquent gesture. "Everything go *poof*!"

Ingersoll nodded triumphantly. "There! There's your proof, Chief."

"Looks like we'll have to list this one as arson, all right," Sullivan agreed. He turned his attention back to the witness. "The man you saw, was he white?"

The Chinese man nodded.

"What did he look like?"

The Chinese man just shook his head and shrugged.

"Well, was he big or small?"

After a moment of thought, the Chinese man said, "Small." He pointed at Ingersoll. "Like him."

Ingersoll's eyes widened indignantly. "What? Is this Chinaman accusing me of burning down my own warehouse?"

"Man I see scurry away fast. Like rat."

Ingersoll's face flushed even darker. Sullivan moved between him and the Chinese elder. "Thanks," he said. "You can go now."

The Chinese man bowed, turned, and walked away at a sedate pace.

Cole said, "He wasn't saying that you burned down your own building, Garrett, just that the arsonist reminded him of you."

"And of a rat," Patsy added under his breath, drawing a scowl from Ingersoll.

"I demand that the police be brought in and that whoever is responsible for this be caught," Ingersoll said.

"The coppers are already here," Chief Sullivan pointed

out. "I saw Inspector Fernack a few minutes ago. I'll find him and let him know about the Chinaman's testimony." He added solemnly, "We'll do everything we can to catch the man responsible for this, Mr. Ingersoll. You have my word on that."

The chief's pledge seemed to mollify Ingersoll somewhat. He nodded and said, "All right," then ran his fingers through his hair again. "I supposed I'd better go see about the insurance claim." Still muttering, he strode off, leaving Chief Sullivan, Lieutenant Driscoll, Cole, and Patsy standing there.

"This is the second fire in a week down here on the docks," Sullivan said. "I don't much like that, boys. Something is starting here, and if we're not careful, it's going to get out of control just like a fire on a windy day."

Cole didn't say anything, but he was thinking about Wing Ko. There had been no evidence found around the warehouse belonging to Brady Enterprises, but maybe that fire had been set, too, and the arsonist had simply been more careful. This fire was definitely arson, but why would Wing Ko have any reason to strike at Garrett Ingersoll?

Maybe the tong was making a move to take over Ingersoll's holdings as well, Cole mused. He was going to have to have a discreet talk with Ingersoll. Cole didn't want to start blaming things on the tong without more proof. If he jumped to conclusions and acted too soon, he might well spark off a war that would spread from Chinatown across the city.

Well, all this trouble had accomplished one thing, he thought wryly as he headed back to the pumper. It had gotten his mind off Annabel Lowell.

At least for a little while . . .

The first step in Annabel's plan was an excursion to Golden Gate Park. Now that she had enlisted Mrs. Noone and Mellisande and Lucius in her effort, they were all eager to help, even Lucius—though he would not have been so undignified as to admit it. He was handling the reins of the buggy horse as it pulled the vehicle along Golden Gate Avenue and into the vast, greenery-filled park. Annabel rode in the back with Mellisande. Mrs. Noone had remained at the house in Pacific Heights, though she had insisted that she would attend the competition itself in a couple of days' time. She had put aside the project of writing her memoirs so that Annabel could devote all of her time to getting ready for the contest.

The park looked similar enough to the way it did in Annabel's time for her to be able to find her way around. None of the art museums and pavilions from her own era had been built yet, but the Conservatory, an elaborate reconstruction of Kew Gardens in London, was already there. Annabel felt a pang of familiarity when she saw it. For the most part, however, the park was just open ground dotted with groves of trees and small gardens and lakes. The largest structure was a band shell where the fire department bands from San Francisco and Oakland would perform.

Canvas tents had been erected in the middle of the park. Lucius brought the buggy to a halt on the path and said, "This will be the headquarters for the competition. One tent for the San Francisco department"—he nodded toward it—"and one for Oakland."

"You're sure about which is which?" Annabel asked.

Lucius shrugged slightly. "I know which one was which last year, and the years before that. They've never changed. However, that is no guarantee they will not this year."

She would just have to be careful, Annabel told herself. She intended to slip into the San Francisco tent, taking advantage of the crowds and the confusion to do so, and outfit herself in a San Francisco Fire Department uniform. Engine companies from all over the city would be taking part in the contests; she would be sure and pick a helmet from some company other than Number Twenty-one. She also intended to avoid Cole as much as possible, since he was the only one of the firemen who might recognize her.

Cole Brady needed to be avoided for another reason, too. Annabel was afraid that the next time she saw him, her mind would be so distracted by delicious memories of his kiss that she wouldn't be able to concentrate on what she was doing.

She had certainly been unable to sleep that night. Instead, she had tossed and turned and carried on an endless debate with herself about whether or not she had done the right thing by pushing him away. Even lying in her bed hours later, she had seemed to taste him on her lips. He filled her senses. The fragrance that was uniquely Cole, a blend of leather and pipe tobacco and bay rum, still lingered, even though Annabel told herself it was just her imagination.

But she hadn't imagined the warm urgency of his mouth on hers, or the way his hands had held her with a mixture of strength and gentleness. Nor had she imagined the feel of his hard-muscled body pressed to hers, molding the two of them together perfectly. As she had tossed and turned and tried desperately to get to sleep, Annabel's body had responded to those memories almost against her will, her nipples hardening and heat pooling and flowing through her body like honey. She wanted Cole Brady, Lord, she wanted him!

But that was only her body talking, she told herself stubbornly. Until he was ready to accept her for who she really was, they could never come together the way she hoped they might. Cole might feel desire for her—Annabel didn't really doubt that for a second—but he didn't respect her.

He would after the fire department competition. She was sure of that.

And after that . . . Well, there was no telling what might happen then.

"Annabel? My dear, have you seen enough?"

Annabel blinked as she realized that Mellisande was talking to her. She nodded and said, "Yes, that's fine."

"The fire wagon race is some five miles long," Lucius commented as he turned the buggy away from the tents.

"That takes them almost all the way around the park. It's quite exciting. The other contests—the ax throw, the hook-and-ladder relay climb, the fire hose battle and the rest—will take place here in the center of the park. The children will be given rides on the wagons around the band shell, and they'll have games of their own. Plus the picnic tables will be filled to groaning. It will definitely be a festive occasion all the way around."

It certainly sounded like it to Annabel. She vaguely remembered Earl Tabor telling her about these old-fashioned fire department competitions, but she couldn't recall any of the details. Wouldn't Earl love hearing an eyewitness account of one of them? she thought.

Thinking about Earl reminded her of the earthquake. For the most part, she had succeeded in putting the future and all the dangers it held out of her thoughts. She had become caught up with fitting in here—and, she had to admit to herself, distracted even more by her budding relationship with Cole Brady.

But the earthquake was still out there somewhere in the future, looming like a great beast that would come in and destroy half the city with one swipe of its deadly paw. There was nothing Annabel could do to stop it. She knew that.

She could flee, though. Mrs. Noone might think it odd, but she wouldn't refuse if Annabel asked to have Lucius take her over to the Diablos so she could search for that mysterious cave. She could still make an effort to return to her own time before the earthquake struck.

If only she could remember the date of the earthquake! Then she could warn her friends when it was closer to the right moment. They would think she had lost her mind, of course, but she might be able to persuade them to take some extra precautions.

No matter how hard she tried, she couldn't dredge that all-important date from her memory. In fact, to her dismay, she was beginning to realize that it was becoming harder and harder to recall what her friends Earl Tabor and Vickie Pasetta even looked like. The longer she stayed here in 1906, the more her memories of her own time faded.

Life here in 1906 wasn't as bad as she thought it would be. This time period had both advantages and problems that were uniquely its own. And Cole was here. Whether Annabel liked it or not, she had to admit that that made a difference.

Enough so that she would be content to stay here the rest of her life? Annabel found she couldn't answer that question, not yet. It would depend to a large extent on what happened during the competition between the fire departments.

And on how Cole reacted when it was all over.

She was ready, Annabel told herself as the buggy carrying her and Mellisande and Lucius rolled away from the park. As ready as she was ever going to be . . .

The day of the competition dawned foggy, as usual, with billows of the white, clinging moisture rolling across from the Marin headlands and engulfing the city by the bay. There was a warm breeze, however, and by ten o'clock, most of the fog had either burned off or been blown out to sea.

Annabel donned a simple dress, one she could unbutton and wriggle out of quickly when the time came. Under it she wore the panties, sports bra, and white T-shirt that had come from her own time. She had the SFFD pin attached to her shirt for luck. On her head she wore a wide-brimmed hat to shield her from the sun. The hat would also serve as a bit of a disguise if anyone caught her when she tried to sneak into the San Francisco Fire Department tent.

Mellisande was going to the park in her own buggy, so Annabel and Mrs. Noone were the only passengers as Lucius drove toward the site of the festivities. Mrs. Noone's lined face was flushed with excitement and anticipation. "I haven't been on an outing like this in years," she said. "And I have you to thank for it, dear."

"I hope you don't intend to overexert yourself, madam," Lucius muttered from the driver's seat of the rig. "You know how delicate you are."

"Nonsense!" Mrs. Noone said crisply. "I feel absolutely wonderful. This fresh air is the best medicine for anyone."

Annabel couldn't argue with that. It was indeed a glorious day.

And it seemed as if everyone else in San Francisco was taking advantage of it, too. The streets were crowded with pedestrians, buggies, horse-drawn wagons, and popping, huffing Model T Fords. The cable cars were packed, with every seat filled, the aisles crowded, and people even hanging on to the outside of the cars. Everyone was converging on Golden Gate Park.

That was all right with Annabel. The more people who were there, the less likely it was that she'd be spotted. Of course, she would still be risking discovery by members of the fire department, but she hoped they would be so caught up in the competition that they wouldn't pay any attention to her.

Skillfully, Lucius guided the buggy into the park, following one of the paths that would take them near the center area where the tents were located. When he could go no farther, he parked the buggy and hopped down from the driver's seat to assist Mrs. Noone. He took her wooden wheelchair from where he'd strapped it to the rear of the buggy, then carefully picked her up and lowered her into the chair. "Thank you, Lucius," she said.

"My pleasure, as always, madam," he murmured. He went behind the chair, grasped its handles, and began rolling it over the grass, picking out the smoothest possible path.

Annabel followed, enjoying the festive commotion all around her. This gathering was part carnival, part circus, part picnic. Crowds of children ran and played, while adults strolled and looked over the fire department equipment on display. A band was tuning up somewhere, the strains of the music floating over the park and providing background for the hubbub. And everywhere, people were laughing happily, adults and children alike. Today was more than an exhibition and competition; it was a celebration.

When they reached the area of the tents, Annabel bent and quickly kissed Mrs. Noone's cheek. "I have to go now," she said.

"I know," Mrs. Noone said. She took hold of one of Annabel's hands. "Good luck, my dear. I hope you get everything you want from this day."

Annabel smiled and nodded her thanks. She knew that if everything worked out as she hoped, things would never again be the same between her and Cole. He would have to look at her in a whole new way.

And what was so wrong with the old way? she suddenly asked herself. There were worse things than having a smart, handsome man looking at you like he wanted to take you in his arms and make passionate love to you. Weren't there?

Annabel gave a little shake of her head as she started toward the tents. She was committed to her plan, and she had never been the sort to back out of something once she had started it. After glancing around to make sure that no one was paying any attention to her, she slipped to the back of the San Francisco Fire Department tent.

Time to go to work.

Chapter 13

THE AX THROW was the first contest, so Cole took his time selecting the ax he was going to use. There were dozens of axes in the tent, and he tried several of them, holding each in his hand to test its weight and balance.

The tent wasn't crowded. There were only a handful of other firemen inside the big canvas structure. Most of the men had already donned the long leather overcoats, high-topped boots, and helmets that would be the day's uniform. Cole was still lingering over his selection of an ax when Patsy O'Flaherty stuck his head in the tent's entrance flap and said in a loud voice, "Sure and they're gettin' ready to start. Ye better get on out here, me boyos."

Cole nodded. He settled on the ax he wanted and carried it over to the entrance. The other firemen in the tent trailed along behind him. None of them looked back.

So none of them saw the slight twitch of the canvas as someone lifted it at the rear of the tent.

Cole strode toward the area where the targets had been set up. The sun was shining down warmly, and he figured the heavy fireman's garb was going to get pretty hot before the day was over. He was accustomed to the heat, however, and knew it wouldn't bother him.

Several men from each company in the department had entered the ax-throwing contest, so there was a large crowd on hand for it. Likewise, the Oakland Fire Department was furnishing a large number of contestants. Friendly jeers—and some not-so-friendly ones—were tossed back and forth by the members of the rival departments as they lined up.

Ropes had been strung up along the edges of the contest area to keep the spectators from wandering into the path of a thrown ax. There was a large open space some twenty feet wide and forty feet long. The competitors stood at one end while wooden targets were set up at the other end. One man from each department stepped up to a line marked on the grass, then took his turn letting fly at his designated target.

Cole was about three-fourths of the way back in the San Francisco line. Like the other competitors, he stretched up on his toes and craned his neck to see how the rest of the contestants were doing. Each time an ax was thrown well, it bit into one of the targets with a solid *thunk!* and cheers and applause came from the watching crowd. Chief Sullivan and the chief from the Oakland department kept track of the scoring.

When Cole's turn came to step up to the line, his competitor from Oakland said, "Hello, Brady. Ready to get whipped?"

"We'll see," Cole said.

"Care to throw first?"

"No, that's all right, you go ahead."

The Oakland fireman grinned and hefted his ax. He was bigger and more muscular than Cole, and the ax looked a little like a toy in his massive hands. Without taking any unnecessary time about it, he lifted the ax and flung it forward. The head smacked cleanly into his target, the ax handle quivering from the impact. The ax had struck well within the circle painted on the target, not more than a hand's span from the edge of the bull's-eye.

The man grinned again as he looked at Cole. "Beat that," he challenged.

Cole didn't believe in boasting and chest-thumping. He toed the line, set himself, and drew back his arm. It flashed forward, sending the ax spinning through the air. It turned so rapidly it was just a blur.

Until it stopped abruptly, the edge of the blade biting so deeply into the wood that it sent a crack splintering up and down through the target from the point of impact. The wood was split so badly that the target broke in half and fell apart . . . but not before everyone there saw that the blade of the ax had hit squarely in the bull's-eye.

A stunned silence fell over the crowd for a few seconds, then it erupted in cheers and shouts and whistles and thunderous applause. Cole's throw was the best one of the day so far, and the points he received for hitting the bull's-eye would give the San Francisco Fire Department an early but solid lead.

Cole glanced at the Oakland fireman who had thrown just before him. The man was still staring at the broken target, amazement etched on his face. He looked at the faintly smiling Cole and just shook his head, as if to say that he gave up, he wasn't going to be able to best Cole's throw. It was doubtful, for that matter, that anyone in either department would.

The San Francisco men who followed Cole didn't fare as well, however, and the lead he had given the department was gradually eroded. Cole shook his head and wandered away to start preparing for the hook-and-ladder relay climb.

The tent had been deserted when Annabel knelt down on the ground behind it and crawled underneath the canvas. She got grass stains and dirt on her dress, but she didn't care. She wouldn't be wearing it much longer anyway.

Moving quickly, she took off the dress, rolled it into a ball, and stashed it and her hat behind some equipment; she would retrieve them later if she had the chance. She bent over, unbuttoned the high-topped shoes, and kicked them off. There were spare uniforms in the tent, because the men would need to change into them later after the fire hose battle, when they would more than likely get soaked. Annabel found a woolen shirt and denim trousers that fit and pulled them on, adjusting the suspenders. Then she stamped her feet down into a pair of boots, glad that she had worn an extra pair of socks so that the boots would fit better. All that was left was the long leather overcoat and the helmet. She shrugged into a coat that was just a bit too big for her, choosing it on purpose so that its bulkiness would help conceal the female curves underneath it. Her hair was already slicked back. She settled one of the helmets on her head. The badge on the front of it indicated that it had come from Engine Company Forty-eight.

Annabel took a deep breath. She wished she had a mirror so she could see how she looked. Lacking that, she would just have to trust to luck and hope that she could pass for one of the firemen.

She went to the entrance, pulled the canvas aside, and peered outside for a moment before leaving the tent. Satisfied that Cole wasn't lurking nearby, she slipped out and headed for the source of the cheers and applause she was hearing.

It was the ax throw, she saw. She sidled up to the rear of the line of contestants from the San Francisco department. Just as she had hoped, no one paid any particular attention to her. She kept her head down so that the short front brim of the helmet would somewhat conceal her features.

She spotted Cole in front of her and was just as impressed as everyone else when his throw not only hit the bull's-eye but split the target as well. She wanted to cheer, but kept her silence.

Things didn't go as well after that. The men from the Oakland department were good, Annabel had to admit. Their throws gradually cut into the lead Cole had established, so that by the time the competitors at the end of the line drew near the front, the two departments were almost even. That was going to put some pressure on her.

Well, she had wanted to perform well in these contests, she told herself. Now she had yet another reason to do so. The honor of the San Francisco Fire Department might wind up resting on her shoulders.

She grinned a little. Pressure had never bothered her all that much. If it had, she never would have become a smoke-jumper.

She was just as glad, though, to see Cole wandering away from the contest area. Since the score was close, if he had remained behind to watch, his attention surely would have been focused on her when it was her turn to throw the ax. She didn't need that.

She hadn't brought an ax from the tent with her, so when one of the men from San Francisco who had already competed came back along the line carrying one of the heavy, double-bladed tools, Annabel held out her hand, lowering and roughening her voice as she asked, "Can I borrow that, buddy?"

"Sure," the fireman said with a shrug as he handed over the ax. "As long as you're going to put it up when you're through with it."

Annabel nodded her agreement, but didn't say anything. She wanted to talk as little as possible. She'd been fortunate that the man from whom she'd borrowed the ax came from a different engine company.

Annabel knew her height wasn't going to give her away; she was just as tall as many of the men around her. And her athletic build helped, too. She hefted the ax. It wasn't any heavier than her Pulaski, and up at smoke-jumper headquarters, they sometimes passed the time by flinging Pulaskis at trees. She was confident she wouldn't embarrass herself in this contest.

Suddenly, it was her turn. As she stepped up to the line, she glanced at the board on which a running total of the scores had been chalked. The San Francisco Fire Department was still ahead, but by the thinnest of margins. If she lost, it would probably be enough to catapult Oakland into the lead.

"No pressure there," she murmured to herself as she lifted the ax, hesitated only a heartbeat, and then let fly.

The ax flew true, revolving gracefully several times on its way to the target. Then the blade thudded into the wood, not in the bull's-eye by any means, but closer to the center than to the outside of the painted ring. The crowd cheered. It was a good toss. The man from Oakland would have to make an excellent throw, almost as good as the one Cole had made, to beat it.

He didn't. His ax blade bit into the outside of the target ring, and a groan of disappointment went up from the Oakland firemen and their supporters. The cheers from the crowd were louder, drowning out the groan. Several San Francisco men clapped Annabel on the back, congratulating her. She kept her head down and didn't say anything, merely nodding in acknowledgment of the accolades.

The hook-and-ladder relay climb was the next contest on the schedule. Annabel drifted in that direction with the rest of the firemen.

This contest would be more difficult for her to enter, since each engine company already had its own team. She might have to be content to observe this one, she decided.

At the beginning of each contest, the ladders on the fire wagons would be down. When the contest began, they would be lifted and extended to their full height, and then each of four men would climb to the top in turn, retrieve one of the brightly colored ribbons tied there, and climb back down. The first team to have all four of its ribbons down would be the winner.

Annabel looked for the Engine Company Twenty-one team and found it after several minutes of searching. Cole was one of the four men standing ready to raise the ladder when the signal came. One of the firemen with him was a small, bandy-legged man with a heavily freckled, pleasantly ugly face. Annabel wondered if the man was Patsy O'Flaherty. She had a feeling he was.

One of the hook-and-ladder wagons from the Oakland department was parked next to the one from Engine Company Twenty-one, and its team was ready, too. The two fire chiefs came over from the area where the ax throw had been staged and explained the rules. Chief Sullivan displayed a starter's pistol loaded with blanks. A shot from the pistol would be the signal for the competition to begin.

When everyone was ready and a large crowd had gathered to watch, Chief Sullivan raised the pistol over his head and squeezed the trigger. The pistol cracked loudly, and the contest was under way.

The firemen sprang to their task. Two of them turned the cranks that lifted the ladder into an upright position, while the other two began sliding out and locking into place the telescoping extensions. When the ladder was at its full extension, Cole began scrambling up, his long coat flapping around his legs as he climbed.

Annabel realized that her pulse was racing with excitement as she watched Cole climbing the ladder. Part of it was from the thrill of watching any sort of close competition, she supposed, but she knew there was more to it than that. She wouldn't have been observing the contest nearly as raptly if Cole had not been involved.

The ladder swayed some under his weight, and Annabel found herself holding her breath at times. Cole was high in the air now, close to fifty feet. A fall from that height could be dangerous, even fatal. And there was no net below to catch him if he slipped.

Annabel glanced at the Oakland hook-and-ladder truck. The first member of the Oakland team had reached nearly the same height as Cole. But Cole got to the top first, snatched free one of the bright red ribbons that was tied there, and started down. He took the descent even faster than he had the climb up, skipping some of the rungs and sliding down with his gloved hands clamped on the sides of the ladder. As soon as his feet touched the platform at the base of the ladder, the second man in the relay started up.

The volume of the cheers from the crowd grew louder and louder as the contest continued. Cole had given his team the lead again, and the second and third men held on to it. Engine Company Twenty-one was ahead by half a ladder-length when the man Annabel had pegged as Patsy O'Flaherty began the anchor leg of the relay.

Patsy scrambled up the ladder even faster than his teammates had, and there was a huge grin on his face as he plucked the last of the red ribbons from the top of the ladder. He came back down quickly and was swamped by his teammates and the other men of Engine Company Twenty-one as he reached the bottom. They crowded around him and slapped him heartily on the back in congratulations. The cheering and applause went on for several minutes, and when it died down somewhat, Chief Sullivan raised his voice and announced the winning time posted by his team, adding proudly, "And that's a new record, folks!"

That brought on more cheering. Annabel drifted toward the back of the crowd while Cole and his companions accepted the accolades. She wasn't sure what was next, but she knew she didn't want to be too close to Cole when the contest got under way.

Suddenly, a nearby fit of violent coughing caught Annabel's attention. She glanced over her shoulder and saw a man about thirty years old standing among the crowd. He was wearing a tweed suit and a straw boater, and in his hand was part of some sort of sausage that he had probably purchased at one of the food stands scattered around the park. His other hand was clutching his throat, and his face was turning a mottled blue and red as he continued to choke and gag. Beside him, an anxious-looking young woman plucked at his sleeve and said, "Desmond? What's wrong, Desmond?" She was holding the hand of a small girl, probably their daughter, who was staring up at the coughing man in a mixture of amazement and fear.

Annabel recognized the problem immediately. Unless someone did something quickly, the man might die right here in the middle of the park on a beautiful sunny day, in front of his horrified wife and child.

Annabel's training took over without her even having to think about it. She took a couple of quick steps that brought her behind the choking man, and her arms went around his midsection. She caught hold of her left wrist with her right hand and jerked back hard, driving her hands into the man's diaphragm. An explosion of air came from his mouth as Annabel executed the Heimlich maneuver. The piece of sausage that had almost killed him flew out of his mouth as well.

Annabel let go of the man and began backing away as he bent over and gasped for breath, drawing in great lungfuls of air. His wife was still hovering around him worriedly, but in between gasps, he assured her, "I'm . . . all right now . . . Who . . . someone grabbed me. . . ."

The little girl pointed and said in a loud voice, "That fireman right there, Papa."

The man started to turn, and Annabel ducked away into the crowd. Heads were starting to turn, and eyes were staring curiously toward the spot where she had been. She didn't want the attention, didn't want Cole noticing the commotion and coming over to see what it was all about. She walked away quickly, not running but not wasting any time, either.

A faint smile tugged at her mouth. She had just carried out the world's first Heimlich Maneuver. Too bad she wouldn't get any credit for it; otherwise, she supposed, it would be called the Lowell maneuver.

Without warning, someone thrust a fire hose in her hands. "Come on," a helmeted fireman said. "We've got to get ready."

She found herself with a large group of firemen from a

variety of engine companies. They were standing beside a pumper with a head of steam up. Across an open space was a pumper from the Oakland department, likewise with steam up and ready to pump. She had stumbled into the fire hose shoot-out, Annabel realized.

She was toward the back of the line of men handling the hose for the San Francisco department. That was a stroke of luck, she told herself; maybe she wouldn't get so soaked that she would have to change uniforms afterward. One thing was certain—no matter how wet she got, she couldn't go into that tent and start taking off her clothes while she was surrounded by firemen.

Cole must not have been entered in this contest. She tried to look up and down the line of firemen without being too obvious about it, and she didn't see him among them. She kept her head down and the helmet tilted over her eyes, just in case he wandered over to watch the competition.

The contest was simple. The teams from Oakland and San Francisco would train their hoses on each other and fire away with the pressurized streams of water until all the members of one team had been knocked off their feet. It made for a wet, messy, muddy, raucous competition, and the crowds loved it, although they had learned to stay well back. Annabel tightened her grip on the hose and swallowed. She had never done anything like this before, but she was confident in her ability to handle it.

Someone gave the signal to start, and valves were opened on each of the pumpers. Suddenly, the hose bucked and jumped like a live thing in Annabel's hands. Even with more than a dozen men hanging on to it, the hose tried to writhe and twist out of their grip from the pressure of the water passing through it. A thick, powerful stream erupted from the nozzle and sprayed across the open area between the two teams. The San Francisco firemen struck first, as their hose began to blast a second before the one attached to the Oakland pumper.

A couple of men in the forefront of the Oakland squad

went down immediately as the stream of water struck them. The other members of the Oakland team, at a quick disadvantage, dug in their heels and tried to control their hose. Water slammed into the men in the front ranks of the San Francisco unit, staggering them. They managed to keep their feet, however, except for one man who slipped and fell. He rolled away and stood up disgustedly, forbidden by the rules of the contest to touch the fire hose again.

One by one, men on each team were knocked down, and with each man who fell and had to withdraw, the hose became more and more uncontrollable for the members of the team who were left. Annabel threw all of her strength into holding on to the thick rubber and canvas hose. She was wet from the spray but not soaked.

When the end arrived it came quickly. The Oakland team, with too few men left to properly control the hose, let it get away from them. It jerked out of their hands and writhed on the ground like a giant snake, spraying water everywhere. The people in the audience laughed and screamed and whooped as they scurried backward out of range of the gushing water. Without having to worry about being blasted themselves, the remaining members of the San Francisco team, Annabel among them, were able to use their hose to knock the rest of the Oakland team off their feet. The men at the valves on both pumpers turned the wheels quickly, shutting off the flow of water.

The victors, who were almost as wet and muddy as the losers, congratulated each other. Annabel was in the thick of it, but there was too much confusion for her to be recognized as not belonging there. She slipped away as soon as she could.

The helmet, high-topped boots, and long leather coat had kept the shirt and trousers underneath from getting too wet. She wasn't so soaked that she would have to change, Annabel decided. She unbuttoned the coat and flapped it back and forth, allowing the shirt and trousers to dry a little in the warm sun.

The fire hose shoot-out was the last contest of the morning. Now everyone would take a break for a few hours and indulge themselves in the picnic lunch. Annabel went to one of the food-filled tables and piled her plate high. She took it and a glass of lemonade and sat down cross-legged underneath one of the trees to eat.

She had been there only a few minutes when she heard one of the passersby saying to a companion, ". . . saved his life, I swear that fireman did. Desmond would have choked to death."

"What fireman?" the man's friend asked.

"Nobody seems to know. He disappeared before anybody could thank him."

"And Desmond's all right?"

"Good as new."

Without looking up, Annabel smiled. She was glad to hear that the man she had helped was all right. That was thanks and recognition enough.

"Yoo-hoo!"

Annabel heard the familiar voice and glanced up to see Lucius rolling Mrs. Noone's wheelchair toward her. It was Mrs. Noone who had called to her. Annabel wasn't sure if the elderly lady had recognized her or not, but from the twinkle in Mrs. Noone's eyes, Annabel assumed that was the case. That didn't bode well, she thought, if she could be picked out from the crowd so easily.

"Hello, my dear," Mrs. Noone said in a loud whisper as Lucius wheeled her up to the tree where Annabel was sitting. "You're doing splendidly."

Annabel smiled. "Thanks. I didn't think you'd be able to spot me so easily, though."

"Don't worry," Lucius told her. "Your disguise is excellent. Mr. Brady won't recognize you."

Annabel felt herself flushing. Had Mrs. Noone and Lucius figured out that she was doing this primarily to impress Cole, to show him that her desire to join the fire department wouldn't be so easily dismissed?

"Are you enjoying yourself?" Mrs. Noone asked.

"As a matter of fact, I am," Annabel replied, and she realized that she was telling the truth. She was no more immune to the lure of competition than anyone else, and it had felt good to do well in the two contests in which she had participated so far. Even without the desire to show Cole he had to take her seriously, she would have enjoyed the challenge of competing.

"Are you going to take part in the fire wagon race?"

Annabel nodded. "I'm going to try." She wasn't sure yet how she was going to insinuate herself among the members of the team, but luck had been with her so far. She would continue to play it by ear.

"We should go find Mrs. Dupree, madam," Lucius said to Mrs. Noone. "You promised to have lunch with her."

"So I did," Mrs. Noone agreed. She held out a hand to Annabel, who clasped it for a moment. "Continued good luck, my dear."

Annabel gave a small wave as Lucius rolled Mrs. Noone away toward the picnic tables. Music welled up from the band shell. The concerts would begin soon, giving everyone a chance to rest and relax before the big race began.

Annabel closed her eyes and leaned her head against the trunk of the tree. She drew a deep breath and let it out slowly, enjoying the moment.

Somebody kicked her foot, and a voice she knew all too well said, "Better not doze off. There's still the race to come."

Cole.

Chapter 14

WITH PATSY HURRYING along beside him, trying to keep up with his longer strides, Cole had been on his way across the huge field when he'd spotted a San Francisco fireman sitting with his back to a tree, head drooping drowsily. The badge on the fellow's helmet indicated that he came from Engine Company Forty-eight. As he and Patsy had walked past him, Cole gave the man's booted foot a light kick and reminded him of the upcoming race.

"Uh, yeah," the man had responded in a low, husky voice, without looking up.

"I figured you wouldn't want to miss it," Cole had said, then he'd moved on with Patsy.

"Have ye seen that gal o' yours here today?" Patsy asked now.

"She's not my gal," Cole said, though a part of him definitely wished that she were. He went on, "And no, I haven't seen her. I thought Annabel might come with Mrs. Noone, but I spotted her a while ago and there was no one with her except Mellisande Dupree and Lucius."

"Maybe since ye wouldn't let her take part in the competition, she's sittin' at home sulkin'."

"That was Lieutenant Driscoll's decision, not mine," Cole pointed out. "All I was supposed to do was ask him about the possibility."

"When the gal asked ye to be fair about it, she may have meant that she wanted ye to be on her side. Women don't always say what they mean, ye know."

"I'll bow to the wisdom of the expert," Cole said dryly.

"Ye think I don't know what I'm talkin' about?" Patsy challenged.

Cole smiled. "I'm sure you do. I've seen you with too many women to think otherwise."

"Sure and that's the gospel truth!"

They wandered on toward the area where the fire wagons were being hooked up to their teams. Each department was racing a steam pumper this year, and Patsy had been selected to handle the reins for the San Francisco entry. Cole thought that was a good idea; no one in the department could handle horses better than Patsy O'Flaherty.

Each wagon would also have a full complement of firemen riding on it, and Cole intended to be one of them on the San Francisco wagon. Several other engine companies would be represented as well.

The fire department bands began playing, performing a concert of marches and patriotic music for the large crowd that had gathered to watch them. The band shell wasn't far from the staging area for the race, so Cole could hear the music quite clearly. The martial strains never failed to affect him. It was good to be alive on a day like today, in a city such as San Francisco, he told himself. There was only one way the day could have been better, he realized.

And that was if Annabel had been at his side.

Maybe Patsy was right. Maybe he should have thrown his support behind Annabel's request. If he had tried, he might have been able to persuade Lieutenant Driscoll to change his mind. Knowing that he supported her might have been just as important to Annabel as actually competing in the contests between fire departments. The thing of it was, that possibility had never occurred to Cole. No wonder she had been angry with him . . .

But there was still the matter of her being a woman, and try as he might, Cole couldn't bring himself to believe that she ought to be part of something like the fire department. Even these contests, as tightly controlled as they were, could be dangerous, and just the thought of Annabel being hurt made him go cold inside and tied his stomach in knots. He didn't want anything bad to ever happen to her. He wanted to protect her and take care of her and bring her all the happiness he possibly could.

And why would he feel like that, he suddenly asked himself, unless he—

"Climb aboard, laddybuck," Patsy said, breaking into Cole's chain of thought. "Time to drive on over to the startin' line."

Cole nodded and reached up to grasp one of the brass grab bars on the side of the pumper. He pulled himself onto the narrow catwalk that ran around the sides of the wagon. Patsy scrambled onto the driver's seat and took up the reins. He flicked them and called out to the horses, and the pumper rolled forward as the team pulled against the harness.

Cole glanced at the other men on his side of the wagon. They were all from other engine companies, and he didn't recognize any of them except vaguely, from having seen them at various fires. He looked over the top of the boiler. The helmets of the men on the other side of the pumper were the only things visible. One of them, Cole noticed, was from Engine Company Forty-eight, and he wondered if it belonged to that sleepy fireman who'd been dozing under the tree. If that was the case, he thought, the fellow ought to be grateful to him for waking him up.

He forgot all about that as the wagon rolled over the smooth, grassy parkland toward the starting line. The race was the highlight of the afternoon and the final contest of the day. It might well determine which of the fire departments emerged victorious. Cole knew that he and his San Francisco cohorts were leading, but there were more points awarded for winning the race than for any of the other contests. With a victory, Oakland could claim the championship.

But that wasn't likely to happen, not with Patsy at the reins. Cole tightened his grip on the grab bar and grinned in anticipation.

Annabel hadn't looked up as she'd mumbled a reply to Cole. It was clear from his tone of voice that he hadn't recognized her, he had thought she was just one of his fellow firemen. She'd kept her head down until he and Patsy moved on.

They had still been within earshot, however, when Patsy asked Cole about his *gal.* The little Irishman was referring to her, Annabel knew. Then had come Cole's response—*She's not my gal*—and Annabel had felt something twist and rend inside her. How could he dismiss her so casually? Had he forgotten all about the kiss they had shared? Annabel certainly hadn't.

She scrambled to her feet and started after Cole and Patsy, keeping her head down as she trailed along in their wake. It took only a few moments for her to realize that they were on their way to the area where the wagons for the race were being readied. She watched, staying back in the crowd where she would be inconspicuous, as the teams were harnessed to the pumpers. Then, as Cole pulled himself up on the left side of the wagon, Annabel moved forward and climbed onto the right side, along with several men from the San Francisco department. No one tried to stop her or seemed to find anything odd in her behavior.

Her heart was hammering with a mixture of expectation and anger as the wagon rolled toward the starting line. Expectation because the race was about to start and she was going to be part of it; anger because of the way Cole had so callously dismissed the idea that she was his girl.

She wasn't anybody's *girl,* she told herself sternly. If she wasn't careful, she was going to allow herself to fall into the trap of thinking like these people did and sharing their old-fashioned attitudes.

But 1906 was where she was, another part of her brain argued, and if she was going to stay here, she couldn't expect everyone else to change their way of life to conform to her ideas.

Annabel took one hand off the grab bar she was holding and used it to wipe away a tear that had welled from the corner of her eye. This mental argument with herself was nothing more than a distraction, and she knew it. She was just trying to keep her mind off the way Cole had rejected her.

When this race was over, win, lose, or draw, she was going to confront him and let him know that she had taken part in the competition after all and had proven herself.

Then she would turn and walk away, and abandon her hope of joining the fire department. She realized now that it wouldn't mean anything.

Not without Cole.

The huge crowd had spread out around the park with picnic lunches. There would be plenty of spectators all along the race course. One of the largest groups was at the starting line, however, which would also serve as the finish line. Cheers rose from the assembled San Franciscans and Oaklandites as the two pumpers drove up to the line. The enthusiasm of the crowd seemed to communicate itself to the horses, who pranced skittishly and pulled on their harnesses, clearly ready for the race to begin. Patsy O'Flaherty and the driver on the Oakland fire wagon had their hands full keeping the teams under control as the band concert wound slowly to a conclusion.

When the music had ended, Chief Sullivan and the chief of the Oakland department, accompanied by an entourage of politicians, wealthy businessmen, and journalists, came over to the race's starting line. Chief Sullivan made a brief speech, then took out his starter's pistol again.

"Drivers and firemen ready?" he called loudly.

"Ready!" came back the shouted reply from the men on both wagons.

Chief Sullivan smiled, lifted the pistol over his head, and pulled the trigger. The weapon cracked, and both wagons practically leaped forward as the horses lunged into motion.

The sudden start jerked Annabel backward, but she was gripping the grab bar with both hands and had no trouble holding on. She came up on her toes just enough to be able to peer over the top of the boiler and see Cole's helmet, its badge emblazoned with the number 21.

The wagons reached a turn in the course and rolled around the curve. Momentum caused Annabel to swing outward a little as the San Francisco wagon made the maneuver. She shifted her weight slightly so as to balance herself and keep her center of gravity stable. Her knees bent in a crouch.

This was something totally new to her. She had thrown fire axes before—well, Pulaskis, but it was almost the same thing—and she had handled hoses with much higher water pressure than the ones in this era were capable of. But she had never ridden on a bouncing, careening fire wagon before. Still, it seemed to be simple enough. The only strategy involved for the riders was to hang on for dear life.

Wind tore at Annabel's face as the wagon raced onward. She kept her head down so that the fire helmet wouldn't be blown off. Of course, even if her masquerade were to be discovered now, it was too late for anyone to do anything about it, she thought. Nothing could stop the race until it was over.

She felt herself starting to slip as the wagon rocked around another turn. Spreading her feet a little wider on the catwalk for stability, she tightened her hold on the brass bar. Suddenly, the wagon hit a rough spot in the path, and the entire vehicle leaped into the air for a split second.

Annabel let out an involuntary yelp as her feet went out from under her.

Her hands clamped like a vise onto the grab bar as she scrambled to get her feet back on the catwalk. For a long moment, she was hanging there on the side of the fire wagon, supported by nothing except her desperate grip. In that instant, she wondered how badly she would be hurt if she fell. If she landed clear of the wagon, she might get by with only a broken bone or two. But if she slipped underneath it, the wheels would surely crush her . . .

Then the toe of her boot caught the edge of the catwalk. She managed to keep that tenuous hold while she got her other foot back on the walk. She pulled herself against the side of the boiler, grateful for its solid support. Her knees were trembling.

The man directly behind her shouted over the thunder of hoofbeats, "Better hang on!"

Annabel nodded. That was exactly what she intended to do.

She looked around, trying to figure out where they were and how much of the race course they had covered. The spectators who lined the route, faceless blurs for the most part at this speed, flashed past her. She couldn't recognize anything. She knew the Golden Gate Park of her own time quite well, but even though the general layout was the same, enough was different that she couldn't tell where they were. The grassy fields, the rolling hills, the gardens, and the groves of trees all looked the same to her. She closed her eyes and leaned against the boiler again. The bouncing, rocking motion was beginning to make her feel a little sick. She wondered if she had gotten herself in deeper than she could handle.

No! That was ridiculous, she told herself. She had faced much worse dangers almost every week of the past few years as a smoke-jumper. She wasn't going to let herself be overwhelmed by a simple thing like riding on an old-fashioned, horse-drawn fire wagon.

The sound of hoofbeats grew louder. She glanced to her right and saw that the Oakland Fire Department wagon was trying to draw even. The San Francisco wagon had been ahead almost from the first, but now the Oakland wagon was cutting into the lead, and she wondered if the SFFD horses were growing tired. She heard the Oakland driver shouting at his team and looked again to see that the rival wagon was pulling even closer.

Patsy O'Flaherty had to be aware of that, too. He was flapping the reins frantically and doing plenty of shouting of his own as he urged his horses on to greater speed.

Though it took an effort of will, Annabel leaned out away from the solidity of the boiler and peered ahead along the race course. She saw another sharp turn coming up, and as the path curved, it went between two stands of trees. The path looked barely big enough for two vehicles side by side. As the wagons drew nearer to the turn, Annabel saw to her alarm that the path *wasn't* big enough for both of them. One or the other of the wagons was going to have to fall back a little.

But neither Patsy nor the other driver showed any signs of doing so. The San Francisco wagon was still in the lead, but only by about half the length of one horse. The Oakland pumper was so close that Annabel could have reached out and touched the leather overcoats of the men riding on the wagon's left-hand catwalk. She could see the tense, grim lines in which their faces were set and knew that she and her teammates had to appear much the same.

She looked ahead again. The hairpin turn was only about fifty yards away now, and neither driver was giving any ground. She heard shouting from the other side of the pumper and came up on her toes again. Cole was yelling something at Patsy, probably warning him. He wasn't even glancing in Annabel's direction. All his attention was focused on the race.

A couple of the firemen on Annabel's side of the wagon waved at the Oakland wagon, motioning for it to fall back.

The Oakland driver ignored them and lashed his team more furiously. Annabel could tell from the set, determined expression on the man's face that he wasn't going to give up. He must have believed that he could pass the San Francisco wagon and reach the turn first.

But there was neither room nor time for that reckless plan to succeed. The horses leaped forward, and both wagons careened into the turn.

Annabel saw the Oakland wagon swaying toward her, and she jerked her feet up so that she was once again hanging on the side of the pumper. The catwalks came together with a grinding crash. Annabel felt the heavy jolt go through the wagon and tightened her grip on the brass bar.

The wagons bounced apart, and the left side of the San Francisco pumper, the side that Cole was on, scraped against the trunks of the trees next to the path. The impact of that collision sent the wagon sliding to the right again, so that it slammed once more into the Oakland pumper. The men on the wagons were screaming and cursing, and Annabel hoped none of them had been hurt. She hung on desperately as both wagons somehow made it through the turn upright. The horses were still running.

The San Francisco team was racing out of control, though, Annabel saw to her horror. Patsy O'Flaherty was no longer on the driver's seat, and the reins had slipped down and were trailing along loose among the flashing legs of the horses. Annabel jerked her head around so that she could look behind, and she saw a huddled shape in a leather overcoat lying motionless on the ground at the edge of the trees. Patsy had been knocked off the seat by the collision.

The San Francisco wagon continued to race out of control. If the horses weren't stopped somehow, there was no telling what catastrophe might occur. The wagon might crash, or it might even go rocketing off the race course into the crowd, where scores of innocent spectators could be trampled by the hooves of the team or crushed by the iron wheels of the wagon.

From the corner of her eye she saw a man start to climb over the boiler toward the driver's seat. With a shock, she realized it was Cole. He was trying to reach the seat, retrieve the reins, and stop the team. His face was set in a resolute expression. Annabel's heart seemed to be in her throat as she watched him inch his way forward, utilizing whatever meager handholds and footholds he could find.

Suddenly, the horses, for whatever reason, veered off the path and started across an open field. Some spectators were nearby, and they scurried frantically for safety, running to get out of the wagon's way. The pumper bounced violently over a rut, causing Cole to slip. Annabel almost screamed as it looked for a dizzying instant as if he would go flying off the wagon.

But then he found a firmer handhold and hauled himself closer to the driver's seat. With a final lunge forward, he rolled over the back of it and fell onto the floorboard. Annabel craned her neck, trying to see if he was all right. A cold, clammy fear filled her.

Then she saw his head as he clambered upright on the seat. He had lost his helmet. He bent forward, dropping out of Annabel's sight again, and she figured he was trying to reach the loose reins.

Abruptly, without thinking about what she was doing, she started to climb. Cole was up there risking his life for all of them, and she couldn't let him do that alone. If it had been Earl Tabor or Captain McPhee or any of her partners from the smoke-jumper unit, she would have gone to their aid without hesitation. Even though she wasn't a member of the San Francisco Fire Department, she found that she could do no less now.

Besides, that was Cole up there. . . .

One of the men beside her yelled, "Hey! Are you crazy?" as she started to scramble toward the driver's seat. She ignored him and pulled herself onto the boiler. If it had been full of water with a head of steam up, there would have been no way she could have done that; the heat would have burned the flesh right off her bones. But for this race, the boilers had been emptied. That was a stroke of luck, and Annabel intended to take advantage of it.

Her heart pounded. She was scared, no doubt about it—scared for herself, scared for Cole, just plain scared. But she knew she could overcome that fright. Only a fool risked his or her life without a little fear. That was what courage was: going ahead despite the fear.

She found a toehold, then a handhold, and pulled herself forward, sliding over the curved top of the boiler.

The driver's seat was only a couple of feet away now. Annabel could see Cole lying on the floorboard, his arm reaching down between the horses as he tried to grab the wildly flailing reins. They whipped back and forth, and Cole strained forward farther and farther as he stretched his fingers toward them . . .

Suddenly Annabel cried out in terror as he started to slip off the floorboard. In another second, he was going to plunge right under the flashing, deadly hooves of the team.

She threw herself forward, letting instinct take over. As she tumbled over the back of the driver's seat, one hand clamped onto the brass railing at the edge of the seat while the other reached for Cole. Her fingers grabbed the back of his coat, bunching up the leather as she fought to hold on to it. As her grip solidified, she shouted, "I've got you!"

Cole managed to grab the trailing reins. He twisted them around his wrist. As soon as Annabel saw that he had the reins secure, she began hauling back on his coat with all her strength. Slowly, Cole rose from his precarious position. He was able to get a hand underneath himself so that he could help lift his weight, and finally he sprawled back onto the floorboard next to Annabel. He hauled hard on the reins, yelling, "Whoa! Whoa!" to the horses. Gradually, as they began to slow down, Cole took up the slack on the reins and brought them under control.

Only when the team had come to a complete stop and

the danger was over did he look over at Annabel, utter astonishment in his eyes.

Well, she thought, it looked like the masquerade was over.

"Annabel?" he croaked, his voice hoarse and filled with disbelief.

Somehow she found the coolness and self-possession to smile slightly and say, "Hello, Cole."

For a long moment, he stared at her without speaking. Then he said roughly, "I've got to see about Patsy." He stood up, looped the reins around the brass railing so that the team couldn't take off again, and dropped hurriedly to the ground.

That was all he had to say to her? After she had risked her life to help him and keep the runaway team from hurting anyone? Annabel scrambled to her feet and jumped down from the wagon, then ran after him, ignoring the spectators and the other firemen who tried to gather around and congratulate her.

Her helmet had stayed on during the commotion. She reached up, unfastened the strap that went under her chin, and took the helmet off. She tossed it aside, no longer caring if anyone realized she was a woman. She increased her pace, but people kept getting in her way and she couldn't catch up to Cole. It was all she could do to keep track of him in the crowd.

A lot of firemen were gathered around Patsy's fallen form. Cole shouldered his way through them, and Annabel finally lost sight of him as the crowd closed in around him. She made her way to the knot of men and said loudly, "Let me through. Let me through, blast it!"

A gap appeared in front of her as some of the men turned. She saw the surprise on their faces and knew it was because a woman was ordering them around. Too bad, she thought. They could just deal with it if their male egos were wounded. She stepped through the opening and saw Cole kneeling beside Patsy.

The Irishman was sitting up, a woozy smile on his freckled face. "Sure and I'm tellin' ye I'm all right," he protested as Cole put a hand on his shoulder to keep him from standing. " 'Twas a patch o' nice, soft ground I landed on. Like fallin' on a feather bed, it was. If I'd only had a lass to fall on it with. . . ."

His voice trailed off, his eyes rolled up in his head, and he went over backward. Cole caught him and lowered him gently to the ground.

With a quick, experienced touch, Cole checked Patsy's arms and legs. "There don't seem to be any broken bones," he said, as much to himself as to the crowd of worried onlookers. "He's got a bump on his head, but it'd take a lot to dent that hard skull. There could be some internal injuries, though."

"There's the ambulance now," one of the firemen said as a wagon with clanging bells drew to a stop nearby. He was wearing the uniform of a lieutenant, and Annabel wondered if he was Lieutenant Driscoll, the head of Cole's engine company.

Cole pushed himself to his feet and looked down at the face of his friend Patsy, who was already coming around again. Cole's expression was so bleak that Annabel's heart went out to him. She stepped up beside him and put a hand on his arm, her touch light and gentle. "Cole . . . ," she said.

He turned his head and looked at her, without speaking. Then he wheeled and stalked away.

Chapter 15

ANNABEL STARED AFTER him for a long moment, shocked and angered by his reaction. His back was stiff and unbending, and as she watched him, anger won out over shock. She broke into a run, ignoring the men who clutched at her sleeve and tried to ask her questions. She didn't stop until she'd caught up with him, grabbed his shoulder, pulled him to a halt, and hauled him around to face her.

"Listen, you jerk," she told him, "in case you didn't notice, I just saved your life back there. The least you can do is say thank—"

She stopped short as she finally noticed the expression in his eyes.

"Cole?" Annabel whispered.

He gave a little shake of his head, like someone coming out of a dream, and the look in his eyes softened a little. But only a little, and his voice was still hard as he said, "What do you want?"

"What do I want?" Annabel echoed. The anger came flooding back. "Well, a little appreciation would be nice."

"Thank you," Cole said dully. "Thank you for making a fool of me."

"What? What are you talking about?"

He gestured toward her fireman's uniform. "Have you been walking around like that all day?" he asked. Then, before she could answer, understanding dawned on his face. "My God, you've been entering the contests disguised as a man, haven't you?"

Annabel's chin lifted defiantly. "I had to show you that I could do what I said. And I have. I did just fine in the ax throw, and I was on the team that won the fire hose battle."

He looked at her, then sighed and shook his head. "It's not about winning," he said quietly. He started to turn away again, then stopped and, choking out the words, said, "When I saw you on that fire wagon and realized you'd been there all along . . . when I thought about what could have happened . . . it scared me. . . ."

Annabel's heart lifted. She could scarcely seem to breathe as she said, "Why, Cole? Why were you scared?"

"Because something could have happened to you. You could have been hurt or . . . or . . . and that was when I knew."

Golden Gate Park and the hundreds of people in it seemed to recede around Annabel. Everything else faded into the background until she and Cole were alone. The two of them were the only ones in the world as they stood there, only inches separating them now, their gazes locked. Something trembled deep inside Annabel, a need that sprang to life, vital but still fragile, and so easily crushed.

"What did you know, Cole?" she whispered.

"That I love you."

The trembling became a full-fledged shaking that went all through her. It drew her toward him, and her arms lifted to go around his neck. His arms folded her against him, strong yet tender, and his mouth came down on hers as he kissed her with desperation. Cole had never felt anything like this before, Annabel knew, because she was feeling the same thing and it was equally new to her. This was love, pure and simple, and though she would have said she had experienced that emotion before, she knew now that she had not. Not like this. *Never* like this.

She had no idea how long they had been kissing when it suddenly occurred to her what their display of affection must look like. To anyone else, she and Cole would have appeared to be two firemen embracing and kissing each other passionately. The thought made her start to giggle.

Cole pulled back, frowning. "What? What's wrong?"

Annabel looked around, and sure enough, there were several dozen people standing nearby watching them, some with smiles on their faces, others sporting confused frowns.

Understanding, Cole muttered, "Oh, good grief." His face started to flush. He covered up his embarrassment by saying, "She's a woman." He looked at Annabel again and added softly, "A woman . . ."

And then he kissed her again.

Well, this had been quite a day, Cole thought a few minutes later. He and Annabel had found a quiet spot near one of the park's gardens. She had taken off the long leather overcoat, and he had draped it over his arm. Despite the fireman's garb, she was beautiful. He missed her long hair, but her brown eyes were as compelling as ever.

He wasn't sure what he felt more when he looked at her: adoration . . . or irritation.

They sat down on a stone bench, and he said, "You shouldn't have tricked your way into the competition like that."

Not unexpectedly, she gave a challenging toss of her head. "What else was I supposed to do?" she demanded. "No one was willing to give me a chance to prove what I can do."

"Why is it so important to you to prove that?"

"Because it *is,*" Annabel said, and Cole knew he couldn't argue with that sentiment.

Nor did he want to argue with her. After what he had

told her a few minutes earlier, he had more pressing worries.

Annabel hadn't forgotten. She said, "Did you mean it?"

"Mean what?" he asked, then regretted it. His feigned ignorance was so transparent it was laughable. Annabel wasn't laughing, though.

"When you said you loved me, did you mean it?"

Cole met her intense gaze squarely and nodded. "Yes," he said. "I meant it."

"I love you, too."

He had thought that he was prepared to hear those words; he had *hoped* that he would hear them. And yet, as he did a shock went through him, a shock as profound as any he had ever experienced in his life. His occasional dalliances with other women had been just that, he realized—dalliances. Pleasant but meaningless. This was completely different. This was the real thing.

He put his hands on his knees and drew in a deep breath. "Well," he said, "what are we going to do about this?"

Annabel looked at him and slowly started to shake her head in amazement. "You . . . you big . . . I don't know what to call you! What do you mean, what are we going to do about it?"

"We can't just ignore what happened here today."

"Is that what you want to do? Ignore it?"

"No, of course not. But . . . it's complicated. I never dreamed you'd dress up like a fireman and sneak into the contests. It's . . . it's outrageous!"

She grinned. "Better get used to it, sweetie."

"And that's another thing. You're so different from all the other women I've known."

"Is that necessarily a bad thing?"

"Well . . . no. I don't suppose it is."

Before he could say anything else, a little girl stopped in front of the bench where they were sitting. She said shyly to Annabel, "Thank you."

"For what?"

"For saving my papa's life."

Cole looked up and saw a young couple standing behind the little girl. The man took off his straw boater and held it in front of him as he said to Annabel, "I just wanted to thank you again, ah, miss."

"And to tell you how excited we were that you did so well in the competition," the man's wife added. "We had no idea you were a woman!"

There was a lot of that going around, Cole thought.

The little girl said, "Maybe I can be a fireman when I grow up, too."

Annabel smiled and nodded. "You just keep on thinking like that, sweetheart." Cole saw satisfaction shining in her eyes.

When the family had moved on, and before Cole could ask her what that had been about, Annabel crossed her arms over her chest and leaned back against the stone bench. "You know, I've got another bone to pick with you. I heard what you said to Patsy earlier."

Cole frowned. "What are you talking about?"

"When you said I wasn't your girl."

"I didn't think you were," he said. "I thought you were a lot more interested in getting into the fire department than you were in me."

"That's crazy! How can you say that after the other day?"

He didn't answer the question, muttering instead, "That was Patsy's fault. He gave me some advice, and I was a big enough fool to follow it."

"Then I owe him my gratitude. You're going to have to introduce me to him so that I can thank him personally."

Cole lifted his head and looked toward the spot where the wagons had crashed together. Worry intruded back into his mind. The ambulance had come and gone, bearing Patsy away to the hospital. "I've got to go see about him," he murmured.

For a second, Annabel looked like she wanted to argue,

but then she nodded. "You're right. We'll go together and make sure he's all right."

Cole stood and held out his hand. Without hesitation, Annabel took it and came to her feet. Hands clasped together, they started walking toward the edge of the park, where they could catch a cable car.

They had gone only a few yards when Cole said quietly, without looking at her, "Thank you for what you did on the wagon. I'd have fallen off if you hadn't been there to catch me."

"It was my pleasure," Annabel told him.

"You know," he mused, "those were good men on that wagon; I'd fight a fire with any of them. But none of them had the presence of mind and the courage to do what you did."

"You started it," she said, sounding a little uncomfortable with the praise. "I saw you going after those reins and knew you might need help."

His free hand clenched into a fist. "I'd like to get ahold of that driver from Oakland. If he hadn't taken such a foolhardy chance . . ." Cole drew in his breath and controlled his anger with an effort. "We probably lost the race because of it, even though I don't really care about that. As long as Patsy's all right, that's all that matters."

"There'll be another race next year," Annabel said. "At least, I suppose there will be."

"I don't know. This may have been the end of the competition."

They walked along in silence for a few moments, then moved off the path as they heard the hoofbeats of a horse coming up behind them. Cole stopped and looked back, seeing a black buggy with brass fittings approaching them. Lucius was at the reins, and Mrs. Noone and Mellisande Dupree were riding inside the vehicle.

Lucius brought the buggy to a halt, and Mrs. Noone leaned out to say, "Hello, my dears." She looked at Annabel and added, "I take it the great masquerade is over?"

Annabel shrugged and smiled faintly. "There doesn't seem to be any point to it anymore, does there?"

"How is your friend, Cole? Mr. O'Flaherty, isn't that his name? The man who was injured in the race?"

"I don't know," Cole said. "We were just on our way to the hospital to see how he's doing."

"We'll take you there," Mrs. Noone offered. "It will be faster than taking a cable car. Annabel, dear, you can ride back here with Mellisande and me, and Cole, there's room on the driver's seat with Lucius for you."

"You're sure about this?" Cole asked.

"Of course! Come along now, time's a-wastin', as they say."

"All right. Thank you, Mrs. Noone." Cole helped Annabel into the buggy, then swung up onto the driver's seat next to Lucius.

"Quite a bit of excitement, eh?" the servant commented as he got the buggy horse moving again.

"Too much," Cole said. "I just hope Patsy's not hurt too bad."

"The way I understand it, there was nearly a riot following the collision of the two fire wagons," Lucius said. He gave a dry chuckle. "It seems that your compatriots from the San Francisco Fire Department were quite incensed at the rather unsavory tactics of the driver from Oakland."

"You're saying a brawl broke out between the two departments?"

Lucius chuckled again. "They say it took nearly the entire police force to bring things back under control."

Cole wondered how he had missed all that excitement, but it was really pretty simple, he decided. Between the concern he felt for Patsy and his declaration to Annabel, there could have been an earthquake going on and he might not have noticed.

I love you. Easy words to say, but when a man meant them, there was nothing more important in the world. He had known that he was strongly drawn to Annabel. Even though he hadn't wanted to admit it, he had felt something for her right from the start. When he had acted on his impulse and kissed her, their mutual response had told him that there might be more to it than a simple attraction.

But it was only today, when he had looked at her after the accident and realized how she might have been badly injured or even killed, that he had started to come to grips with his true feelings for her. He could conceive of nothing in the world worse than something bad happening to Annabel.

Yes, he loved her. There was no doubt of that in his mind. He had finally admitted it, not only to her but to himself as well. And wonder of wonder, glory of glories, she had told him that she loved him, too.

But that left a large question looming in front of them.

What now?

"The sawbones says I hit me head on a tree when I went tumblin' off that wagon," Patsy told them as he sat in his hospital bed, propped up by several pillows. "Ye'd best go back to the park, Cole, and see if the tree's damaged. I'd hate to have the City o' San Francisco dock my pay over it."

"But you're all right now?" Cole asked.

Patsy waved a hand. "Oh, aye. 'Tis fine I am." He leaned forward and added in a loud whisper, "They're only keepin' me here 'cause the nurse there won't let me go. Sure and she's sweet on me, I'm thinkin'."

The nurse, a solidly built redheaded woman in a starched white uniform and cap, snorted loudly and said, "He's delusional. That's reason enough right there to keep him in the hospital for observation." She added to Cole and Annabel, "And I'm afraid I'm going to have to ask you to leave now."

Patsy wiggled his eyebrows. "Is it time for me sponge bath, darlin'?"

The nurse rolled her eyes. "You can come back and see

him again tomorrow . . . if I haven't killed him by then."

Cole and Annabel left the hospital room, and Annabel felt a warm tingle go through her as Cole took her hand while they were walking down the corridor toward the lobby. She had enjoyed meeting Patsy; he was friendly and full of blarney, of course, but she could tell there was a deep, genuine friendship between him and Cole. He had flirted shamelessly with her, calling her "Cole's beautiful Amazon," which had caused Cole to clear his throat and blush. Annabel had enjoyed that thoroughly.

But not as much as she enjoyed having her fingers twined with his now. On impulse, she squeezed his hand, and he squeezed back. The warmth inside Annabel spread.

Lieutenant Driscoll and several other firemen from Engine Company Twenty-one were waiting in the hospital lobby, along with Mrs. Noone and Mellisande. The lieutenant stood up as Cole and Annabel came into the room. "How is he?" he asked.

"As feisty as ever," Cole replied, and relieved smiles broke out on the men's faces. "He's worried, though, about losing the race."

"Well, the next time you see him, tell him not to be concerned about that," Lieutenant Driscoll said. "Chief Sullivan was here a few minutes ago. He told me that the Oakland wagon was disqualified for causing the collision. The race was awarded to the San Francisco department. We won every event this year!"

Cole smiled at the news, but he didn't look as if he really cared all that much about the outcome of the competition, Annabel thought. She could understand that. It was more important to him that his friend was all right.

Lieutenant Driscoll turned to Annabel and grew more solemn. "As for you, young lady, it's a good thing the Oakland department hasn't gotten wind yet of what you did—otherwise they'd probably be yelling that *we* should be disqualified for having a ringer on our teams."

Annabel smiled. "I don't think they'll make too much

fuss, even if they hear about it, Lieutenant. They won't want to draw a lot of attention to the fact that they were beaten by a team with a woman on it."

In spite of his serious attitude, the lieutenant chuckled. "You may be right, Miss Lowell," he said. "Just don't ever try anything like masquerading as a fireman again."

Annabel started to point out that she wouldn't have to masquerade as a fireman if she was actually a member of the San Francisco Fire Department. She reined in the impulse in time. This wasn't the right time or place for such a suggestion—but sooner or later, Cole and all the other firemen would have to deal with the fact that she had done just fine in the competition.

Lieutenant Driscoll turned to Cole and went on, "We'll stay here for a while longer and see if they'll let us in to visit Patsy. Why don't you escort Miss Lowell home, Cole."

Cole looked at Annabel. "I can do that," he said. "That is, unless you've already made other arrangements . . ."

"I'm sure Mrs. Noone would be glad to give both of us a lift," she said.

"Absolutely," the elderly woman chimed in. "Come along, you two. Cole, you'll be dining with us tonight." She held up a gnarled hand to forestall any argument. "And I won't take no for an answer."

Cole smiled. "Guess I don't have any choice, then."

"None at all."

Cole pushed Mrs. Noone's wheelchair out of the hospital. Mellisande said her good-byes to them and went down the street to catch a cable car to her own neighborhood. Lucius assisted Mrs. Noone into the buggy while Cole lifted the wheelchair into the back of the vehicle, then both men climbed to the driver's seat. Annabel had already gotten into the buggy and settled herself next to Mrs. Noone without waiting for Cole to give her a hand. She saw the glance he sent in her direction and instantly regretted that she hadn't given him the opportunity to be chivalrous. Next time she would try to remember to be more of a proper 1906 lady.

She caught herself and asked silently, *Good grief, what am I thinking?* Fitting in was one thing; submerging all of her pride and independence for the sake of a man was another. She wanted more than anything else in the world to have a relationship with Cole Brady, but he was going to have to take her at least partially on her own terms. That was the only way it was going to work.

Lucius piloted the buggy skillfully through the streets of San Francisco toward the house in Pacific Heights. It was late afternoon by now, and Annabel was tired from everything that had happened. At the same time, she was invigorated. She knew Cole had to be wondering what was going to happen next. That was fair enough, because she was wondering that herself.

One thing was certain: Now that their feelings were out in the open, things couldn't stay the same. What was between them would either grow and change—or it would come to nothing.

Annabel wasn't sure she could stand it if that happened.

Lucius drove the buggy through the open gate in the wrought-iron fence around Mrs. Noone's home and took it around back to the carriage shed. As they were all getting out of the vehicle, the rear door of the house opened and one of Mrs. Noone's boarders, a salesman named Davis, came hurrying toward them, an anxious expression on his narrow face.

"Mr. Brady!" he called. "Sir, are you Cole Brady?"

Cole stepped out of the dim interior of the shed and said, "I'm Cole Brady." Dusk was beginning to gather, causing shadows to spread.

"Lieutenant Driscoll from the fire department rang here on the telephone," Davis said. "He told me that he thought you were on your way here. He gave me a message for you."

Annabel sensed Cole stiffening as she stepped up beside

him. Something was wrong, and they both knew it.

"Well, what is it?" Cole snapped.

"The lieutenant said to tell you that you're needed down on the waterfront. There's another warehouse fire."

Annabel caught her breath and started to reach for Cole's arm. She wanted to ask him if he had to go. She stopped short, swallowing the question. Of course he had to go. It was his duty, and Cole could never turn his back when he was needed. Annabel was absolutely certain of that.

She knew that because she was the same way.

She went ahead and touched his sleeve. "Cole . . . I can go with you."

He turned and looked at her for a moment, his face unreadable in the twilight, then he shook his head. "I'd just worry about you," he said. He bent and kissed her, a quick, hard kiss. "I'll see you later." He trotted away, heading around the house and toward the street. There was a cable car stop only a couple of blocks away.

Mrs. Noone rolled up beside Annabel. "Don't worry, dear. I'm sure Cole will be just fine. He's a very good fireman, you know."

"I know," Annabel said softly. But she was a good firefighter, too. She had proven that today, or at least started to prove it.

Still, Cole was right: If she had insisted on going along with him, she would have been a distraction. He would have enough to handle without worrying about her. Having her around probably would have just made the situation more dangerous for Cole, because he would be trying to look after her instead of taking care of himself.

This certainly wasn't the way she had intended for the evening to end. Now that he was gone, she felt an emptiness inside her.

Annabel sighed, and Mrs. Noone said, "Come along inside, dear. There's nothing you can do now."

Annabel frowned slightly. She wasn't so sure there was nothing she could do. . . .

• • •

Once again, Cole had feared that it was one of the warehouses belonging to Brady Enterprises that was ablaze. When he got to the waterfront, however, he found that the pumpers were pouring streams of water into a structure belonging to a man named Tobin. Cole knew him slightly and recognized him as the balding, bespectacled man talking worriedly to Chief Sullivan as they stood a block away from the fire.

So the chief himself was on hand, Cole thought as he hurried over to a hook-and-ladder from Engine Company Twenty-one. He had donned his overcoat and helmet on his way over so he'd be ready to get to work. A hose had been attached to the ladder on the wagon, so that once it was raised water could be sprayed down onto the fire from above. Cole pitched in by helping turn the cranks that lifted the ladder.

Lieutenant Driscoll came over to him and tapped him on the shoulder, raising his voice so that he could be heard over the crackling roar of the conflagration. "The chief wants to see you!"

"Me?" Cole asked. He couldn't figure out why Chief Sullivan would want to talk to him.

Driscoll nodded and jerked a thumb toward the spot where the chief and Tobin were talking. Cole shrugged, moved aside so that another fireman could take his place on the crank, and trotted over to join Sullivan and Tobin.

"Hello, Brady," the chief greeted him. It wasn't quite so noisy here. "You know Mr. Tobin, I take it?"

Cole nodded to the harried-looking warehouse owner. "Of course. I'm sorry about this."

"Maybe you should be," Tobin snapped.

Cole's forehead creased in a frown. "What do you mean by that?" he asked. He had a sudden feeling that he wasn't going to like the answer.

"That warehouse was full of fine textiles," Tobin said angrily, "including some very expensive silk from the Orient. It's going to cost me a fortune to make up this loss!"

"Aren't you insured?"

Tobin shook his head. "Not for the full value of that merchandise. I'll be lucky if this loss doesn't ruin me."

"Like I said, I'm sorry," Cole told the man. "But I still don't see what that has to do with me."

Chief Sullivan put in, "We're pretty sure this fire was arson, just like the blaze that gutted Garrett Ingersoll's warehouse. Inspector Fernack and I have already talked to a couple of witnesses who saw some suspicious characters hanging around here earlier."

"You mean they set the fire in broad daylight?" Cole found that hard to believe.

"The waterfront was practically deserted today," Sullivan pointed out. "Everyone was up in Golden Gate Park."

Now that he thought about it, Cole supposed the chief was right. The neighborhood would not have been as busy to start with on a Saturday afternoon, and on a day such as today, with all the festivities going on in the park, hardly anyone would be around the warehouse district.

He nodded slowly and said, "Arson or not, this fire doesn't have anything to do with me."

"Can you prove that?" Tobin demanded.

Cole felt anger welling up inside him. The warehouse owner was accusing *him* of having something to do with the blaze. He said sharply, "In case you haven't noticed, my job is putting out fires, not having them started."

"No, but you'd know how to go about it, wouldn't you?" Before Cole could make any reply to that outrageous suggestion, Tobin went on, "I've been talking to Garrett Ingersoll. When *his* warehouse burned down, it was full of goods, just like mine. The loss damaged his business, just like this one will hurt me. But when there was a fire at one of your warehouses, Brady, the place was empty. Mighty lucky for you, eh?"

Cole's hands clenched into fists, and he took a step toward Tobin. Chief Sullivan moved quickly to get between the two men. Cole said, "You said it yourself, Tobin. I lost a warehouse just like you and Ingersoll. Why would I have one of my own buildings burned down?"

"Maybe so you wouldn't look suspicious when everybody else along the waterfront started getting hit. Who's next, Brady? Are you going to burn down one of Richter's buildings, or Burke's?"

Sullivan put a hand on Cole's chest. "Hold on to your temper, lad," he cautioned. "It won't help matters if you take a swing at Mr. Tobin."

"Listen, Chief, you know what he's saying is crazy! I'd never have any building burned down."

Tobin pointed out, "You already own more property along the waterfront than anyone else. Could be that you want it all, and what better way to drive the rest of us out of business?"

Cole felt a muscle jumping in his cheek as his jaw clenched tightly. He didn't say anything, but he was grateful to Sullivan when the chief said to Tobin, "You're being mighty reckless with those accusations you're throwing around. Cole Brady is a valued member of our fire department."

"And that's why I'm not going to trust the fire department to investigate this blaze," Tobin shot back. "I'm going to rely on the police. Fernack will get to the bottom of this. I'm going to go talk to him again now."

"You do that," the chief said tightly. "But you'd better be sure of your facts before you go around accusing one of my men of a crime."

Cole and Sullivan stood together as Tobin stalked off. Cole said, "You know I didn't have anything to do with this, Chief."

Sullivan clapped a hand on Cole's shoulder. "I know, lad. You've always been one of the department's best men. But if these fires keep hurting your competitors here on the waterfront, it's going to look bad. For everyone's sake, I hope this is the last one."

Cole looked toward the burning building. Flames still shot up high over the collapsed roof, despite the water being poured onto the blaze. Sparks climbed into the grayish sky, making it look as if the stars had come out early. Cole wiped the back of his hand across his mouth.

"I hope it's the last one, too," he said.

But something inside him feared that it wasn't.

Chapter 16

COLE WAS BONE-TIRED. Annabel could see that in his face as he stepped through the rear door of his house and into the kitchen. He stopped short in surprise at the sight of her standing there.

Back at Mrs. Noone's, she had bathed, washing off the sweat and grime of the firemen's competition, then dressed in a simple beige gown that went well with her dark brown hair and luminous brown eyes. The gown had frills of delicate lace down the bodice and at the cuffs of the sleeves. Annabel had washed and combed her hair, too, so that now it was thick and lustrous as it framed her face. The only jewelry she wore was a gold necklace Mrs. Noone had let her borrow.

"My God," Cole said, "you're lovely." His voice was a little hoarse from inhaling smoke; Annabel's had grown raspy from smoke enough times for her to recognize the sound of it. Cole went on, "But what are you doing here?"

"Well, you didn't get to have dinner at Mrs. Noone's house like you were supposed to," Annabel said, "so I've fixed a meal for you here. Before that, though, there's a hot bath waiting for you upstairs."

"That sounds wonderful," he said with heartfelt gratitude. Then he frowned. "But how did you know when I'd get back from the fire?"

"I didn't."

"Then how did you manage to keep the water hot?"

"I put some on the stove to warm and kept adding it to the tub."

"You shouldn't have gone to so much trouble."

She shook her head. "I didn't mind."

And indeed it wasn't as much trouble as it sounded, Annabel reflected. She'd only had to make a handful of trips up the stairs to the bathroom with the pot of heated water. She had to admit, though, there was a lot to be said for turning a faucet and having hot water come right out of the wall. Amazing the things a person didn't miss until they were gone.

Or hadn't been invented yet.

Cole grinned tiredly. "Since you've prepared all this, I suppose I'd be a terrible ingrate if I didn't take advantage of it. I'll take that bath and be right back down."

"No hurry," Annabel said. "I'll keep the food warm."

She hoped he might kiss her on his way out of the room, but he didn't. Clearly, as glad as he was to see her, he was also distracted. She couldn't help but wonder if it had something to do with the fire.

Mrs. Noone hadn't tried to talk her out of it when she mentioned that she might stop by Cole's house tonight. In fact, the elderly woman had positively sparkled at the idea, suggesting that Lucius drive her over. She probably hoped that something romantic would happen between the two young people.

That was all right with Annabel—she sort of hoped so too. . . .

She had brought food, not knowing what Cole might have on hand. Mrs. Noone had insisted that Annabel take the pot roast that was in the icebox, and now it was staying warm on the stove and being kept company by plenty of carrots and potatoes. Annabel had also baked some bread. She had a bottle of wine waiting on the table in the dining room, along with four candles. She gave Cole a few minutes after he had gone upstairs, then went into the dining room to light the candles. When they were all burning, she turned off the gas fixture and let the soft light illuminate the room.

For a moment, a wicked thought played through her head. She could take that bottle of wine and go upstairs to surprise Cole in his bath. Maybe he'd never had his back scrubbed by a beautiful woman before, and even if he had, she knew a few things she was willing to bet would surprise him. She closed her eyes for a few seconds and let the delicious fantasy fill her senses.

But Cole was an old-fashioned kind of guy, she reminded herself. If she went too fast, she might throw him for a loop and make him think she was some sort of . . . what would they call it in this era? she asked herself. Trollop? Harlot? Soiled dove?

She didn't want to make him uncomfortable. On the other hand, if he wound up kissing her again, there was no telling what might happen. . . .

"You look like you're a million miles away," Cole said as he strolled into the dining room. His hair was still damp from the bath and only roughly combed. He had put on a pair of dark trousers and a white shirt that was open at the neck. The sleeves were rolled up a couple of turns on his muscular forearms. He stopped and looked at the candlelit table, with its Irish linen tablecloth set with fine china and silverware she had found in a glass-fronted cabinet. "This is lovely, Annabel," he said, and his voice was rough—though with emotion this time, not smoke.

"Thank you," she murmured. "I'll go get the food."

Cole stepped forward quickly. "Can I help you?"

She waved him toward the table and said, "No, you just sit down. I'll be right back."

She hurried into the kitchen and returned with the pot

roast. Cole had not taken a seat as she had intended, she saw, but was instead standing with his hands on the back of one of the chairs. He waited until she had placed the platter of roast and vegetables on the table, then pulled out the chair for her.

"There's still bread," she said somewhat awkwardly. "I'll just . . . get it. . . ."

She practically ran to the kitchen and back.

This time, she let Cole hold her chair for her and slide it underneath her as she sat down. He went around the table and picked up the bottle of wine, then worked the cork free with his thumbs. It came out with a faint popping sound. Cole leaned over the table to fill their glasses, set the wine to the side, and lowered himself into the chair opposite Annabel's.

He picked up his glass, and she waited to hear what he was going to say. He hesitated, then finally said, "I'll never be some silver-tongued orator, Annabel, but what I say, I mean." He held the glass out toward her. "To the most lovely woman I know." She smiled and clinked her glass against his, then he added with a smile, "And a pretty dog-gone good fireman, too."

Annabel's heart leaped in her chest. When she'd caught her breath, she whispered, "To the best fireman—and the best man—I know."

Cole inclined his head in pleased acknowledgment of the compliment and tapped his glass against hers again. They each took a sip of the wine, and the glance they exchanged over the rims of the fine crystal glasses was positively smoldering. Annabel knew she certainly felt the heat of it, and from the look in Cole's eyes, so did he.

She took a deep breath and set the glass aside. "We'd better eat before the food gets cold," she suggested.

"Good idea. You went to so much trouble, I'd hate to waste it."

As far as Annabel was concerned, they could leave the food right here on the table and race each other upstairs, tearing their clothes off as they did, and it wouldn't be a waste at all. But she knew Cole had to be starving. It had been a long time since that picnic lunch. And for that matter, she was more than a little hungry herself.

The food was good. Annabel had never prided herself on her abilities as a cook, but from time to time, everything came together just right in the kitchen, and this was one of those times. She found herself enjoying the meal, and as she ate, she asked Cole, "What happened down at the waterfront?"

He sighed heavily, and for a second she thought she had blundered badly by asking the question. But then he said, "I'm glad you brought that up. The whole situation has me bothered quite a bit, and there's no one else I'd rather discuss it with than you."

She felt a warm glow. Being able to share a person's troubles, she'd always known, meant just as much as sharing the good times. She reached across the table and laid her hand on the back of his. "Tell me about it."

Between sips of wine and bites of roast, he proceeded to do so. The longer he talked, the more outraged she grew. Finally, she said, "You mean this man, this Tobin, actually accused you of having the fire at his warehouse set? He thinks you're to blame for it?"

"That sums it up pretty well," Cole said with a nod.

"He's crazy! You'd never do that."

"That's just about what I said, only I was getting ready to take a punch at him while I was doing it."

"Good for you. You should have coldcocked the son of a—" Annabel caught herself and drew a breath before saying, "You didn't get into a fight, did you?"

Cole grinned. "No, Chief Sullivan was there, and he got between us. But I felt like it." He paused, then added, "I don't think I'd have had to take a swing at Tobin if you'd been there—you might have beaten me to it."

"Could be," she admitted, returning the grin. "Obviously, he doesn't know you as well as I do. You're the last person in San Francisco who'd have a building deliberately set on fire. Why did he think you had anything to do with it?"

"Business reasons." Cole drained the last of the wine in his glass. "Tobin's been talking to another man who owns property on the waterfront, a fellow named Garrett Ingersoll. Ingersoll is the one who put the bug in Tobin's ear, I suspect. He and I have never really gotten along very well. Ingersoll has the idea that I'm trying to run all the other warehouse owners out of business so that I can take over the entire waterfront. He thinks I had one of my own buildings torched first to throw suspicion off me."

"That's ridiculous."

"That's what I told Tobin. And I'll tell Ingersoll the same thing the next time I see him." Cole shook his head, frowning in thought. "You know, I had an offer not long ago from someone who wanted to come into Brady Enterprises as a silent partner."

"Who was that?"

"A man named Wing Ko, the leader of one of the tongs here in the city."

Annabel leaned forward. "Could he have had something to do with the fires?"

"It's possible. The Chinese tend to be scrupulously legal in their dealings with the whites, even though the tong members murder each other all the time. But maybe Wing Ko is anxious to expand his power no matter what it takes."

"You should tell the police about this."

He shrugged. "I've got no proof of anything, just a hunch. Inspector Fernack would laugh me out of his office."

"You know, it could be just a firebug setting those blazes."

"A firebug?" he repeated.

"Yes. A pyromaniac. Somebody who gets a kick out of setting fires."

Cole grunted. "A lunatic, you mean."

"Well, somebody who's mentally ill, anyway." Annabel reminded herself that he wouldn't know anything about pyromania or most other mental disorders, not in this day and age. The science of psychiatry was still in its infancy.

"All I know is, whoever's setting the fires has to be stopped. One of these days, a blaze like that is going to get out of control, and we're going to have a real problem on our hands. San Francisco has burned down a couple of times in the past, you know. I don't want to see it happen again."

A pang of guilt went through Annabel. This beautiful city had more than a fire in its future, she knew. But it wouldn't do any good to try to explain that to Cole.

She forced her mind back onto the evening at hand. She shook her head when Cole offered her more wine. "I'd better clear these things away," she said as she got to her feet.

He stood up, too, but he didn't offer to help her this time. "Come into the parlor when you're through," he said.

"All right . . ." She looked at him with a tiny frown, wondering what he was up to, but his face gave nothing away.

She put the cork back in the wine bottle, carried the leftover food into the kitchen and placed it in the icebox, then left the dirty dishes in the sink. Time enough for those in the morning, she thought, assuming that she would still be here in the morning. And she intended to be.

When she came into the parlor, she saw that it was lit only by a small fire in the fireplace. The warmth coming from it felt good. March evenings in San Francisco were quite chilly most of the time, and tonight was no exception.

Cole was waiting by the divan. "Join me?" he suggested, holding out a hand toward her.

Annabel didn't hesitate. She said in a voice husky with emotion, "Of course," and stepped forward to take his hand.

They settled down beside each other, and Annabel discovered that the warmth from Cole's body was even nicer than that coming from the fireplace. He still had hold of her hand. He lifted it and pressed his lips to the back of it, then rubbed it against his cheek. The smoothness of his face told her that he had shaved as well while he was upstairs.

"I know you must be tired," she said. "I can leave and go back to Mrs. Noone's if you'd like."

Please don't like, she thought. *Please.*

"I'm fine," Cole said. "Not nearly as tired as I was earlier. After the bath and that wonderful meal, I feel positively human again."

"Yes, but it's been a long day. . . ." Blast it, why was she doing this? Annabel asked herself. She was practically begging him to kick her out.

"I'm not a bit sleepy," Cole said.

"Well, that's good." Annabel gave an inward wince at the lameness of her response. Maybe, she thought, the problem was that she didn't really feel like talking. So she moved closer to him, feeling the heat of his thigh pressed against hers through their clothes. She snuggled against his muscular torso, and her head rested on his shoulder. It was the most natural position in the world, she discovered as Cole put his arm around her. They fit together as if they had been made for each other.

They were companionably silent for a few minutes as they sat there and watched the fire. Flames like this were so different from the ones she usually dealt with, Annabel thought.

"Annabel."

Cole's voice was little more than a whisper. Annabel lifted her head and turned it toward him. Their faces were scant inches apart now. She could see the muscles in his jaw, the tiny creases around his eyes that came from wind and sun and laughter, the strong line of his mouth, the softness of his brown eyes.

And with that, she pressed her lips to his.

Cole's arm tightened around her shoulders as he pulled her even closer to him. One of Annabel's arms went around his neck. Her pulse seemed like thunder in her head. The sparks that had been smoldering inside her sprang to life, kindling into a heat that would not be denied. Her lips parted in invitation, and when he did not answer it immediately, her tongue darted out to stroke his mouth. He opened in answer to her bold challenge and drew her in. Their tongues met and slid hotly and wetly around each other in a sensuous dance.

Annabel felt a groan of desire welling up inside her, and somehow she had the presence of mind to cup her hand behind his head and hold him firmly in place. Otherwise, she knew he would pull back at the first sound from her, worried that he was hurting or offending her. And that wasn't the case at all.

Her moan of passion was answered by a low growl from him. His tongue had grown more bold, flickering out to explore her mouth. Their bodies were molded together, and Annabel enjoyed the way her breasts flattened against the broad, muscular plane of his chest.

When they finally had to part in order to draw breath, Annabel saw exactly what she had feared she would see in Cole's eyes. He was worried about the impropriety of their being together like this. Respectable women didn't sit in gentlemen's parlors and kiss with such passion and fire. It simply wasn't done in 1906.

Or maybe it was, because Cole asked raggedly, "Are you sure you don't want to go back to Mrs. Noone's?"

"I don't want to be anywhere but right here," Annabel whispered.

"Then stay," he told her in a low, urgent voice. "Stay." And his mouth found hers again.

This time there would be no drawing back, Annabel sensed. And that was fine with her. She and Cole had wanted each other from the first moment they had met.

As they kissed, his free hand stroked the side of her face, then moved down to touch the lace at her throat. An ache sprang up inside her, an almost overwhelming need to be touched. She put her free hand on the back of his and moved it down to her breast. He cupped it through her dress, letting the firm flesh fill his palm. Her nipple, already growing hard, came fully erect at his caress.

He squeezed lightly, and his thumb stroked her nipple. As Annabel sagged against him, her tongue shot into his mouth again. A need to be closer to him, as close as possible, filled her.

The divan wasn't made for this, she realized. Not now, not for their first time together. That required a bed.

She moved her lips from his mouth to his cheek, and then he dipped his head to let his lips trail along her jaw and onto her neck, leaving a line of fiery heat behind them. She closed her eyes and gasped as another spasm of wanting shuddered through her. "Cole," she managed to say hoarsely, "Cole, we should go upstairs."

She felt him nod, heard him whisper fervently, "Yes." Thank goodness he hadn't asked her again if she was sure about this. There was nothing more certain in the world, and they both knew it.

He surprised her, however, by pulling her onto his lap and then standing up with her cradled in his arms. "Cole!" she exclaimed. "Cole, you're going to hurt yourself."

"You're light as a feather," he said as he started toward the foyer and the stairs that led up to the second floor. Passion must have been sending plenty of adrenaline pumping through his veins, Annabel thought, because he seemed to be handling her as if she were indeed no heavier than a feather.

He started up the stairs, carrying her as if he was Rhett Butler and she was Scarlett O'Hara. But *Gone With the Wind* was still thirty years or more in the future, and this wasn't Tara but a mansion on Russian Hill.

Annabel wouldn't have traded places with Scarlett for anything. She was exactly where she wanted to be.

At the second-floor landing, Cole lowered her to the floor. A small gas lamp was burning in the hallway, and it lighted their steps as they went hand in hand to his bedroom. He opened the door and stepped back for her to go first. With a smile, Annabel went into the room. Cole turned on a lamp that sat on a bedside table as Annabel looked around.

The room was a masculine place, all dark wood and leather-bound books and a scattering of papers on a beautiful rolltop desk. A massive four-poster bed filled most of the space.

Cole closed the door, then turned to her. She waited, perfectly willing for him to do whatever he wanted next. What he did was rest his hands on her shoulders and look into her eyes. "I love you, Annabel Lowell," he said. "I've never met a woman like you before."

"And you never will again," she told him, knowing it was the truth. "Are you going to kiss me now?"

"Oh, yes," he breathed.

And as his lips stroked and caressed hers, he put his arms around her and began unfastening the buttons that ran down the back of her dress. Annabel slipped her arms around his waist and leaned against him as he worked his way down. She felt the dress parting and was anxious for it to be completely removed.

Cole ended the kiss and Annabel followed his gentle urgings as he turned her around in his arms. She snuggled back against him, feeling the hard ridge of male flesh against the soft curve of her bottom. She closed her eyes and made a sound of contentment. The reaction wasn't meant to further inflame him, but that was obviously what it did. She felt the response of his maleness. His open mouth came down on the back of her neck. He kissed her there for a moment as he slid the dress off her shoulders.

She cooperated, drawing her arms out of the sleeves and then stepping away from him just enough for her to push the dress down over her hips. It fell around her feet, leaving her wearing only her shoes and stockings and the lacy camisole she had chosen to go underneath the dress.

She stepped out of the garment and turned so that he could look at her, and the heat of his gaze made her tingle as he took in everything from head to toe and back up to her face. "My God," Cole said, "you're lovely."

Annabel reached out and began unbuttoning his shirt. "So are you," she said as she spread it apart to reveal the hair on his chest. It was thick, but not overly so, and tapered into a line that trailed down over his flat belly to disappear under the waistband of his trousers. Annabel finished pulling the shirt off him and dropped it on the floor next to her dress.

Now that he was nude to the waist, she could see just how muscular he really was. She had felt his strength, so she knew what sort of power he possessed, but now she could see it as well. She moved closer and rested her hands on his chest for a moment, looking up into his eyes. Then she could resist the temptation no longer and leaned over so that she could run her tongue around his left nipple.

Cole moaned and stroked her hair as she kissed and suckled first one nipple and then the other. She felt a shudder go through him. He put his hands on her shoulders and thumbed the straps of the camisole down. She straightened so that he could slide the silky garment down her torso. When it was bunched around her waist and her breasts were bare, he returned the favor she had done him and drew each hard nipple in turn into his mouth, then opened his lips wider and took in some of the soft flesh around them. While he was doing that he tugged the camisole down over her thighs, allowing it to fall around her ankles.

She was practically nude now before him, and it felt so right to share herself with him this way. He went to his knees and trailed kisses along her belly, moving tantalizingly, maddeningly closer to the triangle of fine-spun hair that covered her femininity. Annabel closed her eyes and caressed his shoulders as he explored her. His hand cupped her mound and squeezed lightly, and her thighs parted. She was trembling, barely able to stand. He kissed each thigh while his fingers explored their inner softnesses. She longed to feel his tongue on her core.

But not yet; that was something for later. She intended,

in fact, for them to explore every part of each other's body with their lips and tongues and fingers, but right now she wanted something more.

Her hands on his shoulders urged him back up. As he stood, she stepped back and sat down on the edge of the bed to take off her stockings and shoes. When that was done and she was completely nude except for her necklace, she said to him, "Come here."

He came to her, and she unbuttoned his trousers, the task made a little difficult by the erection that was pressing so hard against the front of them. When she was finished, she tugged them down, along with the underwear beneath them, so that his manhood sprang free. She closed her hands around the hard, thick length of it, savoring the feel of velvet steel. Cole's hips pressed forward involuntarily, and as Annabel's fingers slid over his shaft, he groaned.

For a moment, she was tempted to lean forward and take him into her mouth, but she resisted the urge. Again, that would be for later. However, she could not fight off the temptation to plant a quick kiss there. Cole made a sound that was half-growl, half-whimper.

Annabel lay back on the bed and opened herself to him. "I need you," she whispered. "I want you."

"I love you," Cole said.

"And I love you."

He moved over her and poised for a second as she reached down and grasped him lightly to guide him home. She felt his maleness at the gates of her femininity, and then with a powerful surge of his hips, he sheathed himself inside her.

She didn't know if he was expecting her to be a virgin or not. Right now, she didn't care. The exquisite sensation of being filled by him, of joining herself totally to him, was all that mattered to her. For the first time in her life, she truly knew what it meant for two people to become one, to immerse themselves fully in each other, to completely share and devote themselves to the other. This was, at the same time, both the hottest and the most pure passion she had ever experienced. Absolute love and absolute lust coming together in earth-shattering sensations that had Annabel clutching Cole and crying out as he gave himself to her again and again and again. . . .

Until finally, after an unknowable amount of time had passed, he surged deeply within her one final time and held himself there as spasm after spasm of culmination shook both of them. Heat seared through every inch of her being. Her heart swelled, filling to the brim with the love she felt for Cole and he for her.

Then came the long, slow, sweet slide down into the warm afterglow, and Annabel let herself go willingly, knowing that Cole was with her and would keep her safe.

Chapter 17

COLE STRETCHED AND yawned, luxuriating in the sensation of waking up from a long night of deep, restful, dreamless sleep.

Or had it been dreamless? he suddenly asked himself. He remembered visions of pure loveliness, visions of Annabel as the two of them had made love over and over, each time more exciting and fulfilling than the last. All of that *had* to have been a dream.

Then he felt the mattress shift under him, even though he hadn't moved, and a soft warmth press itself against him from behind. Lips caressed his ear in a feather-light kiss, and a sweet voice whispered, "Finally awake again, sleepy-head?"

It took all of Cole's iron self-control not to bound up from the bed and let out a startled yelp. Even more self-control was required when a hand slid boldly over his hip and onto his belly, then went exploring downward. He moaned as the hand cupped the sacs below his instinctively hardening manhood for a moment before shifting to the shaft itself and closing around it in a heated grip.

"Ah, so you're glad to be awake. At least you certainly feel like it."

"Annabel?" he choked out.

Her nude body was pressed against his. She felt her muscles abruptly stiffen as he said her name. "You were expecting somebody else?" she said.

"No, no," Cole said hastily. This was getting out of hand. And that was what he had to do, get himself out of her hand, though he really hated the idea of giving up even for a moment, the wonderfully sensuous feelings she was arousing in him. But he took hold of her wrist anyway, lifted her hand away from him, tried to ignore the pang of loss he felt, and rolled over to face her. Her thick brown hair was tousled from sleep, and she was frowning slightly as she looked at him.

"Who else did you think would be in bed with you this morning?" she asked with a hint of a chill in her voice.

"No one," he said without hesitation. He propped himself up on an elbow and went on, "But I didn't expect to find *you* in bed with me, either."

"You thought I should have left after you went to sleep?"

"Of course not." Blast it, why was she misinterpreting everything he was trying to say? And why was he having so much trouble coming up with the words to make her understand? He took a deep breath and tried again. "I wasn't expecting anyone to be in bed with me. When I woke up, I thought everything that happened last night . . . Well, I thought I must have dreamed it."

"Dreamed it!" she exclaimed. "You didn't remember?"

"Oh, I remember, all right," he said fervently. "I remember just about everything. But it was so wonderful I was afraid it couldn't have been real."

That helped a little. The creases on her forehead went away, and her body relaxed slightly. "It was real," she said quietly.

"I know." Cole leaned over her and brushed his lips across hers in a soft kiss. "Believe me, I know."

"Well, then, I suppose I forgive you for jumping like a

scared rabbit when I touched you. Just don't make a habit of it."

"Do *you* intend to make a habit of it?"

"Of what?"

"Touching me."

She reached for him and breathed, "Oh, yes." Her fingers closed around his manhood again. "As much as possible."

He moved closer to her, but she pressed her other hand on his shoulder and said, "No. Lie back."

He did so, while she raised up and positioned herself above him, straddling his hips. She sat up straight as she lowered herself onto him, and the heat of her femininity engulfing him was almost more than he could withstand. He closed his eyes and moaned as she sank down until he was completely buried within her, as deep as he could possibly go. She put her hands on his chest for balance, then began rocking her hips back and forth, slowly at first, then faster and faster. He opened his eyes and gazed in wonder at her. She was beautiful, her face flushed with passion, her lower lip caught between her teeth, her breath coming fast and hard so that her breasts rose and fell enticingly. He couldn't stop himself from reaching up and cupping them, his thumbs going to the erect nipples to tease and strum.

Annabel cried out and thrust hard at him. This was the fastest, most urgent lovemaking they had shared so far, and somehow, the pace was perfect for this moment. Cole's hands tightened on her breasts. Her fingers dug into his chest. Her hips pushed down against his as she began to let out little panting cries of need.

Cole couldn't hold back. He let go of her breasts and moved his hands to her hips, gripping them firmly as his own hips thrust up. His legs trembled with the need for release. Then his climax washed over him and he held himself still as he emptied what seemed to be his very soul into her. Annabel closed her eyes, tipped her head back, and whimpered as her own culmination shuddered through her.

Then she leaned forward slowly, lowering herself onto his chest until she was cradled there in his arms. Her head rested on his shoulder. Cole reached up to stroke her hair, relishing the feeling of sweet intimacy between them at this moment. They were as together as two people could possibly be, and a part of him wished that they could stay like this forever, that they could forget the rest of the world and just be here with each other. . . .

That was impossible, of course, but for now, it was a dream he was going to hang on to, just as he was holding on to Annabel.

"I'm afraid your cook and housekeeper aren't going to like being sent home like that," Annabel said as she spooned scrambled eggs and sausage from the pan into the plate in front of Cole.

"They'll get over it," he said. "I'll see that there's a little extra pay for any inconvenience."

Annabel put the rest of the food in her own plate and set the pan aside, then sat down opposite him. She had combed her hair and wrapped herself in one of his silk robes, and he thought she looked positively lovely.

He started to eat, enjoying the eggs and sausage and pancakes she had made after he'd sent the servants home. Annabel hadn't come downstairs until they were gone. He hadn't really expected such shyness and modesty from her, especially after some of the brazen things she had done in the past twelve hours. Not that he was complaining about *that,* he thought. It was amazing how things that might seem a bit . . . outlandish . . . became so pure and right, and in their own way almost innocent, when they were being done by two people who were completely, madly in love with each other.

Clearly, Annabel was a woman who had some experience in the ways of the world, he mused as he looked across the table at her and watched her eat. To his surprise, Cole found that this didn't bother him in the least. Some of his friends and acquaintances who considered him straitlaced, even stodgy, probably would have been surprised at his tolerance. Cole didn't care about that, either. He knew when something was right.

He and Annabel were a match, and that was all that mattered, he told himself. He loved her, and she loved him. What had happened in the lives of either one of them before they met was of absolutely no importance.

And it was probably a good thing he felt that way, he thought, because he really knew very little about her. Her life before she had fainted on that ferry dock in Oakland was pretty much a mystery.

She would tell him when she was ready, he decided. Until then, well, maybe a little mystery was a good thing.

"What in the world are you thinking about?" she asked, her fork poised halfway to her mouth with a bite of pancake on it. "You look like you're pondering the mysteries of the universe."

"Something like that," Cole said. "You know, this food is really very good."

"Thank you," Annabel said. "I've had more experience with breakfast than I have with dinner." She glanced at the windows in the dining room. Bright midday light came in through the gauzy curtains. "Even though it's sort of late for breakfast, I suppose."

"Nothing wrong with that. When you're a fireman, you get used to eating meals at different times of the day."

"I know."

So they were back to that again, he thought. He laid his fork aside and said, "We're going to have to talk about what happened yesterday."

"You mean last night?"

"I mean yesterday, in Golden Gate Park. You could have been badly hurt . . . or worse."

Annabel shrugged. "I'm fine. You saw for yourself how well I did in the competition, and I may have saved that man's life—not to mention yours. Nothing else happened.

Well, nothing too bad, assuming that Patsy's all right, and I'm sure he will be."

"I'm not talking about Patsy or competitions or some fellow choking," Cole said. A part of him wished the subject hadn't come up. But he supposed this discussion had to take place sooner or later. "I'm talking about you. You can't take any more chances like that."

"I can't?" she echoed. "Why not?"

"Because . . . because I love you, blast it!"

Annabel threw back her head and laughed, though she didn't really sound amused. "And what about you?" she demanded. "You risk your life every time you answer a fire call, and *I* love *you*! Are you going to give up being a fireman just because you and I are together now?"

He frowned. "I've always been a fireman."

Annabel grasped the edge of the table and leaned forward. "So have I," she said.

Cole closed his eyes and massaged his temples. The situation was deteriorating, and there didn't seem to be anything he could do to stop it. But if he didn't do *something,* Annabel was liable to get mad and leave, and he didn't think he could stand that. . . .

"I'll speak to Lieutenant Driscoll again," he heard himself saying. He lifted his head and met her gaze squarely across the table. His voice grew even more firm as he went on, "I'll tell him that unless the department hires you, I'll be turning in my resignation."

She sat back, her eyes widening in surprise. "You . . . you'd do that?" she asked in a half-whisper. "Why?"

"Because it's what you want," he said simply, "and I love you. I want you to be happy, Annabel."

Even as he spoke the words, he found that he meant them. If she joined the fire department, he would worry about her constantly. But that was a part of life, he realized, a part of loving someone. People had to take their own risks. He had fallen in love with Annabel Lowell, and that meant he loved everything about her, even the more . . . unusual . . . aspects of her personality.

"You'd do that for me?"

"Of course."

Annabel took a deep breath. "Don't say anything to Lieutenant Driscoll. Not yet, anyway."

"What?" She had taken him by surprise yet again.

"I said, don't say anything to the lieutenant. I have to think about this."

"Well . . . all right. If you're sure."

"I'm sure," she said decisively. She reached across the table and took hold of his hand. "But, Cole . . . thank you. Thank you so much."

He wasn't exactly sure what she was thanking him for, but he thought he had enough of an inkling to know that the thing to do now was smile and nod and keep his mouth shut. That seemed to have the desired effect, because Annabel said, "When do you have to be at the firehouse?"

"Not until three o'clock this afternoon."

"Good." Her eyes twinkled with a mischievous passion. "Then we've got plenty of time to finish breakfast and go back upstairs."

Cole smiled and reached for his fork.

Annabel would not have believed that the next few weeks could pass so quickly—or so delightfully. But they did, because she was with Cole, and because the thing that had always been missing in her life, the thing she hadn't even known she needed in order to make herself complete, was now hers. She was in love with a good man who loved her equally in return. That was all that mattered.

Which didn't mean she hadn't been somewhat embarrassed to return to Mrs. Noone's house the day after that first night she and Cole spent together. To Annabel's surprise, she'd found that she was taking on some of the morality of the period, and was worried that Mrs. Noone and Lucius would think that she was now a fallen woman.

As it had turned out, however, Mrs. Noone was delighted for her. "Don't think that just because people put up a façade of so-called respectability, my dear, that we're all hidebound puritans," the elderly lady had said. "Why, things have gone on in this town that would shock you! Cole Brady is a good, decent young man, and you're a wonderful young lady. I think the two of you make an absolutely lovely couple."

"So do I," Annabel had admitted with a smile.

"You'll maintain your room here, of course, for appearance's sake, but don't worry about paying for it. All I want in return is an invitation to the wedding."

Wedding? Neither she nor Cole had mentioned anything about marriage, Annabel had thought. But at the same time, she couldn't imagine ever being separated from him, so she supposed a wedding was an inevitability. And Mrs. Noone didn't seem to doubt for a second that one would take place.

Annabel had smiled and said, "Of course."

She had moved most of her things to Cole's house, Lucius delivering the trunks and telling her somewhat awkwardly, "If that young man ever does less than right by you, Miss Lowell, please inform me immediately so that I may have the pleasure of thrashing him for you."

"I don't think you have to worry about that, Lucius," Annabel had told him with a smile before leaning over to kiss his weathered cheek.

Since then, Annabel had settled in at Cole's house. She had a room of her own on the second floor—again for appearance's sake, for she seldom used it. The cook and the housekeeper had grown accustomed to her being there, and a tentative truce existed between Annabel and the two servants.

As for what existed between her and Cole . . . Well, *that* was a continuous source of wonderment and joy for Annabel.

She had never dreamed of being so happy. Day and

night, her thoughts were of him. He seemed to fill her senses, even when he wasn't there. His presence lingered in the air long after he had gone to the firehouse. And when he came back, she was waiting for him, and the lovemaking was always fresh, spontaneous, and utterly satisfying.

She could get used to this, Annabel found herself thinking on more than one occasion.

As for Cole, he still seemed to be a little puzzled by her decision not to push the issue of joining the fire department right away. Annabel hadn't decided what she was going to do in the long run, but Cole's sweet offer to give up his own career as a fireman had led her to the belief that it wouldn't hurt to postpone the issue for a while, primarily because she didn't want career decisions to interfere with the newfound sensation of being completely in love with a man. She worried a little that the values of Cole's time period were seducing her, but for now, she didn't care all that much. Not as long as she could continue seducing Cole. . . .

The only thing that interfered with this idyllic period was the trouble on the waterfront.

Several more fires had broken out in the warehouse district, and each time at least one building had been destroyed before the fire department could bring things under control. Another warehouse belonging to Tobin had burned to the ground, and the other buildings also belonged to Cole's competitors. In each case, an eyewitness or some other bit of evidence had proven that the fires had been deliberately set. No more of Garrett Ingersoll's warehouses had been targeted, but that hadn't stopped the man from agitating among his fellow businessmen and pointing the finger of suspicion at Cole.

For the most part, Cole seethed in silence, but Annabel knew how much the situation was bothering him. For a fireman to be suspected of being an arsonist was almost unthinkable, and unbearable. Cole knew that Inspector Fernack and the San Francisco Police Department were investigating him and Brady Enterprises, trying to find some link to the fires, and although Lieutenant Driscoll and Chief Sullivan still backed him a hundred percent on the surface, Cole knew that even they had to be growing suspicious of him, thanks to the drumbeat of innuendo that Ingersoll was keeping up.

Annabel was glad that Cole still had Patsy O'Flaherty as a staunch friend and supporter. The little Irishman had spent a few days in the hospital with a concussion before being released. After another few days of recuperating at home, Patsy had returned to Engine Company Twenty-one as good as new. He had been at Cole's side when the company fought several of the fires on the waterfront. Anytime Garrett Ingersoll's name was mentioned, Patsy went into a sputtering, cursing fit, turning the air around him blue with a litany of partially incomprehensible Irish profanity. Annabel had to laugh when Cole told her about Patsy's colorful ravings, even though the subject which had prompted them was quite serious, of course.

A month had passed since Annabel had moved in with Cole, a month that had flown by in a blur of happiness, when he came home one day and, after kissing her, said, "I'd like for you to come to the firehouse tomorrow."

"Why?" Annabel asked with a slight frown. She had avoided going there, for fear that being surrounded by the sights and sounds of a firehouse would be too much for her. They would be different from the way things were in her own time, of course, but she worried that there would be enough similarities to remind her of everything she had lost.

"The company is having a photograph made," Cole said. "I'd like for you to be there to see it."

Annabel shook her head. "I still don't understand."

He reached in his pocket and took out a small box. As he opened it and extended it toward her, he said, "I thought it would be the first outing we'd have together as an officially engaged couple."

A diamond ring, beautiful in its simplicity, rested on the velvet interior of the little box.

Annabel caught her breath. The ring reflected the light from the gas lamps with a brilliant sparkle. A mixture of surprise, joy, and more than a little fear suddenly filled Annabel. "You're asking me to marry you?" she said in a hollow voice.

"Miss Lowell, will you do me the great honor of consenting to be my wife?" Cole asked, the words husky with emotion.

"I . . . Yes, of course!" Annabel's answer tumbled out of her mouth. "Oh, yes!"

Then she was in his arms. The ring box slipped out of his hands and fell to the rug between them, but neither of them paid any attention to it. They were too busy kissing each other with the greatest passion either of them had ever known. . . .

The morning of April 17, 1906, dawned clear and beautiful. Cole was due at the firehouse at noon for the group photograph, so he and Annabel had plenty of time to enjoy a leisurely, early morning bout of lovemaking. They lingered for a long time in bed, each of them using lips, tongue, and fingers to bring the other to the brink several times before backing off and postponing the ultimate pleasure. Finally, when neither of them could stand the ecstatic torture any longer, they joined together, each crying out at the rapturous merging of body and soul.

After breakfast, Cole put on his dress uniform while Annabel donned a dark gray walking dress and a black hat. Her hair had grown back enough that she could sweep it up now if she was careful and pinned it into place.

When Cole slipped into his uniform jacket, Annabel pointed to several ribbons and medals that were pinned to it. "What are those?" she asked.

He shrugged. "Commendations for various things."

Annabel came closer and read the engravings on some

of the medals. "Courage and valor . . . devotion to duty and comrades . . . highest honors . . ." She looked up at him. "You're a hero!"

He looked uncomfortable as he said, "I just try to do my job."

"The City of San Francisco thinks you're a hero," Annabel insisted. She came up on her toes, just a little, and kissed him. "And so do I."

"That means more to me than any of these," he said, gesturing toward the decorations.

It was time to go, so they walked down the steep set of stairs and along the street to the cable car stop. As they rode toward the headquarters of Engine Company Twenty-one, Annabel saw the admiring glances directed at Cole from men and women alike on the cable car. Children gazed up at him in open worship. It was ridiculous, Annabel thought, that a man such as Cole should be suspected of a crime. Her eyes narrowed. Garrett Ingersoll had better hope that he never ran into her in a dark alley. She'd had plenty of martial arts and self-defense training over the years. She would put all that practice to good use.

Another, more likely idea suggested itself to her as she looked again at the medals and ribbons on Cole's jacket. When they reached the firehouse a short time later, she made up her mind what she was going to do. She didn't think that her father would have minded in the least.

The photographer was already there, unloading equipment from the backseat of a Ford Model A. He set up his bulky camera and its black silk drape on a tripod, then took several large, heavy photographic plates from the car. Captain Driscoll was fussily lining up the members of the company. Annabel saw that several of the firemen had brought their wives and families to watch the photograph being made. All of them looked dashing and handsome in their dress uniforms and black caps, she thought, even Patsy, who as the shortest member of the company stood in the center of the group next to the horse-drawn steam pumper around which they posed. Cole, one of the taller men, was placed on the end of the line.

Annabel slipped up to him while the photographer was still preparing for the shot. She took his hand in one of hers and used the other to press something into his palm. "Here," she murmured. "I want you to wear this."

"What is it?" he asked, then looked down at his hand to see the San Francisco Fire Department's eagle-on-a-gold-shield emblem—or at least what would be the emblem of the department someday in the future.

"It belonged to my father," Annabel said, her voice trembling a little. "Captain Mike Lowell. It's his fire department pin. I . . . I want you to have it." She closed Cole's fingers over the pin and squeezed gently.

"But . . . but if it belongs to your father . . ." Cole looked flustered.

Annabel shook her head. "I inherited it."

Comprehension dawned in his eyes.

"He was killed . . . fighting a fire," she was able to go on after a moment.

Cole leaned closer to her. "Annabel," he said softly, "I can't take this. This must be so special to you."

"It is." She managed to smile as she blinked back tears. "But so are you, Cole. Please . . . wear it for me."

He swallowed hard and didn't say anything for a few seconds. Then he asked, "Will you pin it on for me?"

Her smile widened as she took the pin from him and lifted it to his lapel. "I'd be honored to."

She fastened the pin on his jacket and then quickly kissed him, not caring who might see, as Lieutenant Driscoll called, "All right, men, we seem to be ready. Everyone stand at attention now."

Annabel backed off so that she would be out of range of the camera's lens. A small part of her still wished that she could stand among the men as one of the members of the engine company, but she knew now that this could wait possibly forever. She kept smiling at Cole, who stood there with the other firemen looking solemn and dignified. . . .

"Oh, no!" Annabel said. "It *can't* be—!"

Luckily, she hissed the words under her breath as the reaction hit her and the world careened crazily around her. Recognition flooded in on her, and only the self-control she exercised over her muscles kept her from staggering. An annoying feeling of déjà vu had suddenly exploded into a crystal-clear memory. She could see herself standing in the San Francisco Fire Museum with Earl and Vickie, looking at an old-fashioned sepia-toned photograph of an engine company from 1906.

It was this engine company that had been in the old photograph, and today's date had been inked in the corner—April 17, 1906. Earl had said something about it, but Annabel couldn't remember what it was. She recalled the handsome fireman at the end of the line, the man Vickie had pointed out to her. . . .

Cole.

Annabel remembered. He'd had some sort of pin attached to his lapel, and she had leaned forward, there in the museum, to see what it was, only to be distracted before she could identify it.

She knew now that it had been her father's fire department pin, the pin she had just given Cole.

But that meant . . . oh, Lord . . . that meant that even while she was there in the fire museum, in her own era, she had already somehow traveled back in time to give the pin to Cole. But that was impossible, because it had been later that night that she'd answered the call from Captain McPhee to go to the Diablos and fight the forest fire there. How could she have been here in San Francisco *before* she had crawled into that cave to escape the flames?

The unanswerable questions started spinning faster and faster in Annabel's head, echoing so loudly that she barely heard the *whoosh!* of the photographer's flash powder going off, only vaguely noticed him calling to the firemen to stay where they were so he could get another exposure.

Annabel felt her knees buckling. How could it be? *How could it be?*

Unless . . . she really was crazy. Unless she had really been born in this era and everything that she had thought was her life in the future was only a vivid hallucination, a fever dream from a diseased mind. . . .

But there was her father's pin on Cole's lapel, shining in the sun, a relic from a time that had not yet come to be.

Annabel let out a loud moan, and for the second time since she had come to 1906, she did something utterly embarrassing.

She fainted dead away.

Chapter 18

THE FIRST THING Annabel saw when she regained consciousness was Cole's anxious face as he hovered over her and said urgently, "Annabel! Annabel, darling, are you all right?"

She groaned as she caught sight of the pin on his lapel, the pin she herself had fastened there a few minutes ago. Confusion and fear loomed once again in her brain, but she was determined that this time she would not give in to the emotions. Instead she managed to nod and said, "I'm all right. Help me up."

Practically the entire engine company was gathered around her, Annabel saw to her embarrassment. The firemen backed up to give her some room as Cole and Patsy took hold of her arms and assisted her to her feet.

"What happened?" Lieutenant Driscoll asked. "Miss Lowell, do you need a doctor?"

"No, I'm fine," Annabel insisted. "I just felt a bit dizzy for a moment. Perhaps it was the bright sun."

"You're sure?" Cole said.

Annabel nodded. "I'm certain. All of you, go on with what you were doing."

With a dubious look that said he wasn't sure he believed her, Lieutenant Driscoll began herding the rest of Engine Company Twenty-one back into line for the second photograph. Cole didn't want to leave Annabel's side, but she shooed him away and told him to go stand where he was supposed to.

Annabel backed off and tried to unobtrusively lean against one of the hook-and-ladder wagons that was parked in front of the firehouse. She still felt a bit light-headed, but she was regaining control of herself now. She was confident that she wouldn't pass out again.

But she still didn't have any answers to the questions that plagued her. She had read enough science-fiction novels and watched enough movies and TV shows to be aware of such things as time travel paradoxes, and she had a feeling she was in the middle of one right now. It had been conjectured that time and space were both vast loops following similar but not completely congruent paths. That was as reasonable an explanation for the glitch that had sent her back to 1906 as any she could think of. And if the loop theory was true, certain things were obviously going to repeat themselves from time to time, though perhaps with each occasion there would be slight differences. The only way to be sure about that, Annabel realized, was if she could somehow get back to her own time and study that photograph in the fire museum. Perhaps there was one less man in that picture, or someone extra, or some other small discrepancy. Perhaps she herself had caused history to somehow change. There could be infinite time lines diverging into a myriad of alternate universes. . . .

She took a deep breath. Thinking like that was just going to get her in trouble again. She didn't want to undergo the humiliation of fainting for a *third* time.

Besides, there was no point in speculating. She wasn't going to go back to her own time and examine that old photograph in the fire museum. Without even being aware she was doing it, she had come to a decision during the past few weeks. She was going to stay here in 1906 . . . with Cole. He was more important to her than anything she had left behind in her own era, though she still felt bad about the idea of Earl and Vickie grieving for her.

They would get over her apparent death, she told herself. And she couldn't live her life for other people. She had to make the decision that was right for her.

That meant being with Cole Brady. There was no doubt of that in her mind.

Annabel looked on as the photographer finished his work. The engine company dispersed, the men who weren't on duty taking their families and going home, the others heading into the firehouse to change from their dress uniforms into their everyday uniforms. Cole was one of those men; his shift had officially started at noon.

When he came back out of the firehouse a few minutes later, Annabel was waiting for him. He was carrying her father's fire department pin, and he slipped it into her hand. "You'd better take this," he said.

"No, I want you to have it," she protested.

"I know, but something this special, I'll only wear on special occasions—like our wedding."

Annabel smiled at him. "All right. What do you want me to do with it?"

"There's a small jewelry box on the desk in my room. My mother's jewelry is there. Why don't you put it in there."

She nodded as she slipped the pin into one of the pockets of her dress. "All right."

"You're sure you can get home all right?"

Home. That was a beautiful word, and Annabel loved the way he used it now, simply assuming that it meant the place where the two of them would be together. She nodded again. "Don't worry about me."

"I *always* worry about you," he said with a grin. "You're unpredictable. Sort of like a fire. A man never knows what it's going to do next."

She leaned toward him and kissed him quickly. "I think I'd be insulted," she said, "if you weren't so blasted handsome."

He put his hands on her shoulders and drew her closer for a kiss that lasted longer. "I love you," he whispered when he finally pulled back.

"And I love you," she said. Though she hated to leave his embrace, she stepped away from him, then with a cheerful wave turned and headed toward the cable car stop.

Annabel spent part of the afternoon at Mellisande Dupree's shop talking to the older woman, who had become a good friend. Mellisande was thrilled to hear that Annabel and Cole were officially engaged. "It's about time he made an honest woman of you," she said.

Annabel blushed at that comment, well aware that she never would have done so had she still been back in her own time. But 1906 was different, and she reminded herself that now, *this* was her time.

"Does Frances know yet?" Mellisande asked.

"No, I haven't had a chance to tell her yet."

"Then I won't mention it to her," Mellisande said. "News such as this should always be delivered by the bride-to-be herself."

"Thank you. That's awfully nice of you."

"Not at all," Mellisande insisted. "Just don't wait too long, or I shall go mad with impatience if I can't start planning your wedding."

"Cole and I are going to supper at Mrs. Noone's house tomorrow night. I thought we would tell her then."

Mellisande nodded. "An excellent idea."

From the dress shop, Annabel returned to the house on Russian Hill. Mellisande's comment about planning the wedding had started Annabel thinking, and she spent the rest of the afternoon going over ideas in her mind. There would be a great many things to decide between now and the time that she and Cole became husband and wife.

Husband and wife . . . That certainly had a nice sound to it, Annabel thought.

It was evening, and the servants had already gone home for the day when Annabel heard the doorbell ring. She looked up in surprise from the chair in the parlor where she was sitting. Cole's shift at the firehouse wouldn't be over for more than an hour yet, and besides, he wouldn't ring the bell when coming into his own house. Annabel smiled as she realized who the visitor probably was. Mellisande likely hadn't been able to resist the temptation and was here to talk about the wedding.

Annabel went to the front door and reached for the knob, and the thought flashed through her mind that in the era she had come from, she never would have opened her apartment door without first knowing who was on the other side.

She swung open the front door and then jumped back with a startled gasp as the body tumbled through the entrance to sprawl on the floor of the foyer.

It was all Cole could do not to whistle in sheer joy as he unlocked the front door of his house and stepped inside. Until the past few weeks, he had never felt this way about coming home.

Not until Annabel had come into his life.

He shut the door, then hung up his uniform jacket and cap and turned toward the parlor. Suddenly, a dark smudge on the polished wooden floor of the foyer caught his eye, and with a puzzled frown he stopped to examine it. He bent down and touched the smudge with his finger. Whatever it was, it was almost dry, but it still had a sticky feeling to it, almost like . . .

Almost like blood.

Cole shot upright, then called in a strained, urgent voice, "Annabel? Annabel, are you here?"

An answer came back immediately, and in a voice that he recognized with a huge sensation of relief. "In the parlor,

Cole." Thank God, he thought, she sounded like she was all right.

Cole hurried to the arched entrance into the parlor, and was stopped in his tracks. He stood there and stared at Annabel and her visitor.

She was just straightening from the task of tying a bandage around the midsection of a burly Chinese man who was perched uncomfortably on the edge of the divan. The man's face had a grayish hue to it. Clearly, it had been his blood Cole had seen in the foyer.

"Annabel," Cole said in a choked voice, "what's going on here?"

"I'm glad you're home, Cole," she said as she turned toward him. She gestured toward the Chinese man. "This is Mr. Loo."

Through clenched teeth, Cole asked, "What's he doing here bleeding on my divan?"

"He's *not* bleeding on the divan," Annabel said. "I took him in the kitchen to clean the wound in his side and stop the bleeding. I only brought him in here so he'd be closer to the fireplace while I was bandaging him. I knew he needed to be kept warm so that he wouldn't go into shock from loss of blood."

Cole scrubbed a hand over his face. Annabel knew perfectly well what he was asking her, but sometimes dragging information out of her wasn't easy. He said, "Just start at the beginning and tell me the whole thing." He kept an eye on the man called Loo, instinctively not trusting him. This fellow Loo, he figured, might well be one of Wing Ko's *boo how doy.*

"All right," Annabel said. "I was sitting in here a while ago when the doorbell rang. I thought it might be Mellisande—I stopped by her shop earlier in the afternoon to tell her about our engagement—but it wasn't. When I opened the door, Mr. Loo collapsed onto the floor of the foyer."

"I saw the blood," Cole said.

Annabel shook her head. "I haven't had a chance to clean that up."

"Never mind," Cole told her. "Go on."

"Well, he was unconscious and bleeding, and I could see that he was badly hurt. So I took him into the kitchen to see if I could help him."

"Wait a minute. You said he was unconscious. How did you get him into the kitchen?"

"Picked him up and carried him, of course," Annabel said matter-of-factly.

Cole looked again at the Chinese man. Loo had to weigh seventy-five or eighty pounds more than Annabel did.

"Anyway," she went on, "like I said, I stopped the bleeding and cleaned up the wound in his side."

"What happened to him?" Cole asked. "Was he shot?"

At the same time, Annabel and Loo said, "Hatchet."

Cole looked at the man. "You speak English?"

Loo nodded and said, "Some."

"What are you doing here?"

"I come to warn you," Loo said.

"Warn me about what?"

"Wing Ko."

Annabel said, "That's what I was going to tell you. Mr. Loo works for this man Wing Ko. At least, he did—before Wing Ko tried to have him killed."

And here he'd been looking forward to a peaceful evening at home with Annabel, Cole thought. He rubbed his jaw and said, "I think I need a drink. And then I want to hear all about this."

Over the next half hour, Cole listened as Loo explained in broken English how he had worked for Wing Ko since arriving in the United States a few years earlier.

"Not hatchet man," Loo insisted. "Not *boo how doy.* This one carry messages, watch man Wing Ko says to watch."

"You were a spy, in other words," Cole said.

Loo nodded. "This one happy work for Wing Ko, be part of tong, until white man come."

"White man?" Cole repeated in surprise. "What white man?"

"Not know name," Loo said with a shrug. "Him partner with Wing Ko."

Cole frowned. Wing Ko was certainly ambitious; otherwise he never would have taken on a white man as a partner in the tong. Such a thing was unheard of. Wing Ko seemed to have a fondness for breaking rules.

"What does this white man look like?"

Loo shook his head. "Skinny, pale, ugly."

That could have been almost anyone, Cole thought. He said, "What made you decide to betray Wing Ko?" Again, for a member of the tong to turn against its leader was almost beyond comprehension. The fanaticism of the Chinese was legendary.

"White man," Loo said bitterly. "Him tell Wing Ko this one cannot be trusted. Tell Wing Ko he should have this one whipped."

"So that's what those marks were on your back," Annabel put in. She glanced at Cole. "He looked like he'd been beaten within an inch of his life."

"So you have a good reason not to like Wing Ko's new partner," Cole said to Loo. "Or Wing Ko himself for going along with the white man's suggestion. But why did Wing Ko's hatchet men try to kill you?"

"Because this one comes here. *Boo how doy* follows this one, strikes with hatchet when he see where this one is going. This one lucky man. Get hold of hatchet and kill *him.* Then come here."

Cole saw Annabel shudder slightly. She wasn't used to the casual violence that pervaded the tongs.

"I still don't understand why," Cole said. "What does your problem with Wing Ko have to do with me? Why come to my house in the first place?"

"Because of fires," Loo said, his attitude now the patient one of an adult trying to explain something to a child.

Cole stiffened. "What fires?"

"On waterfront. Warehouses burn down. Wing Ko and white man have fires set, then more men who work for tong tell firemen and policemen they see somebody starting fires."

"Good Lord," Cole breathed, thinking back to what he had seen for himself and heard from Lieutenant Driscoll. Many of the witnesses who had come forward to testify that the warehouse fires were the result of arson had indeed been Chinese.

"Cole," Annabel said intently, "didn't you tell me that Wing Ko tried to come in with you as a silent partner?"

"Yes, but I turned him down flat."

"So he found another partner, someone who's just as unscrupulous and ruthless as he is."

Cole nodded slowly. "That's right. And since Brady Enterprises owns more property along the waterfront than anyone else, and since I turned him down, now he's trying to destroy me by having those fires set and making it look like I had something to do with them."

Cole turned toward the telephone. "I've got to talk to Chief Sullivan and Inspector Fernack."

"Fire tonight," Loo said. "That why this one comes here."

Cole stopped short and swung around to face the man again. "Do you mean there's going to be another warehouse fire set tonight?"

Loo's head bobbed up and down. "This one hears Wing Ko giving orders to hatchet men. They start fire."

"Where?" Cole asked urgently.

"Warehouse belong to man named To . . . Tobin."

Cole glanced at Annabel. "Tobin's one of my main competitors. He's lost two warehouses already; if he loses a third, it'll probably drive him out of business. And if Wing Ko succeeds in blaming me for the arson, that'll take care of me, too. Then he and his new partner can come in and take over practically the entire waterfront."

"You've got to stop them," Annabel said.

"Can you show me the warehouse that's going to be torched?" Cole said sharply to Loo.

Again the man nodded. "This one take you there."

Annabel caught at Cole's arm. "Cole, you can't stop this by yourself. Call the police."

"You can do that," he told her. "It's been just blind luck that no one has been killed so far in those blazes. Call the police and have them meet Loo and me on the waterfront."

Annabel looked like she wanted to argue, but finally she nodded. "All right. But be careful."

"I intend to be." He turned to Loo. "Are you sure you're up to going down there?"

Loo rose and pulled his quilted jacket around his bandaged torso. "This one can go," he said.

"All right, then. Come on."

Cole led Loo out of the house. Annabel watched them go, gnawing her lower lip as she did so. A part of her wanted desperately to disregard Cole's wishes and go with him to the waterfront. She had promised that she would contact the authorities, though, so with a sigh she walked over to the small on which the telephone sat.

She picked up the mouthpiece, turned the crank, and when the operator came on the line, asked to be connected to the police department. When someone there answered, Annabel said, "I need to speak to Inspector Fernack." She recalled the name but had never met the man.

"Ain't here right now."

"Well, then, some other detective."

"Detectives've all gone home for the night, miss."

Obviously, police stations were run differently now than they were in the era she came from, Annabel thought. She said, "I need to speak to someone about the arson fires on the waterfront. There's going to be another one tonight."

"Oh, is that so?"

Annabel realized with a shock that the man didn't believe her. His tone of voice was light, almost amused.

"I'm not joking," she snapped. "There really is going to be a fire."

"And how do you know that, miss?"

"I spoke with a man who's involved with the ones responsible for the fires. They're being set by one of the tongs, the one led by Wing Ko." Annabel realized she didn't know the name of the tong itself.

"The Feathered Dragon Society?"

"I suppose so."

"Lady, no offense, but it sounds to me like you don't know what you're talkin' about. Been into the Lydia Pinkham's?"

That was too much for Annabel to tolerate. She blew up and began to chew out the policeman in the same tone of voice she had used on novice smoke-jumpers who fouled up during training. A loud click in her ear stopped her abruptly and told her that the policeman had hung up.

Well, if she couldn't make the police listen, at least she could alert Chief Sullivan. He wasn't available at fire department headquarters, however, and the man who answered the telephone there refused to tell Annabel how to contact him. With her frustration growing, she cradled the mouthpiece, then picked it up again and asked to be connected to Engine Company Twenty-one.

Lieutenant Driscoll was not on duty, but at least Annabel finally got hold of someone who seemed to know who she was and who took her seriously. The man promised to pass on the warning, but then he said, "We can't respond until an alarm has been turned in, though."

"What!" Annabel exclaimed. "I'm telling you about the fire so you can stop it before it gets started."

"We can't do that. Regulations say we can only leave the firehouse in response to an alarm."

Annabel bit back the angry reaction that tried to spring to her lips—yelling at the police hadn't done any good. "Just be ready to roll," she said, then broke the connection.

She had tried, she told herself. She had done the best she

could to go along with what Cole wanted. Unfortunately, it hadn't worked out as he had hoped. So now he needed to know that help *wasn't* on the way to the waterfront. He was down there facing danger with only a wounded man to back him up.

Annabel had to get to him. If anything happened to him because she'd failed to warn him, she would never forgive herself.

She ran to get her coat. It was a cool, foggy night, and it would be even more damp and chilly on the waterfront.

Cole knew which of the warehouses belonged to Tobin. Luckily, they were all in the same area along the docks. He and Loo made their way carefully toward the big, dark, looming buildings. The waterfront was deserted at this time of night. The only noises were the lapping of waves, the rubbing and squeaking of hawsers against pilings, and the distant moan of a foghorn. Cole walked as quietly as possible, and Loo slipped along behind him on soundless feet.

Stopping in the shadows of an alley across from several warehouses, Cole waited for Loo to come up alongside him, then leaned over and whispered, "Which one?"

Loo pointed, and Cole stared intently at the warehouse he indicated. Cole was looking for signs of suspicious activity, but he didn't see any. The place was quiet and seemingly deserted.

He turned back to Loo and hissed, "Are you sure?"

The man nodded emphatically.

"We'd better get over there, then," Cole said. There was very little light, only a faint glow from a gas streetlight two blocks away, and that illumination was diffused by the thickening fog. If they moved quickly, Cole thought, he and Loo could get across the street without being noticed. He took a deep breath, then dashed toward the warehouse, trying to run as quietly as possible.

Suddenly, as he approached the building, figures emerged from the alleys at both sides of the warehouse. As men loomed in the darkness, Cole slid to a stop. He felt his heart sinking and cursed himself for walking into this trap. He spun around, but Loo stood there smiling, and now there was a hatchet in the man's hand.

"They whipped you and then nearly killed you," Cole said.

"All for the glory of Wing Ko and the Feathered Dragon Society."

So he had been right all along about the fanaticism of the tong members, Cole thought. Little good the knowledge would do him now, he reflected bitterly.

But with any luck, he tried to reassure himself, Annabel had been able to reach someone in the police department, and help could be on the way even now. Cole hoped so, because fully a dozen of Wing Ko's *boo how doy* had emerged from the fog and were now surrounding him. There was no hope of fighting his way free.

He took a deep breath as the circle of hatchet men suddenly parted and two more men strolled through the gap. The tall, ascetic-looking Chinese with a thin mustache and a small goatee, wearing an expensive silk robe and a small round cap, had to be Wing Ko. Cole had met with his emissaries, but had never actually seen the man.

The second man, however, was well known to him, and Cole muttered a curse at the sight of Garrett Ingersoll's smirking face. "I should have known," he said.

"Indeed you should have," Ingersoll mocked. "Who would benefit more from having you in jail for arson and your company in ruins? Losing one warehouse full of goods was a small price to pay for what I'll gain in the long run, now that I'm in partnership with my esteemed companion."

"Enough talk," Wing Ko said. He inclined his head toward the warehouse in front of which they all stood. "Take him inside and prepare to start the fire."

"Why are you doing this?" Cole asked quickly as several of the hatchet men started to close in on him. "Wasn't your plan working fast enough to suit you, Garrett?"

"As a matter of fact, it wasn't," Ingersoll said. He moved a step closer to Cole, and Wing Ko motioned for his men to wait a moment. "We lined up enough evidence and witnesses to point the finger of suspicion at you, but even though Sullivan and Fernack investigated, they're still not any closer to arresting you." Ingersoll's voice grew harsh and bitter. "Everyone in San Francisco seems to think you're some sort of hero. The wonderful Cole Brady! Anyone else would have been behind bars by now, but not you. Oh, no, not Cole Brady! If *I* was suspected of arson, they'd lock me up and throw away the key!"

Even under these desperate circumstances, Cole couldn't help but smile slightly as he said, "You know, Garrett, I think you're right."

Ingersoll's hand flashed up and cracked across Cole's face. He cursed and said, "You'll regret that, Brady. But not for long, because you're not going to live long. Poor Tobin's warehouse is going to burn down, but this time there's going to be a difference. You're going to set this fire yourself, instead of trusting the job to your hirelings. But you're going to make a fatal mistake and get caught in the flames yourself." Ingersoll shook his head in mock regret. "Such a shame. But at least now everyone in San Francisco will be convinced that you really were guilty." He stepped back and said to Wing Ko, "Go ahead."

Before any of the hatchet men could grab Cole, another Chinese man came running out of the fog. He spoke quickly to Wing Ko, who listened intently and then smiled. The tong leader snapped some orders in rapid Chinese, and the newcomer bowed and hurried off into the darkness again.

"What's going on?" Ingersoll demanded.

"Change in plans," Wing Ko said smoothly. "We now have another lever to use on Mr. Brady."

"Another lever?" Ingersoll echoed. "What the devil are you talking about? It's over. We're going to kill him!"

Wing Ko shook his head. "Not yet." He snapped his fingers and pointed at Ingersoll. Two of the *boo how doy* stepped up quickly and grabbed Ingersoll's arms.

"What are you doing?" Ingersoll practically howled. "I'm your partner!" He started ranting and cursing.

"We shall see," Wing Ko cut into the tirade. "There will be no fire tonight." He held out a hand and crooked a long-nailed finger in a summoning gesture.

Several men came out of the fog, holding a struggling figure between them.

The blood in Cole's veins turned to ice as he saw the angry, frightened face of the woman he loved in the hands of the hatchet men.

Annabel.

Chapter 19

ANNABEL DIDN'T BLAME Cole for being upset with her. It *had* been a foolish, grandstand stunt for her to hurry to the waterfront after him and then let Wing Ko's men capture her. However, if she hadn't, he would be dead now, his body lying in the smoldering ruin of the warehouse Wing Ko and Garrett Ingersoll had planned to have torched tonight. At least for the time being, Cole was still alive, and so was she.

Of course, there was no guarantee how long that situation was going to last. . . .

They were prisoners, even though they were sitting on a comfortable divan with brocaded silk upholstery. Two hatchet men with cold, hard eyes and expressionless faces stood flanking the doorway that led from the expensively furnished room. If either she or Cole made a move to try to escape, those *boo how doy* would react instantly.

This odd room, with its luxurious furnishings and breathtaking silk tapestries, was somewhere inside a ramshackle building in Chinatown. Annabel and Cole had been bundled inside rolls of canvas and loaded into a wagon to be brought here from the waterfront. Cole had told her to cooperate and go along with whatever Wing Ko ordered for now, until they saw how things were going to play out. There was really no other choice.

From the end of the canvas roll, she had caught a glimpse of the run-down building as they were being carried inside. Then had come a dizzying maze of twists and turns, and finally the canvas had been unrolled and they had been dumped here in this room, onto a fantastically ornate rug. Wing Ko had entered a moment later, as they were picking themselves up, and said, "Please, make yourself comfortable. For the time being, you are my guests and will be well treated, provided that you do not cause any trouble. I will be back later to speak with you."

Wing Ko had been gone for nearly an hour, and Annabel was growing more worried. "When do you think he's coming back?" she asked Cole.

He shook his head. "He's letting us sweat. I don't know what he has in mind, but you can bet that it won't be good." Cole looked at her and asked again, "Are you sure you're all right?"

"I told you, Wing Ko's men didn't hurt me. They just grabbed me as I was coming along the street, and then one of them ran ahead to talk to Wing Ko."

Cole nodded, frowning in thought. "The *boo how doy* recognized you. That means they've been keeping an eye on both of us. I suppose we're lucky Wing Ko didn't just have you kidnapped before now, so that he could try to force me to go along with what he wants."

"Do you think that's what he has in mind now?"

"Could be," Cole said with a shrug.

He was putting up a calm, cool front, but Annabel could see panic lurking in his eyes. He wasn't afraid for himself, she was certain of that; Cole Brady was no coward. However, he could be afraid that something would happen to her. The thought that she could come to harm because of him, she figured, was probably driving him crazy.

But it wasn't Cole's fault, Annabel told herself. The only

reasons they were here were Wing Ko's ruthless ambition and Garrett Ingersoll's treachery.

She wondered where Ingersoll was. Some of Wing Ko's hatchet men had taken him off down the waterfront street, and that was the last she and Cole had seen of him. She couldn't help but wonder if Wing Ko had double-crossed Ingersoll and had him killed. Even now the man's body could be lying in San Francisco Bay.

That thought made Annabel shiver. She reached over and clasped Cole's hand. His fingers closed around hers and squeezed gently, and his touch made her fear subside slightly. She had faced many dangerous situations in her life and come through them all right, she told herself. This one would be no different.

The polished wooden door into the room swung open, and Wing Ko came in. Walking in front of him was a child, a beautiful girl eight or ten years old. With her golden skin, dark, almond-shaped eyes, and long, glossy black hair, she reminded Annabel of a doll. She wore a red silk dress and carried a silver tray with a pot and several small cups on it.

"I have brought tea for us," Wing Ko announced. One of the hatchet men closed the door behind him and the girl. "This is my granddaughter Tsang. Lovely, is she not?"

"Beautiful," Cole muttered.

Wing Ko patted the child on the head. "She is the delicate flower that brings great joy to an old man." He spoke to the girl in Chinese, and she set the tray on a low table and began pouring tea from the pot into the cups. Turning to Cole and Annabel, Wing Ko went on in English, "Now we must discuss business."

"I thought I made it plain weeks ago that you and I don't have any business to discuss," Cole said.

Wing Ko inclined his head. "Indeed you did. But perhaps I accepted your answer too easily. That is why I chose to ally myself with the one called Ingersoll." The tong leader added solemnly, "On reflection, that may have been a mistake. Ingersoll is not one to be trusted. He would betray a business associate if there were more profit in it for himself."

"So you double-crossed him before he could double-cross you."

A faint smile curved Wing Ko's thin lips. "Fate presented me with the key to a more suitable arrangement in the lovely personage of Miss Lowell."

"I'm not the key to anything," Annabel said.

"Oh, but you are," Wing Ko insisted. "Mr. Brady is in love with you, and unless he wishes to see great harm befall you, he will cooperate with my wishes."

So that was it, Annabel thought. Cole had been right. Wing Ko intended to use her as a hostage to make Cole agree to whatever the tong leader wanted. She suddenly felt anger welling up inside her.

"Forget it, Cole," she said. "Don't listen to a thing this second-rate Fu Manchu has to say. I'm not afraid of him."

Cole frowned deeply, clearly confused, as of course he would be, Annabel realized. He had never heard of Fu Manchu, and the sort of tough-guy movie talk she was spouting hadn't been invented yet. She stumbled on, "I mean, I don't think you should cooperate with him."

"I don't intend to," Cole said, looking at Wing Ko rather than Annabel.

"You are making a mistake, Mr. Brady," Wing Ko said. "I do not wish to see anyone come to harm—except, of course, for the enemies of the Feathered Dragon Society. Do not cast yourself in that lot."

"I don't need a silent partner," Cole snapped. "Or any other kind, for that matter. Why do you want to move onto the waterfront? Aren't opium dens and prostitution enough for you?"

Wing Ko smiled again. "There can never be *enough* when it comes to riches, Mr. Brady. I have learned *that* from you Americans."

Cole slumped back against the cushions of the divan. "I guess I don't have any choice, then."

"Yes, you do," Annabel said. She sprang to her feet. "Go to hell, Wing Ko. You can threaten me all you want—I don't care."

Cole reached up, caught hold of her arm, and pulled her down beside him again. "You're not helping," he said under his breath.

Wing Ko folded his arms, slipping each hand inside the robe's opposite sleeve. "I believe I should leave the two of you alone to think on this matter. I shall return in the morning for your decision, Mr. Brady. If you cooperate, Miss Lowell will remain here as my guest for the time being, until our business arrangements are completed, with her every need attended to. Should you not, however"—he shook his head—"it will go very hard for her, I am afraid. Very hard, and very painful." Again he smiled, then gestured at the silver tray and its cups of tea. "In the meantime, please accept my hospitality. I bid you good night."

With a bow, he backed out of the room, the hatchet men opening the door behind him. The little girl smiled at Cole and Annabel, clearly not understanding anything that had gone on, and followed her grandfather. The *boo how doy* left this time, too, and closed the door behind them. Annabel heard the click of a key being turned in the lock.

Cole lifted his hands and wearily rubbed his face. As he lowered them, he asked in a bleak voice, "Well, what do we do now?"

After a moment, Annabel said, "I know one way we could pass the time, but considering that Wing Ko probably has spies watching us through peepholes, I doubt that you'd want to."

Cole stared at her in amazement for a moment, then threw back his head and laughed. "My God, you never give up, do you?" he asked as he slipped an arm around her shoulders and snuggled her against him.

"You can't just give in to Wing Ko's demands," Annabel said without looking at him.

"I don't see that I have any choice."

"You can't trust him. Look how quickly he turned on Ingersoll."

"That's true. But as long as he has you . . ." Cole shrugged and left the rest unspoken as he reached up with his other hand to stroke Annabel's hair.

She rested her head against his shoulder, and to her great surprise had to stifle a yawn. In such desperate circumstances as these, how could she be getting sleepy? And yet there was no denying that she was. She closed her eyes, telling herself it was just for a moment. . . .

When she awoke, Annabel had no idea how long she had been asleep. From the stiffness that pervaded her body as she tried to shift in Cole's arms, she figured it had been several hours, at least. He was asleep, too, breathing deeply and regularly. The delicate cups of tea sat untouched on the silver tray nearby.

Annabel was able to slip out of his embrace without waking him. She stood up, stretched, and looked around the room, wondering if Wing Ko did indeed have spies observing them. She wouldn't have put anything past the tong leader, not after everything she had seen the night before.

Suddenly, something nagged at the back of her brain. The day before had been April 17. She and Cole had been captured by Wing Ko during the evening. They had been brought here and had waited for quite a while before Wing Ko came to talk to them. Then they had both dozed off, and more time had passed. It had to be well after midnight by now, maybe even close to dawn on April 18.

April 18 . . . April 18, 1906 . . . Why did that date practically scream out in her mind as having some sort of important meaning . . . ?

Annabel's eyes widened in horror, and she breathed, "Oh, no. No, it can't be."

But she could hear Earl Tabor's voice as clearly as if he were in the room with her, saying as he had on countless occasions when talking about the history of San Francisco, *It was just after five o'clock in the morning on April eighteenth, 1906, when the great earthquake hit. . . .*

Now she also recalled what Earl had said in the fire museum about the photograph's having been taken not long before the earthquake. . . .

Annabel spun around and lunged toward the divan. She knew Cole carried a pocket watch in his trousers. Her hand dug in the little pocket just below his belt and closed around the smooth surface of the watch case. Cole jolted upright, startled out of sleep, and exclaimed, "Wha—Annabel? What are you doing? What time is it?"

That was just what she was trying to find out. She struggled with the catch on the watch, but finally the case sprang open, revealing the face of the timepiece. The hands stood at 5:05.

Her voice trembled as she asked, "Is this watch right?"

"Of course it is," Cole said. "Annabel, what's going on? How long have I been asleep?"

"We've both been asleep all night," she said. "And now it's too late."

"Too late?" Cole stood up from the divan and gripped her upper arms. "Annabel, what are you talking about? Has Wing Ko been here again?"

A laugh that bordered on hysteria bubbled out of her mouth. Wing Ko was the least of their worries now. "Cole," she said hollowly, "there's going to be an earthquake."

"An earthquake?" he repeated. "How do you know?"

She laughed again. "Trust me. *I know.* And it's going to start any minute now."

He was looking at her the same way he had looked at her on the ferry dock in Oakland a month or so earlier, and on several other occasions since then: like she had lost her mind and gone stark raving mad.

She fought down the hysteria and found herself growing

calm again. An eerie self-possession crept over her. It was coming, and there was nothing she could do about it.

"Listen to me, Cole," she said. "Please."

After a second, he said quietly, "I'm listening."

"No matter what happens, always remember that I love you. You've made me happier than I've ever been in my life, happier than I ever dreamed of being."

"Nothing's going to happen—," he began.

She stopped him by laying a fingertip against his lips. "Listen," she said again. "It took a . . . a miracle of sorts to bring us together, but it was meant to be. It was always meant to be. You and I were made for each other."

"Yes," he said huskily. "Yes, I think we were. I love you, Annabel."

"And I love you, and that's all that matters." She slipped her arms around his neck and drew his head down to kiss him. Their lips met, warmly and tenderly stroking, and neither of them even thought about the fact that they might be being watched. All they could think of was each other. All they *needed* to think of was each other. The kiss deepened, grew stronger and more passionate. . . .

The earth moved.

Literally.

Annabel cried out in shock as the floor suddenly leaped and bucked under their feet as if it were alive. She grabbed hold of Cole for support, but he was thrown into the air, too. Both of them fell, sprawling on the rug. They were thrown violently back and forth, and a huge, grinding roar slammed into their ears. The room's expensive furnishings were flung around wildly, and the silk tapestries fluttered and flapped on the walls as if a strong wind were blowing. Cole tried to climb to his feet, but he was thrown down again as another strong shock hit.

Annabel wound up lying on her stomach with the rug bunched underneath her. She lifted her head and looked toward the door. It had been wrenched from its hinges and hung at a cockeyed angle. She reached out, caught hold of

Cole's sleeve, and shouted over the rumbling, "Look!" She pointed at the door.

Cole made it to his feet on his second attempt, and he took Annabel with him, grasping her arm to pull her upright. The floor wasn't shaking quite as much now. Both of them stumbled toward the door. They had to get outside, Annabel knew. They wouldn't necessarily be safe, but they would be better off out in the open than in this building, which had not been constructed to withstand such violent tremors.

Cole grabbed the doorknob and wrenched it to the side. One of the hatchet men was suddenly in front of him, weapon upraised to strike. Even in the middle of an earthquake, Wing Ko's *boo how doy* were going to follow their orders.

Before the hatchet could fall, Cole's fist shot out and slammed into the man's jaw with stunning force. The guard went backward, bouncing off the opposite wall before falling unconscious in the doorway. Cole took Annabel's hand and stepped over the man.

Once they were in the corridor, they saw that the other hatchet man had been trapped under a collapsing ceiling beam. Annabel knew at a glance that he was dead, his skull crushed.

Cole bent over and scooped up one of the fallen hatchets. "How do we get out of here?" he shouted. The noise of the quake wasn't as bad now, but it was still painful to the ears.

Annabel glanced around desperately. She had no more idea than he did which way led out of the mazelike warren of corridors and chambers inside Wing Ko's house. Another tremor hit, throwing Cole and Annabel into each other's arms. They hung on to each other tightly until the aftershock passed.

These *were* aftershocks now, Annabel knew. She had lived through the quake in '89, plus dozens of smaller ones. She knew the first shock was usually the worst, but the smaller ones that followed could be almost as devastating. This one, in fact, had caused the wall at the end of the hallway to collapse, and grayish dawn light flooded in from outside.

Cole saw the opening at the same time as Annabel, and he began racing toward it, tugging her along with him. He didn't have to tug very hard—she wanted out of here as much as he did.

Annabel pulled back slightly as they neared the gaping hole in the side of the building. She didn't want them to run out blindly and perhaps plummet into a fissure that had opened up in the earth. Cole must have thought of the same thing, because he said, "I'll take a look."

"I'm going with you!"

He didn't argue. They stepped cautiously to the edge, where the hallway had snapped off as if broken by a giant, careless child. The floor now slanted up at about a twenty-degree angle.

The drop to the ground outside was only four feet. Cole said, "Come on," and hopped lithely to the surface. Then he turned back and helped Annabel down. As they swung around, away from the house, they got their first good look at the general damage.

"Oh, my God," Cole breathed. Annabel knew the words were intended to be a prayer, because she was echoing them in her mind.

The destruction and chaos were incredible.

Everywhere they looked along this Chinatown avenue, buildings had either collapsed or were canted sideways at perilous angles. Cracks ran through the street, some of them narrow fissures only a few inches wide, others gaping abysses that spanned several feet. Steam spouted into the air from some of the fissures. In other places, water fountained high above the street from pipes—previously under the surface, but now exposed—that had buckled and broken as the earth shook.

The street was full of people running and screaming,

shouting curses and questions, crying desperately for loved ones from whom they had been separated. Most were in nightclothes, though some had hastily and haphazardly pulled on regular garb and others were practically naked. Nearly everyone was in bare feet, and since there was so much broken glass lying scattered in the street, people also cried out in pain as their soles were slashed.

Cole put his arm around Annabel and pulled her tightly to his side as they stared at the wreckage of an entire city. Annabel had known, of course, that this earthquake was destined to be a bad one, but knowing something in a textbook sort of way was entirely different from witnessing the calamity and its accompanying human misery.

When Annabel looked up at Cole, he seemed dazed, as he must have been. What he was seeing here was completely unexpected to him. Annabel's brain was stunned, too, but she knew she had to snap out of it—and quickly.

"Cole," she said. "Cole, we have to get away. Wing Ko and his men could still come looking for us."

He gave a little shake of his head as he came out of his horrific reverie. "You're right," he said. "Let's go." Then he added in a bleak voice, "But where?"

Annabel cast her mind back to Earl's good-natured lectures and the things she had learned in school about the Great San Francisco Earthquake. As much death and destruction as the monster tremor itself had caused, the fires that followed it had been even worse.

"The firehouse," she said. "We need to get to Engine Company Twenty-one."

Cole nodded in agreement. Now that they had a plan and a goal, Annabel could almost see him growing stronger. He took his arm from around her shoulders and grasped her hand instead. "Come on," he said determinedly.

Annabel wasn't exactly sure where they were, and all the destruction around them made it even harder for them to orient themselves. But Cole seemed to have at least an idea of the right direction, and as he held Annabel's hand, he started trotting down the street and around a corner. They pushed their way through the press of panicking people, hanging on tightly to each other's hand so they wouldn't get separated. Cole angled toward the middle of the street, getting them as far as possible from the buildings they passed. That was smart, Annabel knew, because there was a strong possibility that some of those walls could collapse, and they didn't want to be trapped under tons of falling brick and mortar.

Suddenly, the screaming in front of them intensified and the flow of people in the street changed course. Cole and Annabel were almost knocked off their feet by the sudden shift in the human tide. They staggered out of the way of the worst of the stampede, and as the crowd around them thinned somewhat, they saw what had prompted the change.

About fifty yards ahead of them, a huge black bull was charging back and forth in the street and tossing its massive head wildly. Clearly, the animal was crazed from everything that was going on around it. Annabel had no idea where a bull had come from in the middle of Chinatown—from someone's backyard, perhaps—but it was unquestionably here and just as certainly dangerous.

Movement seen from the corner of her eye caught Annabel's attention. A little girl, her face contorted by crying, stumbled out into the rapidly emptying street. The red silk dress was familiar, and Annabel recognized the girl as Wing Ko's granddaughter. She came to a dazed stop between Annabel and Cole and the maddened bull.

Suddenly, the bull swung its head toward the child. It pawed the broken street, then charged. The little girl had her back to the animal and was so frightened by everything else that was happening that she had no idea of the danger bearing down on her like a runaway locomotive.

"Tsang!" Annabel shrieked, plucking the girl's name from her memory of the night before. The girl looked in her direction but otherwise didn't budge.

Cole lunged forward, breaking into a run toward Tsang. He was closer to her than the bull, but the bull was faster. The broken paving of the street made it even harder for Cole to run. Annabel watched in horrified yet hopeful suspense as Cole and the bull galloped toward each other on a collision course, with the little girl in between.

As he left his feet in a dive, Cole's arm shot out and looped around Tsang, jerking her to the side. He twisted in midair while pulling the girl to him so that when he fell to the street, he protected Tsang's body with his own. They rolled away as the bull thundered past, missing them by scant feet.

Annabel ran onto the buckled sidewalk, giving the bull plenty of room to gallop on past her and down the street; then, when it was safe, she hurried over to Cole and Tsang. Cole was getting to his feet. He had the little girl cradled in his arms. Her arms were around his neck, and she was sobbing as she clung tightly to him.

"Cole! Are you all right?" Annabel asked as she came up to them.

He nodded and met her eyes over the little girl's shoulder. "I'm fine, and so is she. But what do we do with her now?"

Several figures loomed behind him. Annabel could see them, but Cole could not. He saw her eyes widen in surprise, though, and he stiffened.

"Wing Ko?" he asked.

The tong leader, his round cap gone and his silk gown disheveled, stepped closer and said, "I will take the girl." Behind him were several of his hatchet men, but they didn't look quite as threatening as they normally did. In fact, they were wide-eyed with barely controlled fear.

Cole swung around slowly. Wing Ko stood there with his arms outstretched. Cole handed Tsang to him, and as Wing Ko took the girl, he spoke to her in rapid Chinese. Her sobbing intensified, but she was clutching her grandfather and clearly glad to be back with him.

Wing Ko stared at Cole for a moment and then said in a stiff, oddly formal manner, "I saw what you just did for my granddaughter. What was between us is no more, Cole Brady. Never again will you or those you love have reason to fear the Feathered Dragon Society. The tong no longer has any interest in your business."

"What about Ingersoll?" Cole asked.

Wing Ko shook his head. "Do not trouble your mind about him. He is less to you than a gnat to that bull from which you saved my beloved granddaughter."

Annabel felt a shiver go through her at the merciless tone of Wing Ko's voice. If Ingersoll wasn't already dead, his odds of surviving for very much longer ranged from slim to none.

"I don't want him killed," Cole said harshly.

A faint smile touched Wing Ko's lips. "I have no control over this. . . ." A sweep of one of his long-nailed hands indicated the aftermath of the earthquake around them. "But I can say that he will come to no harm at the hands of me or my *boo how doy.* However, if he survives, evidence will soon come into the hands of the police indicating that he was responsible for the wave of fires on the waterfront. This is justice, is it not?"

Not really, Annabel thought, because Wing Ko would go unpunished for his part in the arson. However, there were times when you had to take what you could get, and clearing Cole's name was the most important thing, anyway.

Cole nodded his acceptance of Wing Ko's proposal. Wing Ko inclined his head and said, "We will part now. I wish you and Miss Lowell the utmost happiness in your life."

Cole put his arm around Annabel again as the tong leader, his followers, and the little girl faded back into the shadows of an alley. "Will they be all right?" Annabel asked.

"Men like Wing Ko have a knack for survival," Cole said. "Whatever happens next, he and the girl will come through it." He looked down at Annabel. "You knew the earthquake was coming. Maybe it's better that I don't know how you knew. But what about now? Do you know what's going to happen?"

Annabel took a deep breath. "Fire," she said. "Cole, San Francisco is going to burn."

Chapter 20

AND SO IT did. San Francisco burned for three days and three nights, from early in the morning of Wednesday, April 18, 1906, to the morning of Saturday, April 21. The destruction was immense, with the earthquake itself responsible for only a portion of the many lives lost and buildings destroyed. By the afternoon of the 18th, much of the country already knew that one of the worst natural disasters in history had occurred on the West Coast—and it was just getting started.

Cole's instincts led him and Annabel unerringly through the nightmarish chaos to the firehouse where Engine Company Twenty-one was headquartered. Along the way, they saw pillars of black smoke climbing into the air all over the city and bright red flames leaping from the ruins of destroyed buildings. It took them almost an hour to make their way from Chinatown to the firehouse. When they reached it and saw that the redbrick building was still standing, a wave of relief went through Cole. The windows were broken and a few cracks ran up the sides of the building, but that appeared to be the extent of the damage. Those who had been on duty at the firehouse had probably come through the quake unharmed.

The big front doors were open, and the pumpers and the hook-and-ladder trucks were gone. They were already out fighting the many fires, Cole thought. Holding tightly to Annabel's hand, he stepped inside and called, "Patsy! Lieutenant Driscoll! Anybody here?"

A pathetic meow from above answered him. Cole tipped his head back and looked up at the living quarters on the second floor. The black-and-white cat, Fulton, stuck his head over the edge of the balcony-like structure.

"Fulton!" Cole said. "Come on, boy!"

Fulton launched himself out from the second floor, and Cole let go of Annabel's hand so that he could catch the cat. Fulton's claws dug through his shirt and into his skin, but Cole didn't care. He was glad to see that the engine company's mascot was all right.

"Fulton, meet Annabel," he said as he turned so that Annabel could pet the fuzzy feline. "Where is everybody?"

The only answer forthcoming was a loud purr as Annabel scratched Fulton's head between his ears. When after a moment she tried to take her hand away, he put out a paw and batted at it, as if commanding her to continue petting.

"I have to try to find the company," Cole said. "The way the fire is spreading, I'm sure they could use the help."

"We'll both help," she said.

Cole started to frown, then shrugged instead. After the dangers they had already faced together, it seemed a bit futile to argue with her now about staying out of harm's way.

"Fulton will be all right here," he said as he put the cat on the floor. "The building doesn't seem to be in any danger of collapsing, and I don't think there'll be any more aftershocks." It had been quite a while since any tremors had been felt. They were still possible, of course, but the likelihood of their occurring was growing less with each passing hour. Cole took Annabel's hand again and turned toward the big doors in the front of the building.

Before they could leave, one of the pumpers rolled into the firehouse, pulled by a team of wild-eyed horses. Patsy O'Flaherty was at the reins, sawing on them as he brought the team to a halt. "Cole!" he cried as he dropped the reins and leaped down from the seat. "Ye're all right!"

Cole threw his arms around his friend and pounded Patsy on the back. "What about you?" he asked.

"Sure and I'm never better!" Patsy's expression, jubilant over his seeing Cole, now fell as he thought about what else was going on. "But I can't say the same about poor old San Francisco. The whole blessed town seems to be ablaze, and there's no water!"

Cole gripped Patsy's arms. "No water?" he repeated. "What do you mean, there's no water?"

"The new mains were all busted by the earthquake! We've got little or no water pressure anywhere in the city. We used what was in the tanks of the pumpers mighty fast, and once 'twas gone, we couldn't refill 'em!"

Cole wasn't able to stop himself from letting out a groan. "How can anybody put out the fires without water?"

Patsy shook his head. "The lieutenant says the rumor is that the army's comin' in from the Presidio. Says they're going to try to blow out the fires with dynamite."

"It won't work," Annabel said.

Both Cole and Patsy turned to look at her. "What do you mean?" Cole asked.

"It won't work," she said again. "Dynamite won't put out the fires. They're too widespread. And the explosions will just scatter burning debris and make the fires worse."

Cole looked at her for a long moment. He had no explanation for her uncanny ability to predict what was going to happen. But the important thing was, so far she had been right. She probably was about this, too, he figured. If they could get to the authorities in time to warn them about the dangers of using dynamite—

In the distance, a dull boom sounded, followed by another and then another. Too late, Cole thought. Too late. The blasting had already started.

Patsy must have read the grim expression on his face, because the little Irishman said gently, "Och, they probably wouldn't have believed ye anyway, lad. The best thing ye can do now is to see to you and yours."

Cole nodded slowly. Patsy was right. Cole looked at Annabel and said, "I'd like to check on my house, and I'm sure you want to see if Mrs. Noone is all right."

"Yes, I would," she said. "But the fires . . ."

"We couldn't stop them by ourselves. And they won't be put out anytime soon. We'll still have our chance at them."

Patsy said, "The lieutenant sent me with this pumper t' see if by some miracle we had pressure back here at the station. Let me check on that, and if there's no water to be had, I'll take the two o' ye up Russian Hill 'fore I head back."

"Thanks, Patsy," Cole said. "Let's go check that water main."

Unfortunately, only a few drops of water trickled out of the main when Cole turned the valve to open it. Patsy shook his head. " 'Tis like that all over the city. How in Hades can anybody fight a fire without water?"

The explosions were still going on in the distance. According to Annabel, the dynamite was doing more harm than good. But Patsy was right: The army officers responsible for the decision to use explosives in an attempt to snuff out the blazes would not have listened to any warnings once their minds were made up.

Cole, Annabel, and Patsy climbed onto the pumper, and Patsy took up the reins once more. He backed the horses out of the firehouse and hauled them around so that the pumper was soon rolling toward Russian Hill.

"Gone, all gone," Cole muttered as he stared at the flattened wreckage of what had once been his house.

Patsy had let them off at the base of the steep steps that led to the top of Russian Hill. That was the quickest way to reach the street where Cole's house had stood—until a little after five o'clock this morning.

Annabel touched his arm, knowing that he had to be feeling pain at the sight of his destroyed home. The house had been home not only to Cole, but to his mother and father as well. Cole had grown up there, had never really known any other place to call home. And now, like he said, it was gone forever.

Abruptly, he turned to Annabel and put his arms around her, drawing her into a fierce hug. "Cole?" she said, her voice squeaking a little because he was holding her so tightly.

"I'm so glad you followed me last night," he said in a hoarse whisper. "If you hadn't, you'd have been here when . . . when . . ."

He couldn't make himself go on. He was realizing just how close he had come to losing her.

"I'm here, Cole," she whispered back to him as she returned his hug. "I'm here with you, and I'll always be here."

She lifted her head, and his mouth found hers in a kiss that blended love and sorrow and relief. They stood there like that for a long moment, clinging to each other in front of the ruins of the house that would have been home to both of them.

The house could be rebuilt, Annabel thought as she gloried in the warmth and strength of his embrace and his kiss. As long as they were together—that was all that really mattered.

Patsy had promised to wait for them. They turned away from the wreckage and went back down the steps. As Patsy looked at them inquiringly, Cole said in a taut voice, "The house is gone."

"Sure and it's sorry I am," Patsy began.

Cole shook his head. "I'm just glad Annabel and I

weren't there, and the servants wouldn't have been there so early this morning, either. Now, let's go see about Mrs. Noone."

The streets were still crowded with refugees from the catastrophe, but Patsy rang the bell on the pumper and made a path for the wagon to follow. He had to steer around places in the road where the pavement had collapsed or thrust up, so it was slow going as he and Cole and Annabel made their way toward Pacific Heights. A black pall of smoke hung over the entire city now. It might have been dusk, rather than midday. People shuffled pitifully along the ruined streets, coughing from the smoke, their eyes dull and lifeless and bereft of hope. Annabel's heart went out to them.

She knew this stunned state of mind wouldn't last. Within a few days, people would begin making plans to start their lives over. San Francisco would rise again, a phoenix from the ashes, as it had always done before. But for now, for many people, it was as if the world as they knew it had come to a final, irrevocable end, and Annabel could not help but feel sorry for them.

The fires had not yet reached Pacific Heights, and many of the fine houses were still standing with only minor damage, Annabel saw to her relief as Patsy drove toward Mrs. Noone's. The gate in the wrought-iron fence out front stood open, and Patsy sent the wagon rolling up the driveway.

Lucius must have seen them coming. He trotted out to meet them. "Miss Lowell!" he cried as Patsy brought the wagon to a stop. "Thank God you're all right! And Mr. Brady, too."

Annabel hopped down from the pumper without waiting for Cole to give her a hand. She quickly embraced Lucius, then asked, "What about Mrs. Noone?"

"She was quite upset, of course, and greatly worried about you, but she insists that she's fine. She says that she's been through earthquakes before and will no doubt experience them again."

Annabel smiled a little. That sounded like Mrs. Noone, all right.

"The fires may spread up here," Cole warned. "You'd better be ready to move fast if you have to."

Lucius nodded. "Indeed, sir. I already have some supplies loaded into the buggy and the horse ready to hitch up if need be. If worst comes to worst, we can depart from here in a matter of moments."

"Good. Keep an eye on the fires." From up here, practically the entire city was visible, spread out below. At the moment, however, there wasn't much to see except billowing clouds of black smoke.

Cole turned to Annabel and asked, "What now?"

"I'd like to see about Mellisande."

He shook his head and pointed toward the downtown area. The smoke was as thick there as anywhere else. "We wouldn't be able to get anywhere close to Market Street."

Annabel knew he was right, but she still felt a pang of regret. If only she could have remembered earlier when the earthquake was going to occur . . .

And what would you have done? she asked herself. *How do you stop an earthquake, even if you know it's coming?*

The answer was simple: She couldn't have done a thing to prevent the quake. But she might have been able to see to it that her friends were in the safest possible place.

There was no guarantee anyone would have believed her, she reminded herself. It was the same as the army using dynamite and having the plan backfire. History had to run its course.

"I think we should go back to the engine company," Annabel said. "Maybe there's not much we can do, but at least we can try."

Cole studied her intently for a moment, then nodded. "You're right. We have to do what we can."

From the driver's seat of the fire wagon, Patsy said, "Ye're daft, both o' ye! Ye're out of it. Why not stay somewhere safe until 'tis all over?"

Cole put his arm around Annabel, and she saw that from somewhere, he had summoned up a grin. "Because we're firemen!" he said, then glanced at her. "Better make that firefighters."

"That's right," Annabel heard herself saying, and incredibly, she was grinning, too. "So let's go fight those fires."

Patsy rolled his eyes and shook his head, but he said, "All right, then. Climb aboard."

And as the wagon rolled down the hill toward the spreading flames, he chuckled and muttered once again, "Daft . . . the whole lot of us!"

In the end, what saved the city was a shift in the wind and the waters of San Francisco Bay. As the flames were blown toward the waterfront, the area available for burning was gradually pinched down, and at the suggestion of some unknown fireman, water from the bay was used to fill the pumpers so that eventually they were able to bring the various blazes under control. Several times during the three days following the earthquake, the authorities announced confidently that the crisis was over, only to be proven wrong as the conflagrations began to rage once more. By Saturday morning, however, the fires really were under control.

Fire Chief Dennis Sullivan, much beloved by not only the men in his department but by the population at large, was trapped in the collapse of one of the firehouses, in which he had been sleeping at the time of the earthquake. Severely injured, he was finally pulled out of the wreckage, but he never regained consciousness and died shortly after one o'clock on Sunday morning, never knowing what had happened to San Francisco. Sullivan, a canny man when it came to fighting fires, might have stopped the army from using dynamite and making the situation worse, but there is no way of knowing that.

Mellisande Dupree also died, though whether in the earthquake itself or in the fire that ravaged the downtown area afterward, no one was ever able to determine. Her funeral was held on Monday, one of hundreds, perhaps even thousands, that took place on that grim day. Cole Brady and Annabel Lowell were in attendance.

Garrett Ingersoll was never seen again, although whether he died in the natural disaster or met some other fate could not be determined. However, a few weeks later, a known arsonist confessed to starting the warehouse fires along the waterfront and told police that he had been hired by Ingersoll in an attempt to damage his competitors and frame Cole Brady for the crimes.

Much of the civilian population of San Francisco was evacuated during the fires that raged for three days, but when the blazes were finally put out, people began to drift back into the city. Annabel's prediction proved to be true: While some people gave up and never returned, most San Franciscans soon rolled up their sleeves and went to work rebuilding their homes and businesses. The smell of smoke was replaced by the scent of raw, freshly cut lumber as new buildings began to rise.

Most important, the city learned from the cataclysm that befell it. The new buildings were stronger, designed to better withstand the shock of an earthquake. The water system was repaired and improved, as was the fire department's alarm system, which had proven to be sadly inadequate during the crisis.

For his service during the fire, Cole Brady was awarded a commendation by the fire department. He was one of many to win such an honor, and as the ribbon was being pinned on his uniform by the new chief, Patrick Shaughnessy, in a large ceremony several weeks later, Shaughnessy looked with interest at a small pin attached to Cole's lapel.

"An eagle, eh?" Shaughnessy grunted. "I like that. May have to give some thought to redesigning our insignia. Where'd you get that pin, lad?"

Cole was standing at attention. He said, "My wife gave it to me, sir."

"Wife, eh? Be sure and give my compliments to the lady."

Cole smiled. "You can give them to her yourself, sir, along with her commendation. You're about to give her an award for meritorious service."

Shaughnessy's eyes widened in surprise as he looked at the fireman standing next to Cole. Sure enough, he—she!—wasn't a fire*man* at all, even though she wore the uniform and the round black cap with the badge from Engine Company Twenty-one on it.

"A . . . a lady fireman!" Shaughnessy sputtered. "Why wasn't I told about this?"

"If I were you, sir," Cole ventured, "I'd get used to it. After the way she performed during the fire, we couldn't refuse her a place in the department." He cast a meaningful glance at Annabel, who continued to stare straight ahead—though with a sparkle in her eyes. "But she's agreed that she'll retire when it comes time to start our family."

Chief Shaughnessy drew a deep breath. "Yes, well, you'd better get to work on that, son. Yes, indeed." He stepped over in front of Annabel and lifted the ribbon he held in his hand. "In the meantime, I'm proud to present this commendation for meritorious service. . . ." Then he hesitated, unsure where to pin the ribbon.

Cole saved him any further embarrassment by taking the ribbon from him and pinning it on the breast of Annabel's uniform jacket.

Then, in front of the whole crowd, he leaned over and kissed her.

Patsy O'Flaherty, on Annabel's other side, put his fingers in his mouth and let out a whistle of approval, then began to applaud. Soon, everyone else in the crowd was doing the same.

• • •

Summer in the Diablos was beautiful, Annabel thought. As Cole handled the reins of the team and guided the wagon along the trail, Annabel cradled little Michael in her arms and pointed out the tall pine trees and the snowcapped mountains and the colorful birds that flitted through the blue sky. Of course, at only two months old, he wasn't very interested in such things.

Annabel's career as a fireman hadn't lasted long. She had honored her promise to Cole and retired as soon as she knew for sure that she was pregnant. Her service with the San Francisco Fire Department—this time around!—would be only a brief historical footnote, if that much. It was entirely possible, she knew, that history might forget about her entirely.

But that was all right. And although she sometimes missed being a member of the department, being retired was all right, too. She had Cole, and she had Michael, and they were the two most precious things in the world to her.

But who knew? Maybe someday, when Michael was older . . .

"I'm glad you came up here with me," Cole said. "I could have gone to the sawmill to see about buying lumber for the new warehouse by myself, but it wouldn't have been nearly as enjoyable a trip."

"It felt a little strange, riding the ferry across to Oakland and stepping out onto the dock," Annabel admitted. "I couldn't help but remember when we first met there." Even though that fateful day was fifteen months in the past, her memories of it were still quite vivid. "You must have thought I was insane."

"The thought crossed my mind," Cole said dryly, then he went on, "No, not really. All I could really think about was how beautiful you were, and how your eyes were the most compelling eyes I'd ever seen." He looked over at her. "They still are, and you're still the most beautiful woman in the world. You always will be."

She smiled and leaned her head against his shoulder.

There was nothing wrong with contentment—as long as she didn't ever allow it to make her complacent.

Not likely, she thought.

At the sawmill, Cole struck a deal for the lumber that would go into his new warehouse. The time would come, Annabel reflected, when this whole area would be a park and logging would no longer be allowed. That was good, but it was still in the future. She had learned to accept that about a lot of things.

And to tell the truth, though she still had some memories from her previous life, most of the time it seemed like she had been here in the first decade of the twentieth century forever. Cole was responsible for that. She still had no real answer to the riddle of how she had been transported back in time, but she firmly believed it had to do with the fact that the universe meant for her and Cole to be together. Some things just had to be, and the laws of time and space and physics didn't mean a thing in the face of true love.

She had packed a picnic lunch before they left the house on Russian Hill that morning—the *new* house—and Cole found a good place for them to stop and eat on the way back from the sawmill. It was a grassy, flower-dotted meadow at the base of a hill. Cole stopped the wagon and took a large quilt from the back. He spread it on the grass, then took the picnic basket when Annabel handed it down to him. He placed it on the quilt and reached back up to take Michael.

There was nothing Annabel liked better than watching Cole hold their son, she thought as she joined the two of them on the quilt and opened the picnic basket. Cole was talking nonsense to the baby, and he had Michael laughing and cooing. Michael had only recently started doing that, and Annabel loved the sound of it.

Cole and Annabel ate the fried chicken, biscuits, and fruit from the basket, then she unbuttoned her dress and took Michael so that he could eat, too. Cole stretched out, leaning on an elbow, and grinned across the quilt at them as he watched. "Some picnic, eh, lad?" he asked. Michael didn't say anything in reply.

Later, after Michael had finished nursing and Cole was holding him again, Annabel stood up and fastened her buttons. "I believe I'll take a walk to the top of the hill," she said.

"Go ahead. I think Michael's getting sleepy, though."

"Just sit there and rock him. He'll doze off soon."

"Well, all right. Are you sure you don't mind going for that walk by yourself?"

Annabel smiled. "What's going to happen to me?"

She turned and started up the hill, enjoying the sight of the flowers waving in the gentle breeze. When she reached the top, she stood and took a deep breath of the clean air. At this elevation, it was crisp and almost cool, even in summer.

The view was breathtaking. Mount Diablo rose in the distance. Annabel looked along Mitchell Canyon toward the peak and thought that sometime in the next few decades, a resort hotel would be built up there. She would probably even live to see it, though not the way it would be just after the turn of the millennium, when a certain fire would break out here in the Diablos and smoke-jumpers would be summoned to help battle it. . . .

She froze suddenly as the familiarity of her surroundings came crashing in on her. Slowly, she turned, and there it was in the hillside, partially screened by brush now, the dark, irregular opening of the cave into which she had crawled over a year earlier, seeking shelter from the flames. *Over a year earlier?* Over ninety years in the future!

Annabel realized she was having trouble breathing. She squeezed her eyes tightly shut, then opened them again. The entrance to the cave was still there, inviting and mocking her at the same time. The thoughts that went through her head now were the same ones she had when she first crawled out of that hole in the hillside. If she crawled back in, would the mysterious forces that had brought her here take her back to her own time? Or would she find herself lost in yet another era, another island in the stream of time?

She took a step toward the cave. . . .

Then stopped, and turned, and looked down the hill. Cole still sat there below her, holding Michael, and as Annabel watched, he lowered his head and tenderly kissed the head of their sleeping son. Slowly, Annabel's lips curved in a smile.

Then she walked down to rejoin her family, and not once did she look back at the dark hole in the hillside behind her.

Author's Note

THE SAN FRANCISCO Earthquake of 1906 and the great fire that followed it actually occurred, of course, including the bull that rampaged through Chinatown. Certain minor historical details have been slightly altered in this story for dramatic purposes. There was an actual Engine Company Twenty-one in the San Francisco Fire Department, but the characters I have placed in it are entirely fictional.

As always, I love to hear from my readers. You can contact me at P.O. Box 931, Azle, Texas 76098, visit my web page at http://www.flash.net/~livia, or E-mail me at *livia@flash.net.*